Life,
Loss,
and Puffins

Life, Loss, and Puffins

A Novel

Catherine Ryan Hyde

LAKE UNION
PUBLISHING

Published by Lake Union Publishing, Seattle

www.apub.com

Amazon, the Amazon logo, and Lake Union Publishing are trademarks of Amazon. com, Inc., or its affiliates.

ISBN-13: 9781662504419 (hardcover)
ISBN-13: 9781662504433 (paperback)
ISBN-13: 9781662504426 (digital)

Cover design by Shasti O'Leary Soudant
Cover image: © Wendy Stevenson / Arcangel; © Denis Belitsky / Shutterstock; © Guang Cao / Getty

Printed in the United States of America

First edition

Life,
Loss,
and Puffins

Chapter One

Chicken Livers, Water Chestnuts, and Bacon

Sit down, girls. Just sit on the couch there. And please don't roll your eyes. I mostly mean you, Tess, because you're doing it right now, but the request really applies to both of you. I'm going to do that thing grown-ups do where they tell you a very long story, and there's really no way out.

We've known each other for a couple of weeks now, so that's why I'm about to begin oversharing. Or I'm sure it will seem so to you.

Let me start with my odd name. In case you were wondering.

Even though I never use anything but Ru, and would figuratively shoot anyone who tried to do otherwise, I'm sure you've figured out by now that my real full name is Rumaki Evans. My mom didn't even give me a middle name. If she had, I would certainly go by it.

She'd been in the hospital after having me and probably on a lot of drugs and whatnot, and somehow she got it in her head that Rumaki was the name of some famous Japanese warrior or philosopher or some such. Which is already a little odd on the face of the thing, because we're not Japanese. But I wouldn't have minded going through life with the name of a proud and brave Japanese person from history. Not even a little bit. It wasn't until after the ink dried on my birth certificate that she found out rumaki is actually an hors d'oeuvre people make for parties with chicken livers, water chestnuts, and bacon.

This is where my mom and I parted ways in our approach to life. Sure, we all make mistakes. Anybody can make a mistake. But I figure, go back and fix it. You can change a name, you know.

You would have to have known my mom. She was . . . different. In a lot of ways. She did things her way, and any and all external feedback regarding whether it was the right thing to do never made a dent. She cared what people thought of her. A lot. She agonized over it. She just never changed.

Once she went with something, that was it. No backing down.

Now *I'm* the one who has to go through life with the name of a chicken-liver appetizer.

I suppose I could have changed it when I got older, but I didn't. And by the time I get more of this story out of my system, I think you'll understand *why* I didn't.

Anyway, I've barely started telling it and I'm already off on a tangent.

Now that you know my bizarre name, the next important thing to say, though you must know it already, is that I'm freakishly smart. Those are not my words. I overheard my mother telling someone that about me when I was five. For eight years I wore it as a badge of shame, telling no one that my own mother had said I was a freak.

And then came the start of college, and Gabriel. Everything changed with Gabriel.

Oh. I know what else I forgot to say. On this fabled first day of college I had just turned thirteen.

Freakishly smart. Like I said.

But before I tell you about starting college, I have to tell you about my grandma Mimi. Trust me, it's all related.

There's so much I could say about her. It's almost hard to know where to begin.

I'll start here: My mom called her Screaming Mimi, but as far as I know she never raised her voice in her life. At least not in *my* life. And yet, if you knew her, you'd understand what that all means.

She wasn't a cruel or dangerous woman, my grandma Mimi. I liked her. She just had a way of cutting through you. First with her eyes, then with her words. She was something like a truth bomb. No, not a bomb. A bomb is messy and inexact. More like a truth laser. If she saw something inside you she viewed as a cancer, she could go in and excise it without taking a millimeter of healthy tissue in the effort.

I wasn't afraid of her. I was a fan of all that. But my mom was afraid of her. And I was a little bit afraid of my mom, so maybe it's all part and parcel of that mom thing. I've only had the one, so I'm not sure.

Anyhow. About five weeks before the beginning of the semester, Grandma Mimi had a stroke. It was bad. It was very upsetting all around, for everybody. She was in the hospital, and then she was in this rehab facility that I thought was suspiciously like a nursing home. One side of her face drooped, and her speech was hard to understand.

Sometime during her time in the nursing home—er, rehab facility— she told my mom that I was not to attend community college. I wasn't there, so I don't know her exact words. I only know what my mom told me about it. But Grandma Mimi said something along the lines of "My granddaughter's intelligence is a miracle and you will not be wasting it."

Okay. Background. Sorry.

My mom wanted me to go to a community college because it was less than ten miles from home. So I could live at home, and she could go on being my mom in a way that felt familiar and normal to her. But I had been accepted to a pretty prestigious university. Full-ride scholarship. But that prestigious university was a little over a hundred and fifty miles away. My mom had a job she loved, managing an art gallery, and was not willing to move. And she thought I was too young to be away from home. So she wasn't going to let me go.

Even after Screaming Mimi told her she had to, she wasn't going to let me go. She was going to go see her mother—Mimi—on the following Monday and tell her no deal. The university thing just wasn't on the table. It would have been the biggest, toughest, most dramatic example of standing up to her mother that my mom had experienced in her entire life.

It never happened.

That Sunday night Grandma Mimi had a second, larger stroke and passed away in her bed at the nursing home.

And that's at least some small part of how I came to be enrolled at the university. Because it became something like Grandma Mimi's last wish.

Also I wouldn't put it past my mom to be afraid Mimi would come back and haunt her. I think she'd been less afraid of Mimi when she was alive. At least back then she had some idea where her mother *was*.

It turned out there was more, reason-wise, but it was purposely being kept from me at the time.

———

I can't tell you how anxious I am to jump straight to Gabriel, but a good storyteller doesn't leave gaps. To me, life only got interesting after I met him, but I know you'll probably ask me how we got thrown together in the first place.

It started in the office of an adviser for the university. Something like a guidance-counselor person would be in high school, but as you rise through the levels of your education the titles of the people who serve you elevate as well.

My mom was talking to the adviser, whose name was Rita Wilson. I remember that, because I remember everything.

I was looking out the window at the sun in the trees, watching this noisy red-breasted bird hop around, and doing a math problem in my head. Not anything hard. Just enough of a problem to keep my brain on track but not enough to challenge me. Once I told my mom one of the problems out loud, just so she could see it was easy, and her eyes rolled back in her head. I was surprised. Back then I thought everybody would think it was a simple enough thing.

Did I mention I get bored easily? I've developed coping mechanisms over the years.

Then I came back into the moment, where I looked over and saw my mom twisting the strap of her purse.

She was pretty aggressive about gestures like that. She twisted until that leather strap looked like it would break under the strain. Until her fingers looked weirdly white. Like white-knuckle stuff, as the old saying goes, but it wasn't her knuckles. She had the ends of her first two fingers wrapped up tight.

Every one of my mom's gestures was part of a language. I can even translate her into English for you.

"Oh dear. Someone wants me to do something I don't want to do. Of course I'm not going to do it, but now this person will think badly of me and accuse me of being a bad mother. Not out loud, of course, but *there*. Right in *there*, behind her eyes."

Okay, maybe I embellish a little, because embellishment is my style. But trust me, that's the gist of the thing.

"What are we talking about?" I asked, and they both stared at me.

"Ru drifts away when her brain is not engaged," my mother said. "It's why I really can't take a chance on just moving her along with more jumps in grade level. Even though that might be better for her socially."

I thought that was an odd thing to say because, other than occasionally hanging out with my science teacher during lunch, I had no social life and she knew it.

More silence.

"So you're just not going to tell me?" I asked.

Rita Wilson stepped in.

She was a really tall, stunning Black woman with her hair in neat little braids that all merged into one long braid at the nape of her neck. She wore half glasses whose frames seemed to shimmer when the light hit them just right. Her lipstick was this spot-on perfect dark red.

5

"I was telling your mother that we have some families who will take in students in a more comprehensive sort of way. Rather than just renting out a room, they treat their boarder more like a member of the family. In other words, they would serve you family meals, drive you to campus . . . not just leave you on your own the way they might with an older student. And I even know for a fact that one of these families has a vacancy. A mother and son. Paula Gulbranson is the woman's name. Only about four miles from campus."

"But not part of the full-ride scholarship," my mom said, strangling her purse strap again.

"I'm afraid not," Rita Wilson said. "It would be an extra expense, if you can manage it. But I can tell you it's worked out well in the past."

That seemed to get my mom's attention. I could tell because she left her purse strap alone for a few seconds.

"Oh, so this has come up before? Other students my daughter's age have attended?"

"Well . . . ," Rita Wilson began. "No. Not during my tenure here. I won't say it never happens, but it's unusual. The students who roomed with this family in the past had physical disabilities that caused them to require additional support to attend."

More silence. More violence aimed at the strap of my mother's purse. I mean, lots and lots of silence and violence.

I was just about to leave in my head again when Rita Wilson said, "Why not just meet with this family? You've driven all the way here. I'm guessing you'll at the very least want lunch before the long drive home. Let me just see if they're available."

That was when my life got interesting. I thought the lunch would be hopelessly boring. I'm not wrong a lot, but occasionally I can be spectacularly wrong. In this case, I really had no idea how wrong it was even possible for a person to be.

———

The weird thing about the first time I met Gabriel is that my initial impression of him was not good at all.

He was sitting across the table from us. Next to his mom. I'll get to her in a while.

We weren't at the cafeteria on campus. We had decided to go to a little sidewalk café about a five-minute walk away because Gabriel's mom said the food was good there. I thought it was just okay.

I was watching him, and he never seemed to look up. He kept his eyes down, running one thumbnail along the gap where the aluminum edging around the tabletop met the table itself. His hair was just on the dark side of blond, longish, and combed back so it only looked long at the nape of his neck. He looked kind of clean-cut. Scrubbed, actually. Like someone had cleaned him till he was shiny.

But he wouldn't look up.

I thought, *What is wrong with this kid?*

I guess it's weird that I called him a kid in my head, because he's nearly five years older than I am. I'm not sure how to explain it, except that I sort of didn't think of *myself* as a kid—and, coincidentally, neither did anybody else.

I watched him for a long time, wondering what his problem could be.

And then, just like that, he looked up. Right into my face. And he smiled. And that smile was everything. It just utterly changed my world.

Don't get the wrong impression here. There was nothing even the tiniest bit romantic between Gabriel and me, and there never will be. In fact, there was nothing even the tiniest bit romantic *about* either Gabriel or me. Toward anyone. I think that was part of why we clicked so well. We were both missing that piece, which seemed to help our other pieces, our friend pieces, click.

But back to that smile.

It was shy and conspiratorial, all at the same time. It was contagious. I swear it made me crack a smile as well. It was as though he already liked me, and had decided to share a secret message with me. And the secret message was . . . *Life is fun.*

It had never occurred to me that life could be fun until I met Gabriel. It honestly never so much as crossed my mind.

———

The second time I met Gabriel was the same day, but later toward evening. My mom had taken us to his mother's house, where we had been invited to see the living quarters that would be mine if she agreed to this thing. Which we both knew she wouldn't.

My mom and Gabriel's mom were talking as if I weren't there. As if I didn't exist at all. Or at the very least as if I had no say in any of this. *Welcome to your childhood, if you didn't know already.*

"Go on upstairs," Gabriel's mom said after a time. When she noticed I did indeed exist. "It's the second door on the right."

I walked up the hardwood stairs, but I didn't go to the second door on the right. Because, as I passed the first door on the right, I could hear Gabriel singing. It wasn't loud, but it was definitely *out loud.* Not under his breath or anything like that. I just stood there for a few seconds, wondering how much confidence a person would have to have to sing in any manner that anyone else could even potentially overhear.

If the door had been closed, I wouldn't have knocked. I would have just walked on by. But it was standing wide open.

"Hi," I said.

He stopped singing and said, "Hi," in return. Then he went back to singing.

I wasn't sure what the song was. The tune was nothing I recognized, and I could only make out about half the words.

I just stood there until he ran out of song.

Then he said, "You can come in, you know."

"Oh," I said. "Actually, I didn't know."

"Well, you can."

I walked into his room.

He was sitting on the window seat, and the window was open. The panes opened out in two vertical sections, and there was no screen. He was half leaning out and looking down at the street. It was pretty dark in there. Just the spill of light from the hallway.

I walked over and sat next to him, and we looked down together.

The house was in a dramatically urban setting. Practically downtown. There was no front yard or anything. Just people walking up and down the sidewalk under his window. I thought the sun was nearly down, though it was hard to tell, because the sky had clouded over and begun threatening rain. You could see it might let go at any minute.

My eyes began to adjust to the light, and I looked over at him. And he looked back. And he smiled again. It wasn't the exact same smile I told you about before, but it was another one, and it was also good.

I noticed two things that struck me as a bit unexpected.

One, he was wearing eye makeup. Hard to say how much in that light, but definitely eyeliner and shadow, and possibly mascara.

Two, he had an old-fashioned watering can sitting next to him. The kind with a handle and a long spout with a big disk diffuser at the end that allowed the water to come out in separate drops. More like a shower and less like a stream.

"Whatcha doing?" I asked.

"I'll show you."

We waited a minute, apparently for a person to come by under the window. Then he picked up the can and sprinkled a few gentle drops of water down in that person's direction.

It appeared to be a young woman. She stopped. Held out her hand to see if there were more. Then she walked on. She never looked up for the source of the drops. Then again, why would she? Drops come from the sky, especially when the clouds are dark, and threatening rain.

"You're watering *people*?"

"Something like that."

"Wouldn't it be better to just fill some water balloons or something? She hardly even noticed."

"No," Gabriel said. "That's not what it is at all. I'm not trying to hit anybody with something to shock them or upset them. I'm just making them think it's started to rain. To see how they react to that."

We sat silently until a middle-aged man in a nice suit strode by under the window. Gabriel released a few drops. Without so much as pausing his quick steps, the man opened a black umbrella.

"There," Gabriel said. "See?"

I did not see.

"Well, now I know *what* you're doing, all right. The next word that comes to mind is *why?*"

"It's just a little experiment," he said. "It's just a way of seeing if you can change what people do. They always say you can't change the people around you. I think they must mean you can't change really deep things about their nature, and you can't make them change in just the ways you want them to change. But it seems to me you can't *help* but change the people you come in contact with. It might be small changes, but their lives can't possibly be just exactly what they were if you had never been there at all. Get it now?"

"Not really," I said.

I'm not sure if I mentioned it yet, but I'm a very honest person. As in, to a fault.

"It's something I got from my mom," he said, "when she drives. She doesn't speed. She drives the speed limit. Not under, but not over either. She says there's never enough money and a speeding ticket is a stupid thing to waste our money on. But it brings out the worst in other drivers. They tailgate her to the point where it's dangerous. So she does this thing she calls training the guy behind her. If he gets too close up on our tail, she'll take her foot off the gas and just slow down by two or three miles per hour. Then if he backs off a little she'll speed up again. Maybe she'll even do a mile over the limit just for that minute. And this goes on for a while, and he starts staying back because he doesn't want her to slow down . . . but what I always wonder is whether he consciously realizes what's going on. Kind of an impossible question to answer, since we'll never meet him, but I tend to think no, he doesn't. Because if people realized, I think some of them would honk or flip her off or try to pass. I think it's so subtle that it stays subconscious. That's my theory anyway. And just like that, she changed somebody. Kind of a heady concept, don't you think?"

I realized as I listened to him that Gabriel was also very smart. Maybe not like me, because hardly anyone was a freak like me, but much, much smarter than your average seventeen-year-old boy.

"Get it now?" he said.

"Yeah, I think so. It's about feeling like you have some control over something."

"Maybe," he said. "Maybe, yeah."

"You must do this a lot," I said.

"No, I never tried this particular experiment before."

"Then why do you have your own watering can?"

"It's just the one my mom uses on the houseplants."

I might have forgotten to mention that there were a lot of house-plants. It was a real rainforest in that house.

We sat quietly for a time, and nobody walked by under the window.

Then a bunch of people headed our way, but before they drew level with Gabriel's building the rain let go for real. They all popped open their umbrellas, except for one woman who didn't seem to have one. She covered her head with what looked like the evening paper and ran in spite of high heels.

"Experiment over," I said.

"I guess."

"Why do you wear eye makeup?" I asked.

Maybe I shouldn't have asked, but I was just curious. I hoped I hadn't sounded like I was judging. I was just curious.

"It's just me. It's who I am. It makes me feel more like myself. You know? Why? Does it bother you?"

"No, not at all. Why would it bother me? I was just curious because you weren't wearing any before. You know. At lunch."

"My mom told me I couldn't."

"Oh. She thought I would care?"

"I think she thought your mother might mind. And we really need to rent out that room. We need the money."

"Oh. That must be weird to have somebody tell you not to do a thing that makes you feel like yourself."

"It is," he said. "It's also the story of my life."

A moment's silence, punctuated by the sound of heavy rain.

Then he said, "Would your mother have minded?"

"I don't know," I said. "I'm not sure. We never talked about makeup on boys. Probably not. She probably only cares about the things that challenge her personally."

Then the two mothers in question came up the hardwood stairs, and my second meeting with Gabriel was over.

Maybe just as well. One side of us was starting to get a little bit wet.

———

It was a long drive home. An hour and a half. A long time to watch the windshield wipers swish back and forth, just at the edge of being unable to keep up.

For most of it, my mom and I didn't talk.

Then I decided that not talking was stupid at a time like that.

"Are you going to let me do it?"

"You're thirteen," she said.

For maybe half a minute I just watched the streetlights flash by through the rain-spotted windows, and the lights of oncoming cars, because I was too mad to answer.

"I hate it when you do that," I said at last.

"Do what?"

"State an obvious fact like it's some kind of argument."

"I think you already knew the answer to the question before you ever asked it," she said.

We drove for a few minutes in that silent rage that was so familiar to us. Such a natural part of our interactions.

"You know it was Grandma Mimi's last wish," I said.

"Don't do that."

"Do what?"

"Play the Grandma Mimi card."

"It's not a card," I said, raising my voice for the first time. "She wasn't a card. She was my grandmother. She was your mother."

"Now who's stating the obvious like it's some kind of argument?"

I never answered, because of the irritating factor of her being right.

———

The following morning she went out without telling me where she was going. Then she came back midafternoon without telling me where she had been.

Over an otherwise silent dinner she said, "We'll try that thing with the Gulbransons' house so you can attend the university. We'll try it for a semester and see."

I asked no questions, because I had what I wanted and didn't want to risk it. I just let my imagination run wild, thinking what it would be like to live in that house, with that interesting boy, and attend a university with a curriculum that didn't make me want to stare out the window and do math in my head. It sounded so heavenly that I didn't fully believe it was coming. It seemed too good to be true.

It would be months before I learned what had caused her sudden, dramatic, and uncharacteristic change of heart.

Chapter Two

The Point of a Study on Pointing

I begged my mom to take me there at least a week early, so I'd have time to unpack and get to know the Gulbransons before the semester started. I made it sound like a mental health request—like I needed it for my security—because she responded to that. In reality she was driving me up the wall with her nervousness about my going, and I knew I'd be happier somewhere else. Anywhere else.

She ended up driving me there just in time for Sunday dinner. I had to be at the university first thing Monday morning.

"Do you have your phone?" she asked.

She was biting her thumbnail. She'd never bitten her thumbnail. Not once in all the time I'd been alive to know her.

"Mom."

"What?"

"When do I ever not have my phone?"

"I'm sorry. I'm just . . ."

"You're just what, Mom?" I asked when I got tired of waiting for her to tell me.

"I feel like this is it."

"Like this is it for what?"

She sighed deeply and dramatically before answering.

"For your childhood, I guess. I feel like your childhood is ending."

"Interesting," I said.

"You don't agree?"

"That it's ending now? No. I don't agree. I think my childhood ended when I was five."

When I got to kindergarten. That was when I realized that kids were one thing and I was something else. Everyone else started catching on soon after.

"I'm sorry if I made mistakes," she said.

And I said, "I'm not sure if there was anything you could have done. I think the situation just is what it is."

———

Dinner in the Gulbranson household was surprisingly quiet. Almost stately.

I was served a stuffed zucchini with salad and bread on the side. The zucchini seemed to be stuffed with a generous helping of sausage, tomato, cracker crumbs, and parmesan cheese. Which meant Mrs. Gulbranson actually cooked.

It was pretty good, if you liked zucchini.

My mom's idea of dinner was to overcook some meat and serve it with side dishes straight out of a can. Corn, or that slimy gray, bitter version of spinach.

So I decided I would eat Mrs. Gulbranson's dinner, despite not being a huge zucchini fan. It was my version of giving her an A for effort.

She watched me eat for a few minutes off and on. Then she asked an odd question.

"Ru. Are you nervous about tomorrow?"

I looked up into her face and finished chewing before answering. I was not raised in a cave or a barn. I can be civilized.

"No. Why would I be nervous?"

"Well, it's . . . it's all new. A big university. Lots of changes."

"But it was made for people just like me. So I'm not sure what wouldn't fit."

She nodded too many times and remained silent after that.

See, this was the moment. This was that inevitable intersection between me and everybody else. That moment when I let somebody see in, even just the tiniest bit, and they realize I'm not like them. Not like anybody they're used to dealing with. Once I found it quite troubling, but now I'm pretty used to it. Why go through your life troubled over something that's not going to change? Suck it up and move on.

I guess I promised to say more about Gabriel's mom, didn't I?

She was short, and a little bit plump, and had rosy cheeks. Actual rosy cheeks, like Mrs. Santa Claus. That is, it didn't look like rouge. Could have been rosacea or a blood-pressure thing, or maybe she was Mrs. Santa Claus in disguise. Her hair was always done up just so, and she doled out smiles like she was paying debts, not like they had spontaneously erupted from within her. Just the opposite of her son.

Speaking of her son, he never said a word during dinner. He did smile those wonderful smiles at me. Three times. As it turned out, we would have plenty of time to talk later.

———

I was lying in bed that night, and I wasn't sleeping. Which is interesting, because usually I sleep. I had no special thoughts about that at the time.

I heard a voice, and it made me jump. It sounded like somebody right there in the room with me, which was a startling development. Like they were standing between the bed and the wall, which was impossible because the bed was right up against the wall. But anyway, that was how it sounded.

"Are you asleep?" the voice said.

It was quiet, but it was a voice. So it was startling. As I said.

"Gabriel?" I said, my heart feeling kind of poundy. "Where are you? Are you in my room?"

"No, I'm in *my* room," he said, still sounding like he was in mine.

"Why am I hearing you so well?"

"Two reasons. The walls are really thin, but that's not the main thing. There's a ventilation duct between the two walls. Right under the beds. But I won't talk to you if you don't want—if you want privacy or you just want to sleep."

"I don't mind talking," I said. We lay in the dark for a minute, and didn't. Then I said, "Did you talk through the duct to the other people who roomed here?"

"No," he said, and his voice was soft and sounded genuinely regretful. "They wanted privacy and sleep. Are you really not nervous about tomorrow?"

"I don't think so," I said. "I mean . . . how would I know?"

"Not sure how to answer that," he said. "I might not understand the question. I mean, when you feel something, it's just there. You just know."

I wanted to tell him that feeling things was not a specialty at our house, but I didn't want him to think I was weird.

"*I'm* nervous," he said. "Even though I only got into the state university."

"Oh, you're not going to Wellington? I didn't know that. I thought we were riding there together."

"I have to drop you off there and then drive another twenty miles."

"I'm surprised you didn't get in. You seem so smart."

"They say I just missed the cutoff. One more place and I would have had it."

"Oh, no," I said.

"What?"

"I took your place."

"I don't see it that way. I mean, they accepted a lot of people. Not just you."

I thought he was being too generous, but I didn't say so, because if someone is being too generous toward *you* I think it's best to keep your mouth shut.

We were quiet for a minute or two.

Then I said, "I just figure, the university is set up for people like me, so why be nervous? In fact, probably most of the people who go there are not as smart as I am. But I don't mean that the way it sounds."

"How do you mean it?"

"It sounds like I'm being braggy, but I'm really not. I mean, being smart is good, but only to a point. And I think I passed the point."

I waited, but he said nothing. So I continued.

Honestly, I don't know why I said what I said next to Gabriel. I mean, it was true. It had been true since I was five; I just don't know why I said it. I never had before. Somehow it just took no time at all for me to find a home in Gabriel and know I was safe there. But I can't explain how or why.

"When I was five," I said, "I overheard my mother talking to a friend of hers. Talking about me. She told her friend Donna that I was 'freakishly smart.'"

I paused, but nothing happened. I want to say I could hear him waiting, but I worry it'll sound daft. I felt like he didn't know the right thing to say yet, because he didn't yet know what I meant, so he was hoping I would go on. Yes, I understand that's too much to know through a wall, however thin, but that's how it felt.

"She thinks I'm a freak," I said.

"Oh, I don't think that's how she meant it."

"There's no other way to mean it."

"She meant your intelligence. Not *you*."

"But I *am* my intelligence. You can't separate us out."

"I don't think that's true," he said. "Here. Do a little experiment with me. Just try this. Point to yourself."

"Point to myself?"

"Just go with me. I have my reasons."

I sighed, but I did as he asked. In the dark, I could feel the tip of my index finger press into the spot between my eyebrows.

"Now what?" I asked him.

"Now tell me where you're pointing."

"My forehead."

"Really?"

"Yes, really. Why? Where am I supposed to be pointing?"

"It's just that they did this study. And everybody points to their heart. *Everybody.* Well. I guess not everybody, but . . . that's just . . ."

"Weird?" I asked. "Freakish?"

"I was going to say 'interesting.'"

But he might have been toning it down for me.

"I'm different, all right," I said. "You'll learn that about me after a while. But anyway. Listen. What was that study all about, anyway? Why would somebody do a study on where people point when you ask them to point to themselves? What's the point of that? No pun intended."

"It was in a bigger context," he said. "It was about heart transplants. And about how people will tell you they're their brains but if you ask them to point to themselves they'll point to their hearts. They'll also tell you they don't believe in cellular memory, and they don't think a human heart carries anything over to the recipient during a transplant. But then the vast majority of people say they wouldn't want a heart from a murderer. So I just thought that was interesting."

"You don't need a heart transplant, do you?"

"Oh, no. I'm fine. I just find stuff like that fascinating."

We didn't talk for a time.

Then he said, "I don't think your mom meant any harm when she said that."

I was thinking that people do harm all the time without meaning any. But that wasn't what I said.

I said, "It's just hard when your own mother thinks you're a freak."

"Smart is good," he said.

"To a point. But I think I passed that point."

Right, I know. I said that before. But anyway, I said it again.

I don't remember anything more from my talk with Gabriel that night. It could be because I was getting sleepy, but I doubt it, because I have an eidetic memory and hyperthymesia—which is an unusual combination and pretty much another way of saying I don't forget anything, ever—and they seem to work under all conditions. More likely I fell asleep without even realizing it, and not another word was said.

———

I knew everybody would want to know how my first day of college went. Believe me, I knew. Because those were the first words out of everybody's mouth. Even Gabriel, and he didn't usually ask the more obvious questions.

I'll tell you girls what I told him, and hopefully that will be enough. I'm not going to get into a whole long story about it because—spoiler alert—it was boring. Why tell boring stories?

Stop rolling your eyes at me, please. We talked about that.

He picked me up in front of the student union. It was a deal my mom had insisted on, quite sure I would be kidnapped and killed if I walked from campus out to the street.

Gabriel drove this car . . . How do I describe this car?

It was older. Oh, who am I kidding? It was old. From the '90s, I think. A Nissan. It was yellow. But I don't just mean yellow. I mean *so, so* yellow. Blindingly yellow. It ran really well, though, despite its age, because his father had put a brand-new engine in it before giving it to Gabriel for his sixteenth birthday. He ran a mechanics shop, Gabriel's father, but he was pretty much estranged from the family because Gabriel's mother couldn't stand him.

I got in and put on my seat belt, and we headed toward home.

"How was your first day?" he asked.

I was surprised because, like I said, he tends to ask the more skate-under-the-radar questions. The ones other people miss.

"Before I tell you," I said, "I'll ask you the same question. It was your first day of college, too. So . . . how did it go?"

"It was . . ." He paused for a time, as if the right word was escaping him. "Kind of . . . wonderful."

"Oh," I said. "That's nice to hear."

At least one of us had had a good experience, so I was glad of that. We drove without talking for a few seconds.

His hair was freer. More *down*. Not slicked back. It fell all around his head and shoulders like the mane on a lion, and it was wavier than I had realized. Almost at the edge of soft curls. I noticed that he had put on blue nail polish for his first day, but not all the same color of blue. Three different shades, distributed seemingly at random on his various fingers, which were graceful and long. Almost chiseled looking, like something a really good sculptor would carve out of marble.

He noticed me noticing.

"I hope nobody gave you a hard time about the nail polish," I said, so he would know it wasn't my own reaction I was worried about.

"Not at all," he said. "That's one of the things that was so wonderful about it. In high school most people were too caught up in their own drama to care, but there were always those times when the jocks would have nothing better to do than make my life miserable. But in college . . . it's like people aren't so . . . it's not like a small town. Not that this is a small town, or like my high school was one. It just had that kind of vibe. But the university was more . . . I want to say cosmopolitan, but I'm not sure that's the right word. Sophisticated? Is that the word I'm searching for?"

"I don't know," I said. "But it must at least be close, because I know what you're saying. I had a peer group too, so I get it. They thought I was from outer space. Not that I care. Well. Maybe I care. Maybe I don't care now because I gave up, but maybe I cared at the time."

"Your turn," he said.

"Oh. Right."

I sighed.

"Not good?" he asked.

"No. Not very."

He didn't ask any more questions. He just waited while I put my thoughts together, which was an experience a little like the proverbial herding of felines.

"All the time I've been in school," I said, "I've been bored. No matter how many grades they skipped me over, it was still a matter of instantly getting what was being taught and then staring out the window and figuratively drumming my fingers until everybody else got it. All day, every day. Waiting for the rest of the world to halfway catch up. Everybody talked to me like the university would be some kind of panacea for that. I guess I let them oversell it to me. I thought I'd be all tingly with educational stimulation and excitement because I was finally in an environment where the learning was happening at my level. But I'm not sure why I let myself believe that, because I told you last night that I'd be smarter than most of my fellow students. Again, not meant to be braggy. At least they don't have to feel like freaks. Anyway. This is probably more than you wanted to know. Perfectly simple question. How was my first day? It was just like all the other days. It was . . . basic."

"Wow," Gabriel said. "That's too bad. I wonder how you solve a problem like that?"

"I'm not sure you do," I said. "Trigonometry was pretty acceptable. And I mostly enjoyed Introduction to Astrophysics. I made a friend of my astrophysics teacher. I think there's a chance she might meet with me privately and tutor me at a higher level."

"That's something," he said.

"Yeah. That's something."

We stopped at a light, and waited, and I watched the way the red disk of stoplight reflected in the hood of his very yellow car.

"I'm beginning to wonder what it's all for," I said.

"Life?"

"That too. But I meant education."

"Oh. Well, I guess that depends. I figure it's to get you where you want to go in life. What are you studying to be?"

"I'm going to go to medical school," I said. "But I don't picture myself being your friendly local physician. I haven't got the bedside manner for it. I figure I'm better suited to medical research."

He tapped his fingers on the steering wheel, but didn't answer. Then the light changed and we drove again.

"You didn't say it," I told him.

"Say what?"

"'Maybe you'll discover the cure for cancer.'"

"That's setting you a pretty high bar."

"I suppose. But that's not what bothers me when people say it. It's the sheer repetition. There's nothing wrong with the sentiment, and the people who say it mean no harm. But anything that's said to you hundreds of times, always in the same words . . . it's going to get old."

"I guess," Gabriel said. "But anyway, you need education to get there. So that's what it's for, right? To get you to medical school."

"But there's a bigger question," I said. "Do I *want* to get to medical school? Or is it just assumed that I'll get there because I can? Because I'm smart enough?"

To his credit, Gabriel didn't try to answer that clearly unanswerable question.

———

When we got home, Gabriel's mom stuck her head out of the kitchen with her eyes shiny. With that bright face. I wondered if she was really as happy as her face wanted the world to believe. If anybody possibly could be.

She looked to me before her own son.

"How was your first day?"

I sighed inwardly, but I made sure it didn't come out into the world to be heard.

"Fine," I said. "It was fine."

"Your mother called. She wants you to call her back as soon as you get home."

I walked off into my room to do that while Gabriel's mother presumably asked her son the same dreaded question. Except it wasn't dreaded to him, because his first day was cosmopolitan and sophisticated and wonderful.

"Hey, Mom," I said when I heard her pick up.

"Hey, sweetie. How was your first day?"

I sat with my eyes closed for a second or two, once again trying to keep my sigh silent. It wasn't as though I hadn't seen the question coming.

"Fine," I said. "It was fine."

Honesty didn't feel like an option, because she would have loved an excuse to bring me home. Or so I thought.

"Good. I'm glad. So, listen. Honey. Slight change of plans. I'm not going to be able to come get you and bring you home this weekend. Something came up."

I waited, figuring she would tell me what. Not that I cared. I was happy to stay there with Gabriel. But people like to say things like that out loud, so I gave her the space to do it.

"A work thing," she said after too long a pause.

I knew she was lying. I just didn't know why.

When you've lived with someone all your life, you know how to read them. For all there was to be said against my mom, she did have her good qualities. And one was honesty. She was mostly honest. So when she lied, she did so awkwardly, probably as a result of not enough practice.

I wasn't answering, and that seemed to make her nervous.

"I'm so, so sorry," she said. "Your first weekend and all. Are you feeling homesick?"

"Mom."

"What?"

"You dropped me here, like, twenty-four hours ago."

"Right, right. But you'll have all week, and then the weekend, and then another whole week."

"It really doesn't matter, Mom. I'm fine here. I'll be fine. I have Gabriel to talk to, and I'll probably have to study all weekend anyway."

See? I can lie, too. I should be so lucky that I had to study to keep up in my classes.

"If you're sure," she said.

We chitchatted about this and that for a few minutes.

I hate chitchat.

While we were talking I kept wondering why she'd really canceled the weekend. All I could think was that she was back in touch with her father, my grandfather, and she didn't want anyone to know about it. Maybe she was visiting him in his nursing home. I'm not sure why that thought came into my head, except that Grandma Mimi had just left us, and that was a reunion Mimi would not have tolerated well while she was alive.

"I'll *call* you on the weekend," she said.

"That's fine," I said without much enthusiasm.

We hung up the phone.

I sat on the bed for a minute or two, just staring at the screen of my phone.

Then I said, out loud, "Fine. Don't tell me. See if I care."

———

"Maybe she has a boyfriend," Gabriel said.

Oddly, it was an idea that had never crossed my mind.

We were lying in the dark, each in our own room, talking quietly through the ventilation duct. There was a tree outside the window— one of those small, scraggly things that cities allow to grow up out of a square hole in the sidewalk—and the streetlight just beyond it threw shadows of its lightly blowing branches onto my wall. It was nice.

"That's hard to picture," I said. "She hasn't had any men in her life since the divorce. But I guess anything's possible. She could tell me that, though. I mean, why keep it a secret?"

"Sometimes when a relationship is new people want to keep it to themselves until they're sure it's really going somewhere."

"Maybe," I said. "I guess she's sort of an empty nester now. Maybe there are all kinds of things she's been wanting to do while she was too busy raising me."

Still, I couldn't think of a one. Not a single, solitary one. Or why she would need to keep any of them from me.

It was a good thing I fell asleep and didn't waste too much time on theories, because, looking back, I wasn't even close. I wasn't even in the right neighborhood.

It was just not the kind of thing a person tends to imagine.

Chapter Three

An Inch from the Flat-Earth Theory

I was talking to my new school friend—my Introduction to Astrophysics teacher. Her name was Ms. Stepanian, and she was young, as professors go. She was tall and slim and wore jeans but with really nice blazer-type jackets on top. Nice blouses, too—pure silk and such. It was like she was always dressed up on top but the part of her below the waist didn't get the memo.

"Here's the thing about astrophysics," I said.

"Okay. Tell me the thing about astrophysics."

"You kind of know that everything you're learning is wrong."

We were in her big auditorium-style teaching room. Or whatever you call that in college. Sorry. What can I tell you? It was only my second day. There were never any windows in those rooms. I guessed they were cracking down on my one remaining defense mechanism for boredom. And everybody else's, of course—it wasn't like I thought they removed all the windows just because I was about to attend.

"Extrapolate," she said.

"Science is always learning something new."

"Which is a good thing."

"But then we find out that what we used to believe about the universe was wrong."

"Sometimes. Not always. Sometimes new discoveries disprove previous theories. Other times they confirm them and go on to expand on them."

"The new space telescope," I said. "The James Webb. They should have named it after someone else."

I was going off on a tangent with that last sentence and I knew it. But I couldn't stop myself.

"I hear you," she said.

"But that was not my actual point about the JWST."

"I didn't figure it was."

"My point was that we welcome it, even though it's probably going to show us that a lot of what we believed about the universe was wrong. Even the people who came up with the theories that might be about to explode into dust. They welcome the JWST."

"They're scientists."

"And you're a scientist, right?"

"I'd like to think so," she said.

We were sitting on her desk, and she was eating a Cobb salad out of a bubble-shaped plastic container. I watched her pick around in there with a disposable fork.

"So," I said, "I guess my question is . . . how do you do that?"

"Welcome the very thing that might disprove your theories?"

"Right. That."

I was eating a meatball sub. I'd said that last thing while my mouth was still a teeny, tiny bit full, which made me feel like she would think my mother raised me wrong. Maybe in a barn or something.

I looked up at her face. I'd been looking down to make sure I didn't get marinara sauce on my shirt and then have to walk around like that for the rest of the day. She had one eyebrow arched upward. Like she was trying to figure me out. Distill me into something that made sense.

"You don't like to be wrong?" she asked.

"No, it's not that."

"Okay . . ."

Then she just waited. Chewed, and waited.

"It's more like . . . I like things that hold still. When you look at reality and accept it as reality and then you find out the whole thing was a misperception . . . it's like an earthquake."

Having lived every day of my life in California, I felt qualified to say so. But it was clear by her face that she wasn't getting me.

"How is it like an earthquake, now? Explain that to me."

"The ground under your feet is supposed to be solid. It's supposed to be something you can count on. I mean, once upon a time the best scientific minds of the day thought the Earth was flat. But more recently. Like, 1917. Einstein's static universe. And then Edwin Hubble came along with the redshift relationship and demonstrated that the universe is constantly expanding. And of course we're so proud of all we know now. Like we've come so far from there. But have we? What if we haven't? What if we're something like an inch from the flat-Earth theory and thousands of miles from where we need to be?"

"Always a possibility," she said.

"Learning facts that might not be facts at all feels like walking around on shifting sand. Like there's nowhere to stand. It makes me uneasy. So I'm going to ask again. How do you do it?"

She set down her salad. Put the bubble-shaped bowl on her desk near where she was sitting, dropped the fork into it, and wiped her mouth on a tiny, skimpy paper napkin. Carefully, more like blotting, so as not to smear her lipstick. Or so I assumed.

"And I will answer that. But first I want to ask *you* a question. What do you like to do for fun?"

This absolute silence rang out. Both in the room and inside me. I just felt blank all over, from my brain down to my toes. I could not have been more stunned by the question. She might as well have thrown a glass of ice water in my face.

Time stretched out, and I wasn't answering.

"Just as I suspected," she said.

"What did you suspect?"

"That you would have no answer. That you wouldn't know."

She waited for a reaction from me, but I still had nothing. So she went on.

"You hear the word, and you know what it means in a purely intellectual sense. But you don't really know what people mean when they say it. You don't know how they *feel*. You watch people have fun and it's like listening to a conversation in a foreign language."

I realized as she spoke that my mouth was open. Thank goodness there was no meatball sub in there at the moment.

"How did you know all that?" I asked.

"I was an intellectually gifted child myself."

I mulled that over for a time. Took another bite, chewed it thoroughly. Swallowed.

Then I dove in.

"So if you have brains you can't have fun?"

"No, of course you can. And many gifted students do. Some are very balanced and rounded. But I've noticed that when a child has a big, obvious gift, sometimes the people around that child focus on the gift to the exclusion of everything else. Anyway, I just wanted to get you thinking about that."

I thought about it for a while. Several minutes. And we didn't have a lot of time left. In a mere seven minutes her next class would come in, and lunch would be over. And our talk would be over.

"I have a new friend," I said. "I feel like I have fun when I'm with him."

"What do you two do that's fun?"

"Just talk, mostly. Once we did an experiment to see if we could change people's behavior in a small way." I paused, feeling bad because I figured it was not enough. "Does that count?"

"Sure," she said. "Of course. Everything counts."

I glanced at the clock again. Six minutes.

"You haven't answered my question," I said.

"Right. Okay. And I will. Here's the answer. Here's how I do it. I love the vast reaches of the universe *because* it's so completely beyond us, physically and otherwise. I love it *for* that, not in spite of it. Its impenetrable nature makes it something like a higher power to me. I study at its feet. I never expect to really know or understand it. I never strive to be equal to it, because such a thing would be patently impossible. The very nature of it stretches my brain almost to the breaking point, and that's pretty much the textbook definition of awe, in my opinion. And awe is good. If you want a piece of advice, always choose to live your life in a way that promotes awe. Forget the solid-ground thing. It doesn't exist anyway. Go for the awe. Revel in the feeling that a thing is so big you can never know it. Know what you can about it, but love the fact that it can't truly be known, because that means it's so vast and complex that it's almost like what people talk about when they talk about God. Why would you want to bring that down to our size just to help yourself feel secure? Then nothing so awe-inspiring would exist."

Just as she finished the last sentence, the first of her students wandered in. A bored-looking girl with her long hair falling over her face. She sat in the very back. The farthest corner. Why did people do that? I always sat in the front row to soak up as much as I could.

"That," I said, "is a really, really . . . *really* . . . good answer."

Finally. Finally somebody was speaking to me at a level that didn't make me want to stare out the window.

———

Dinner that night was a chile relleno casserole. All the ingredients of a good chile relleno but baked together in layers in a casserole dish instead of fried. Gabriel's mom served refried beans on the side. I like refried beans.

"What did you learn in school today?" she asked.

As usual, she was looking at me.

You would think she'd be more interested in what her son was learning. But she seemed to think she owed me the attention as part of the rental agreement. As though curiosity about my studies was one of the things my mom was paying her for.

"All of it?" I asked. "It took me over six hours to learn it all. I could tell you every word of it, but I don't think it would fit into dinnertime."

She laughed nervously. Uncomfortably. See? I knew she was not as happy as her face wanted the world to believe.

"Well, maybe not every word of it," she said. "Maybe just the most important thing."

"How do I know what's important?"

Honestly, I wasn't trying to be difficult. I wasn't giving her a hard time on purpose. I was just pretty literal at that age, and not very much into nuance.

"I guess . . . ," she began, "maybe just the thing you found most interesting."

Once again I mentally doubted the value of this game. But I answered the question.

"I learned that awe is more important than solidity."

"Awe?" she asked.

"Yes," I said. "Awe."

"That's not the usual type of thing they teach in a university."

"Right," I said. "True. It's not. That's probably why it was the most interesting thing."

I looked up at Gabriel, and he gave me another of his signature smiles. Small but wonderful. It was a lot like the first one. The "life is fun" one. But this one was more like "Ru is fun." So that made me feel good. That made it my favorite of all the Gabriel smiles, and that's not the easiest contest in the world to win.

———

I was lying in bed talking to Gabriel when he asked me this question.

"What made you want to take astrophysics, anyway? You don't need it for medical school."

"No."

"I just wondered."

"I had to take something that was just for me. That I might actually find interesting."

"Right," he said. "I agree. I just wondered why that one."

I lay quietly for a minute and listened to the music downstairs. Gabriel's mother was into vinyl. Actual old vinyl records that you needed a phonograph to play. The current selection was some kind of swing or big band music, though I'd never heard the band. Why would I know anything about swing music? I was thirteen. People were always forgetting that, but it was true.

"My father used to take me camping," I said. "Before he passed away."

"Oh. I didn't know your father died. I'm really sorry."

"Thanks. We would go off just the two of us. He would take me but not my mom, because he told me once 'I could hold a gun to your mother's head and tell her "We're going camping or else" and she would say "Fine, go ahead and shoot."' He liked to go places where the stars were really clear at night. One time he took me to Kelso Dunes in Mojave—in that preserve in the Mojave Desert. It was November. Really cold at night. We were sitting outside in camp chairs and I was all wrapped up in two blankets. I was six. All of a sudden we started seeing all these Leonid meteors. They just exploded out from a single point like a fireworks show. And the stars were so bright and clear behind them. The moon was down and the sky was so perfectly dark except for the natural light show. I just always remember that."

"You remember everything," he said. "You have an eidetic memory."

"Right, but when I remember this, I *enjoy* remembering."

We lay there in silence for a couple of minutes. The music had changed. Now it was the soundtrack from *Oklahoma!* Not that I really knew much about that old musical, but it was right there in the lyrics they were singing.

"I want to say something about that," Gabriel said. "But I don't want you to think I'm judging or criticizing."

"I wouldn't think that about you. It's just not who you are. Go ahead and say what you're thinking."

"It sounds like you had this *feeling*. This really wonderful *feeling* experience about being out under the stars. And somehow you managed to turn it into an intellectual exercise. Your reaction to that beautiful feeling was to decide to study the formation of the universe and how stars and planets are born and die. You made the whole thing academic."

"Of course I did. That's what I do."

He didn't answer.

"I mean . . . should I do something different?"

"I can't decide that for you. But it's something to think about."

So I thought about it.

I thought about it so much that night that I only got a couple hours of sleep and I was super tired in all my classes the next day.

But here's the problem: I *thought* about it. I thought about how I have a problem with thinking too much.

Leave it to me to think I can solve a thinking problem by thinking.

———

When I came down the stairs for breakfast the next morning, Gabriel's mother was on the phone. But I had no reason to think that had anything to do with me, because why would I think that? Why *would* it?

I do realize I'm not the center of the universe.

I could smell oatmeal, and that's one of my favorites. Throw in milk and lots of brown sugar, and that's just about the world's best breakfast, especially on a cool fall morning.

Gabriel was still upstairs brushing his teeth. I knew because I heard him as I walked by the upstairs bathroom. He was a very noisy tooth brusher. I have no idea how a thing like that works, but it's true.

Just as I was about to take that last step into the kitchen I heard Gabriel's mom say something into the phone, and it caught me.

"Yes, of course. I'm clear on whose daughter she is."

At that moment it *did* dawn on me that the call might have something to do with me.

Of course I stopped walking and did not step into the kitchen.

"Well, I certainly don't mean to step on your toes, and I do understand it's not really my place. But with a thing like this . . . Well. My grandfather had this old saying about advice. He always said you should never give advice unless it's life or death, or the person asks for your advice. And of course you didn't ask."

A pause while the other person was—apparently—talking. It certainly crossed my mind that the other person was my mom. Then again, Gabriel's mother might have known other people with daughters. It was not a unique situation.

"I guess not for *her*," she said.

More pausing.

"It's not that I don't understand why you feel that way, but children can handle a lot of honesty. More than we give them credit for, I think. We think the truth will hurt them, but the truth always comes out in the long run, and then there's damage from the fact that they weren't told the truth right out of the gate. But of course it's your decision."

Even more pausing.

"I'm sorry you feel that way. It won't happen again. I give you my word. From now on I'll keep my thoughts to myself."

Just at that moment Gabriel popped up behind me, out of nowhere. At least, it felt like a popping-out-of-nowhere thing.

"Hey," he said.

It startled me, and I jumped a step forward, and this weird little sound came out of my throat.

"I have to go," Gabriel's mother said.

And she very quickly hung up the phone.

So by then I was pretty much thinking it was about me.

———

We had been sitting down to breakfast for maybe a minute when my phone rang. Maybe two minutes as an outside guess.

I looked down at the phone and saw it was my mom calling.

"Oh," I said. Mostly to Gabriel's mother, though I wasn't looking at her. "I shouldn't get this during a family meal. That would be rude."

"No, go ahead and take it," she said. "Just this once."

As though it was important. As though she already knew it would be.

I clicked to accept the call.

"Hey, Mom," I said.

"Hi, darling," she said, and she sounded terrible. Like she was sick and had not one ounce of energy.

"You sound terrible," I said. "No offense."

"None taken," she said. "I have the flu."

"Oh. I'm sorry. Are you okay there by yourself?"

"Yeah. Of course. I'll be fine. But I don't think I should drive out there and pick you up next weekend either. I'm so sorry to let you down, but I'm not even sure I'm safe on the road when I'm this sick, and besides, no point passing it on to you."

"Sure," I said. "I get it. It's okay."

I glanced up at Gabriel's mom, who would have been the world's worst poker player, and once again I got the distinct impression that she knew something.

———

While Gabriel was driving me to the university, I said, "I think your mom knows what my mom's big secret is."

"Why do you think that?"

"I heard her talking on the phone this morning. I could be wrong. It could have been somebody else with a daughter."

"Want me to feel her out about it?"

"Would you?"

"Sure, of course. But I have to warn you, it's not likely to get me far. If she's been sworn to secrecy about something, you couldn't pry her open with a crowbar."

Unfortunately, he turned out to be right.

He kept after her for days, poking and hinting. But if she knew anything about my home situation, she never gave it up.

Chapter Four

When a Toucan Met a Penguin

It was between my mom's fourth and fifth cancellation that I decided to enlist Gabriel's help.

We were driving home in the afternoon. His phone was sitting on the car's console between us, and honestly, that was only a distraction at this juncture of events, because his lock screen was an image of an Atlantic puffin.

"Oh my gosh!" I said, loudly enough to startle him halfway into the next lane. Which fortunately was empty.

Kind of a quaint, colloquial expression on my part. "Oh my gosh." But my mother had taught me not to throw God's name around in conversation. She was not religious at all, and she didn't care about it for herself, but she said I would never know who I might offend. It wouldn't have been Gabriel, but the whole thing was force of habit by then.

"What?" he said. "You scared me."

"Sorry. But you have a puffin on your phone."

"Because I love puffins," he said.

I pulled my phone out of my pocket, swiped away the messaging app, and showed him my home screen image. It was . . . wait for it . . . an Atlantic puffin. But Gabriel's puffin was flying low, coming in for a landing on some presumably Icelandic cliff. Mine was just standing there on those odd duck feet with a mouth full of those little fish puffins like. A line of them, drooping in an orderly fashion from his wildly colorful beak. Still, the coincidence was pretty astounding.

"*I* love puffins!" I said. No, not quite accurate. I didn't *say* it. I squealed it. Shrieked it. Fortunately this time he was prepared to drive right through my enthusiasm. "All my life I've been trying to get my mom to take me somewhere where they have Atlantic puffins. But she hates to fly. She never says straight out that she has a phobia about it, but it's really the only explanation at this point. She offered to drive me up the coast of Oregon. They have tufted puffins up there. But a tufted puffin is not the same."

"*So* not the same," Gabriel said.

"An Atlantic puffin is so whimsical."

"They look like cartoon characters," he said.

"They do! I always think they look like a cross between a penguin and a toucan."

"Wow," Gabriel said. "I never thought of it that way. But now that you say it, it's so true."

Unfortunately, by this time I was beginning to remember the mental agenda that had been so clearly planted in my brain when I climbed into his car. Too bad, because it was not nearly as much fun as an Atlantic puffin.

Then again, what is?

"I apologize in advance for the sudden change of direction," I said. "But I want to ask you a big favor. If my mom cancels one more time for this weekend, will you take me to see her?"

"Well, sure," he said. "I mean, if it's okay with my mom. I mean . . . didn't your mom say not to come, though?"

"She did. She said she didn't want to give me the flu. But that was weeks ago when she first got it. How can she still be contagious?"

"I guess we can ask her again."

"Not really what I had in mind," I said. "I was thinking more that we could . . . sort of . . . surprise her."

"Oh," Gabriel said. And, for a full minute or so, nothing more.

"I realize it's a big ask."

"No, it's fine," he said. "You need to know what's going on. We'll make up some kind of story for my mom. We'll say she wanted you to come. We'll just do it."

———

She canceled one more time for that weekend.

———

I stood on the front stoop of our house and knocked, even though I—of course—had a key. But it's one thing to unexpectedly find someone at your door and quite another to unexpectedly find them standing inside your house. The latter would just about be enough to give a person a coronary.

I heard the sound of footsteps coming to the door.

Gabriel was standing about three steps behind me on one of the stone stairs. I turned halfway around and smiled at him, and he gifted me with one of those wonderful Gabriel smiles in return.

"That's a good sign," I said. "She's well enough to come answer a knock."

The door swung open.

Standing in the entryway was my aunt Bitsy. Not my mother. My aunt Bitsy.

"You're not supposed to be here," she said. She looked past me, narrowing her eyes at Gabriel suspiciously. "And who are *you*?"

My aunt Bitsy was a gigantic woman. Not overweight at all—that's not what I mean. Tall, with big bones and broad shoulders. Wide hips. Just a lot of woman, imposing and intimidating, with small, close-set eyes and unpleasantly coarse hair. And we had never gotten along. My mother had often said it was because we each took stock of the other and cited irreconcilable differences. I had always thought it was because she was horrid.

"What are you doing here?" I asked her.

"I was just about to ask you the same question," she said.

I lived there, but I wasn't sure it was the best answer right in that moment.

My aunt Bitsy lived in Kentucky. *Kentucky.* And this was California. I did mention that this was California, right? I think I did. If not, sorry.

"She didn't tell me you were coming for a visit," I said. "Also you never come for a visit."

"It's because she isn't feeling well," Aunt Bitsy said.

She still had not stepped out of the doorway to allow us in. To my own damned house.

"It's two thousand three hundred and three miles," I said.

"You and your photographic memory," she said, even though I'd told her many times that that's not what it's properly called. I always thought she did that on purpose. Also, she said it as though she found it personally inconvenient that I knew things.

"Isn't that a long way to travel," I said, "just because your sister has the flu?"

She opened her mouth to blast something back at me, but nothing came out. Whatever she was about to say seemed to get stuck. She closed her mouth again. Glanced down at the welcome mat.

Then, finally, she stepped back out of the doorway to allow us through.

"Well, you're here," she said. "So I suppose you might as well come in."

I think that was Aunt Bitsy's version of a warm welcome, but it's hard to know for sure.

My mom was in bed, and she looked like death itself. Her hair was limp and lifeless, her face deadly pale. She barely looked like my mother. It was alarming. She looked up at me like I'd surprised her while she was robbing a bank.

"What are you doing here?" she asked.

I opened my mouth to say something polite and conciliatory. Something about how I'd been concerned about her welfare. Before it could make its way through my brain and out my mouth I contracted a bad case of the honests.

"I guess I'd had just about as much as I could take of secret keeping," I said. I almost said "being lied to," but I softened it at the last moment.

I was standing in her open bedroom doorway. I could feel the big shadow-presence of my aunt Bitsy behind me. Gabriel, being a wise person, had opted to wait outside. He had a way of knowing when he was not welcome. So did I, but I didn't care.

"I have no idea why you would say a thing like that to me," my mother said. Even her voice sounded lifeless.

I opened my mouth to say something, but I swear I don't know what it would have been. I guess I was willing to allow my words to surprise me.

I never got that far. Aunt Bitsy beat me to it.

"Oh good heavens, Mitzy!" she bellowed. "Just tell the girl the truth!"

I might've forgotten to mention that my mom and her sister were named Mitzy and Bitsy. If they had been identical twins, it would have been so cute you could lose your lunch over it. But they weren't any kind of twins. Bitsy was four years older, and they were of such different statures that it raised eyebrows about Grandma Mimi's fidelity to my grandpa.

But I don't mean to digress. We were right in the middle of an important something, weren't we? When the heat is on, my mind tends to flit around.

"I can't," my mom said, and her voice was so hopeless and devoid of energy that it was barely a voice at all. "I just can't. I can't bring myself to do it."

"Want me to do it?" Aunt Bitsy asked.

For what seemed like a long time, my mother offered no reply. I couldn't tell if she was thinking or had just run out of the initiative one needs to say words.

Meanwhile my mind was flitting. Hopping here and there like a little birdie on some kind of speed-type drug. In retrospect I call that fear. I had no idea what to call it at the time.

Then my mother nodded just the tiniest bit.

"Come downstairs," Aunt Bitsy said to me. "I'll make us a cup of tea. We'll talk."

———

"What on earth is the story with that boy?" she asked while the kettle was heating.

"He's my friend," I said.

"He seems a bit odd."

"He's not odd at all. He's one of the best people I know. If not *the* best person. And I will not take kindly to anything said against him. And, also, I can't believe you're keeping me waiting on this thing by talking about something completely unrelated."

She sat down at the table with that deep grunting sound people make when they're old. Except she wasn't old. Well, I guess what I mean is that she *shouldn't have been* old at her chronological age. But she was.

"It's not the flu," she said. "It's lung cancer."

"Oh."

That wasn't much of a response, but in the moment it was all I had. Looking back, I think I was in a little bit of shock. At the time I only knew I was missing what it took to really meet that moment.

No one said anything for a truly bizarre space of time.

The kettle whistled while we weren't saying anything, and Aunt Bitsy got up and made us each a cup of tea, set them on the table in front of us, and sat down across from me again.

"My mother doesn't smoke," I said.

"No," Aunt Bitsy said. "She doesn't."

"You think she smoked and we didn't know it?"

"No. She didn't smoke."

"You can get lung cancer if you never smoked?"

"Yes," Aunt Bitsy said, blowing on her hot tea. "It's less common. But it happens."

"How long has she known?"

"She went to the doctor not long before your semester started. She didn't want to tell you because she thought you'd delay your education if you knew."

I never answered that. My brain spun with answers, but I think they all tripped over each other in there and fell down. Or something like that.

I thought, *Of course I would have delayed college. Who wouldn't?* I thought, *Would that really have been so bad? I'm thirteen. I'm starting college at thirteen. I'm five years ahead of the crowd and that means we're in a hurry . . . why?*

I didn't say any of it.

Instead I geared up for something far more important. Far more difficult. It took me a minute, but I pulled myself together and got it done. I'm good in crisis, probably because I make everything cerebral.

"Prognosis?"

"Months."

"Months?"

"Not very many months at that."

"Wait," I said. "Wait. Wait."

"I'm not sure where you think I'm going."

"You can be fine enough that you don't even know you have a problem, and then go to the doctor and find out, and then only have *months*?"

"With lung cancer, yes you can. It can go very fast."

"And she robbed me of a few weeks I could have spent with her."

"That's exactly what I tried to tell her," Aunt Bitsy said. "But you know how your mother is. She's a very stubborn woman."

I jumped to my feet and said, "I have to go."

I hadn't known I was about to jump to my feet. I hadn't known I had to go. All of life was a surprise to me in that moment. Nothing was anything that could be seen coming.

"What about your tea?" Aunt Bitsy asked.

"I just have to go."

"I could put it in a travel cup."

"Okay. Sure."

"Is there anything you'd like me to tell your mother?"

I almost said, "Tell her I'll never forgive her for this." I came very close to saying it. But those are the kinds of things you regret after somebody is gone. Not that I honestly believed, accepted, or even had absorbed that my mother was about to be gone. But I had the thought. So I guess it was in there somewhere.

"No," I said. "There's nothing I'd like you to tell her."

———

Gabriel and I were driving out of town, headed back to his mother's house, when I said, "I think I'm really angry with her for stealing this time from me. Even though I sort of know I wasn't acting like I wanted it. But looking back it feels stolen."

He kept his eyes on the road while he answered. I noticed that his voice was soft. Then, and also always. But then more than usual. His voice was . . . I want to say "small," but that sounds pejorative, and I'd never mean it that way. It was small in a way that made him seem bigger. I guess that made no sense at all, but that was how I felt. Maybe "gentle" is more the word I was searching for. Or if "strident" had a suitable antonym.

"Because she didn't tell you for weeks?"

"Right," I said. "And that's time I could have spent with her. And she stole it from me."

At first I thought he wasn't going to answer at all. Then after a minute or two he found a place to pull over to the curb. He shifted the very yellow car into "park" and pulled on the hand brake, which squeaked.

"What?" I said.

"I was just thinking . . ."

But he trailed off without telling me what.

"What? What were you just thinking?"

"I was just thinking . . . aren't you kind of . . . stealing more time from yourself? By stomping off like this? It's not a criticism. I just don't want you to be mad at yourself later."

For a time we only stared straight forward, through the windshield, without speaking. I wasn't really thinking, either. At least, I don't think I was thinking. I think I was just staring.

"Turn around?" he asked after a while.

"Yeah," I said. "Turn around."

And we drove back to my mother's house in silence.

Chapter Five

Plausible Deniability

We were lying in bed that night. No, scratch that. It was a highly inaccurate statement, which is generally unlike me. I was lying on the living room couch. Gabriel was lying in a sleeping bag about seven feet away.

I couldn't have my room because Aunt Bitsy had long ago staked her claim to it. There was no guest room.

I think when the sleeping arrangements were decided that day, there had been some derogatory sentiments aimed at Gabriel. Not to his face, but that might be worse. They were vague statements that left room for plausible deniability, but I'm not stupid. That much we've established.

He'd been outside getting the last of our things from the car. We had packed for the idea that we might stay the night or the weekend. I'd been downstairs, but I heard my mom say, "A teenage boy and girl sleeping in the same room together?"

Aunt Bitsy laughed, and the laugh was the worst part of it.

"*That* boy?" she said to my mom. "Have you *met* that boy?"

I'd trotted upstairs and stuck my head in the room and said, "I can hear you, you know."

Aunt Bitsy stopped talking but did not apologize.

I shook my head and trotted back down the stairs, half wanting to say more. But I couldn't get the "more" to come together in my head. No matter how many times I told it to be coherent, it refused to obey.

The gist of it was this: I worry about a world where it's an insult to a boy to suggest he wouldn't try to rape a girl. I'd like to say I only worry about my aunt Bitsy, but there's a lot of that going around.

But I'm digressing again.

We were lying in couch and sleeping bag but obviously not asleep.

I said, "It was nice of your mom to let you stay."

He didn't answer. Instead he just made a sound I couldn't quite interpret.

"She did say you could stay," I said. "Right?"

"Not exactly. She insisted I come home. She wanted me to leave you here and drive back and pick you up on Sunday night. But I told her you needed support. She pretty much just accepted that I was going to defy her. I wouldn't exactly call it nice on her part. I'm getting really tired of obeying her. She makes too many demands, and I keep going along, and it's not really me, and I'm getting to the end of that rope. I can feel it."

"Oh," I said. "Well. Anyway. Thank you."

"You're welcome," he said.

Then we didn't talk for a time.

"You know I'm not going back to the university," I said.

And Gabriel said, "Yeah, I do know that."

"I don't mean I'm not going back ever. Just . . . you know . . . until this thing with my mom . . ."

At the time I'm sure I would have sworn I was handling all this beautifully, but for a beautiful handler there sure were a lot of things I couldn't bring myself to say.

"I knew what you meant," Gabriel said.

That might have been the beginning of a pattern I had with him. I would say something, then clarify the something, only to learn that he'd understood perfectly all along. Probably because I was so used to saying things that hit other people like a complex alien language. But Gabriel got me. Always did. Right from the starting gate.

I may have been deadly serious about staying and not going back to school, but my confident proclamation was spoken like a person who had never met my mom.

———

I was sitting by my mom's bed, helping her drink tea through a straw. It was just the two of us in the room.

Aunt Bitsy was downstairs in the kitchen, cooking. Or baking. Or something. Gabriel was somewhere, but I didn't know where. He had a way of making himself fade away. Almost disappear. Or it seemed that way to me, anyway. In cases like this he did it to be kind and stay out of the way, but I think it was developed as a safety strategy. Just a hunch.

I didn't know why my mom couldn't drink the tea without me. I had to hold the cup out near her face and tip the straw until it was almost to her mouth. Then she would put her lips around it and sip. I wondered if it was the chemotherapy draining her so she couldn't move, or if something was making it hard to lift her arms. The radiation treatments, maybe? Or it was possible she'd even had surgery and didn't tell me. Anything was possible. Nobody was telling me anything.

I could have asked, of course. But that might have resulted in details, and the details were very hard for me to bear.

"I want to ask you a question," I said, "but I worry that it'll sound like a judgment or a complaint. And I really don't mean it that way. I'm just curious, and I want to ask you before . . . you know. While I still can."

"Go ahead and ask, then," she said, in that voice that made it sound like a simple breath was more than she could afford.

"Why didn't you teach me to have fun?"

She made an odd little sound that I thought, at first, might be pain. Only a few seconds after the fact did it occur to me that it might have been a faint bark of laughter.

"Is that something you need to teach?" she asked in that light breath of almost-voice.

"Well . . . I don't know. I only know that I don't know it."

"Kids play," she said. "They gravitate toward fun. Nobody has to show them how. They just have it in them. You didn't seem to have it in you." She paused to breathe and maybe gather strength. "You never showed any inclination toward playing or having fun. This is the first I've heard that you were even interested in it. Remember that toy you had when you were two? The one that made barnyard sounds when you punched the pictures of the animals?"

To any other child this might be an odd question, but to a child with an eidetic memory it was perfectly valid.

"Sure," I said.

"Instead of playing with it, you took it apart to see how it worked. I think you wanted to know if there were really animals in there."

"No," I said. "I knew there were no animals in there. Come on. It was like a foot by six inches. I knew there was no cow inside."

"But you were two."

"But I was me. No, I took it apart to see how they did that."

"Which is not nearly the same as playing with it."

We fell silent for a minute or two, and I helped her sip more tea.

It felt almost like she was blaming me for the problem, which didn't seem right, but I wasn't sure how to go about saying so. And, even if I had known how, I still wouldn't have belabored the issue, because there was only just so much you wanted to challenge someone who couldn't even raise her arms to sip a cup of tea.

And yet, even as I had that thought, something came up that I couldn't stop myself from saying.

"Why didn't you stand up for Gabriel?"

Her face looked confused.

"Stand up for him?"

"Aunt Bitsy was being mean about him and you didn't say anything."

"What would you have had me say?"

"Anything!"

"Well, honey. You must admit it *is* a bit odd the way he wears makeup."

"No, I don't have to admit that. Why is it odd? Why are you judging him?"

"I'm not judging him, honey. I really don't care how he wants to look."

"Then why didn't you say something?"

She sighed, and it was a thin little thing without much conviction.

"She's my big sister, honey, and she's something of a steamroller. I don't say much to contradict her if I can help it."

That seemed sad, but not like a problem we could solve in that moment. And, anyway, it was honest. And it did answer my question.

So I took the conversation in a completely different direction.

"I want to stay at the Gulbransons' . . . after . . ."

I couldn't bring myself to say after what. But it wasn't like we didn't both know.

"That won't be possible, honey. If they're not being paid they'll want to get another paying tenant in that room."

She sounded a bit stronger, but I guess I was forcing her to be. I wasn't allowing her the luxury of being tired and weak.

"You could just set aside that money to pay her. You know. Until I'm eighteen."

"Oh, honey."

"What?"

"You have no idea how fast our money is disappearing with all these medical bills."

"But you have insurance."

"Insurance doesn't pay a hundred percent."

"So I have to live here and commute to school?"

It was not a well-thought-out question. The house was a rental. It would be considerably more expensive than my room at Gabriel's. Somehow my mind simply refused to go to the plan she had in mind.

The one that was just about to burst out into the light.

"You'll go to Kentucky to live with your aunt Bitsy."

"No!" I said. Shouted, actually. I jumped to my feet, spilling some of the tea. "No, I won't. I can't. I hate Aunt Bitsy!"

"Honey, you're shouting, and she can probably hear you."

"I don't care. I won't go. I won't live with her. I won't."

I set the tea roughly on her bedside table and stormed out.

As I was running down the stairs a voice in my head said that a good daughter would have stayed and helped her drink the rest of the tea. But I couldn't go back.

I looked for Gabriel in every room of the house but the kitchen, but I didn't find him. I knew he wouldn't be purposely hanging out in the kitchen with Aunt Bitsy—nobody in their right mind would—so I figured he must be in the backyard.

I stomped through the kitchen to the back door.

Aunt Bitsy was making a pie from scratch. Rolling out dough to make a top crust, with a big wooden rolling pin I hadn't even known we had. Her hands were covered with flour and she had a smear of it on her cheek. Her face looked dark. Mood-wise, that is. There was a ton of light in our kitchen.

"I'm not your biggest fan, either," she said.

I didn't bother answering. I just stepped out into the yard.

Gabriel was lying on his back on the grass, under our big oak tree. He had his hands laced behind his head.

I walked over and sat down next to him, and he somehow read my energy without even looking.

"Whoa," he said. "You okay?"

"No."

"I'm sorry."

I stretched out next to him in the grass and laced my hands behind my head, just the way he was doing.

"What are we looking at?" I asked.

"I think there must be a nest up there. I can't see the nest, but this adult bird keeps coming back to the same spot in the tree with stuff in its beak. Bugs, and once a big long worm."

"I don't see any of that."

"Well, the bird is gone right now. Probably out looking for more food."

"Can I ask a favor of you?"

"Sure."

"Can you go upstairs and help my mom finish her tea? You have to hold it near her face and tip the straw so it's practically right in her mouth. I stormed out of there before she was finished with the tea and now I feel bad because she can't drink it on her own."

"Sure, no problem," he said. He got up and brushed grass off the seat of his jeans. Shook off the back of his shirt. "I'll be right back."

While he was gone I waited, and watched, but the mama bird never came back.

That's pretty typical, I thought. *The world puts on shows like that for Gabriel, but not for me. It's just something about him, and something* not *about me.*

Then I started thinking about what would happen if the mama bird never came back. What if something happened to her? What would the babies do? Were they even old enough to survive on their own?

After a minute I realized I was crying, which was utterly weird, because I never did. Maybe when I was a baby-baby, but even when I was a toddler, I just never cried. But that day I did, and over some baby birds I couldn't even see. Except it wasn't really about the birds. Any idiot could figure that out.

Gabriel came back after a while and lay down in the grass beside me, and we stared up into the tree together. He didn't ask me why I was crying, which was part of what I loved so much about him. Anybody else would have said "What's wrong?" Which is a perfectly stupid thing to say to someone whose mother is . . . you know. I mean, it's more than obvious what's wrong. It's just a question that doesn't need asking.

"Did she say anything about me?" I asked him after a time.

"She says she feels bad that she didn't encourage you to play more. She asked me if I could help you have fun."

"Oh," I said. "Okay."

I had almost asked the same question of Gabriel once. The night after I had that talk with Ms. Stepanian, I had almost asked Gabriel to teach me to have fun. But I hadn't asked. Not because I didn't feel like I could talk to him, and not because I wasn't confident I could ask him anything. Because I realized that he had already started. He had been teaching me to have fun in odd, small ways ever since the day he and I first met. And it didn't seem right or even necessary to ask for something a person has been giving freely all along.

Chapter Six

The O Word

It was late Sunday afternoon when I decided to break it to my mom that Gabriel was leaving for the week but I was staying. Or, more accurately, that I thought I was.

As it turned out, I never got the chance.

Aunt Bitsy was in the kitchen washing up the dinner dishes, and I thought she couldn't hear us, so I told Gabriel I was going to go tell my mom I wasn't going back to the university. That old Bitsy-bat had sonar, let me tell you.

Well. Very good ears, anyway.

She came out into the living room drying her hands on a dish towel.

"Let me show you something outside," she said.

"Okay," I said, and got up off the couch.

"No, both of you. In the front yard. It's important."

We rose and followed her outside, where she closed the door behind us and turned to address us on the front stoop.

"You're out," she said. "Go back to school. Your mother's orders. We thought you might try something like this, and I have strict orders to make sure it doesn't work."

"You can't stop me from being with my mother," I said.

I was nursing this big ball of what felt like rage in my throat, and it was hard to talk around it.

"*I'm* not stopping you. *She* is. She wants you in school. You can come back next weekend, but right now it's my job to throw you out. She hasn't got that kind of energy. Even just talking to you this weekend used up more energy than she's got to spare."

My ball of rage was melting in my throat, morphing into abject panic.

"But what if something happens and I'm not here?"

"If things take a bad turn I'll call you. But you have to let people die the way they want to die. Now respect her wishes and go."

It was the first time that word had been spoken out loud—I myself had been studiously avoiding the word—and I deeply resented it.

"Our stuff is inside."

I confess it was a ruse to get back in—one that was apparently completely transparent to Aunt Bitsy.

"You wait here on the porch," she said. "I'll pack up your things and bring them out."

And with that she stepped back inside the house and closed the door. Halfway to slamming it, really. That was followed by some sounds I couldn't quite interpret. It sounded like she was scuffing her feet on the foyer carpet, though it made no sense that she would.

I stood for a moment, feeling mostly blank. I could feel Gabriel near my right shoulder, which was nice. It was the only thing about the moment that was.

"I have a key," I said.

I dug around for it in my jeans pocket. Pulled it out and looked at it in the fading light, like there was something interesting to observe about it.

I put it in the lock and turned it. And it turned. But the door would not open. It was as though something was blocking it.

"Hmm," Gabriel said. "She must have wedged a chair under the knob or something."

I collapsed onto the top step in utter defeat, and he sat next to me, pulling his knees up to his chest and wrapping his long arms around them.

It was chilly, and my jacket was inside. But that was the least of my worries. It registered, but was overwhelmed by bigger problems.

"Is this just the damnedest thing?" I said.

"It's pretty cold," he said. And I didn't think he was referring to the autumn evening. "In general I share your thoughts about her. But she does seem to genuinely care about your mom. You know. In a gruff sort of way."

We sat without talking for a time, and I could feel myself begin to shiver.

"I'd give you my coat," he said. "If I had it."

"I'm fine," I said.

But I was anything but fine.

I took a deep breath and said something that was very hard to say. If it had been anybody but Gabriel sitting next to me, I just know I would have kept those thoughts to myself.

"My father is gone."

"I know," he said. "I'm sorry."

"I'm going to be . . ." I paused for a silly length of time. "You know. The O word."

He seemed to take a minute to think about that.

"An orphan?" he asked after a while.

"Shhhh. Just because that's what I'll be doesn't mean I want to say it. Or hear anybody else say it."

I'm not sure what he was going to say in reply, if anything, because before he could answer, we heard a scraping at the door behind us. I turned my head just in time to see the door open a couple of feet and our overnight bags dropped onto the stoop.

"See you next weekend," Aunt Bitsy said.

And she slammed the door hard. Much harder than necessary.

We sat a moment longer and listened to more of the scraping noises that could only be the sound of Aunt Bitsy wedging something under the doorknob. Aunt Bitsy didn't mess around when it came to having her way. Sure, she said it was my mother's way, and I have no doubt that was true to a great degree. But my aunt really seemed to enjoy being the enforcer.

———

On the drive back, which was mostly silent, Gabriel said something odd.

He said, "Would you mind if I did a little experiment?"

I shook myself out of my dark orphan thoughts and looked at the side of his face.

"What kind of experiment?"

"Well, you know me. You know the kind of experiments I like to do. This is maybe not the best moment, and you can just say so. But I thought it might be interesting."

I really didn't have the energy to object. I felt like an overcooked noodle.

"Sure," I said. "Whatever."

"Point to yourself."

In the swirl of clouds obscuring my brain, I looked down to see that I was pointing at my torso. Not exactly my heart. A little lower. Somewhere between my heart and the spot in my gut that had been roiling and aching all weekend.

"Huh," I said. "You were right. That *was* kind of interesting."

"See, that's the thing about grief. When things are really terrible, we come down out of our heads."

"Wow. Even me."

He let that go by.

"Not to say that makes it a good thing," he said. "When things are terrible, they're terrible. But it just seems like bad things have something they bring along that's . . . well, not good exactly. But, I guess . . . useful."

I just stared out the window and thought about that. Except I wasn't thinking, really. My brain felt cool and stalled. Very still. I think I was just feeling the idea settle.

"I hope it's okay to say that," he said.

"Sure. Why wouldn't it be?"

"I don't mean to make it sound like there's anything good about this. I hate it when people do that. I just thought it was interesting. How we change when we go through something like that."

"I'll take it," I said. "If there's anything even the slightest bit useful about any of this, I'll take it. Because, I've got to tell you, the rest of this absolutely sucks."

———

I saw my mom again the following weekend, and I think it's fair to say I was brought down hard by my own expectations.

I had this silly, idealized imagining of how things would go.

I thought I would apologize for the worst thing I'd ever done to her. I hate to even admit what it was, but I will. It had been shortly after my dad passed: we'd had a bitter fight, and I'd told her in a roundabout way that I would rather have kept him and lost her. Though it was true, I had never shaken my sense of shame and ill ease about the incident, and now that I really was losing her it only loomed more prominently in my gut and at the back of my brain. In fact, I thought it was just about the worst regret a person could possibly harbor.

The old and highly ungrammatical phrase "You ain't seen nothing yet" comes strongly into play here, but I don't want to jump ahead.

Then I figured she would apologize for every unfortunate error she'd made in raising me, starting with my given name. In my simultaneously advanced and adolescent brain I saw this pretty much taking all weekend.

And somehow, in my wild imagination, this exchange would make it all okay. Our meeting of minds and hearts would cause everything to feel resolved, and her loss would move from the realm of the intolerable to the gentle land of the bittersweet.

And it would all be manageable.

Then Gabriel drove me there.

I walked upstairs into her room and she was, for all intents and purposes, already gone from me.

Her eyes were closed. She didn't open them when I spoke to her. She seemed unresponsive. She was on supplemental oxygen, and her breathing was so labored that it hurt to watch her struggle.

"Mom?" I asked.

I waited. Nothing.

"Mom? It's me. Ru. Can you hear me?"

Nothing.

And, just like that, I knew it was already too late. I watched my lovely daydream of the meeting of our minds and hearts slip away. I felt her imminent leaving shift back from bittersweet to intolerable.

In addition to the pain of watching her struggle for breath, struggle to cling on to the very idea of life, I was pained by the near complete unfamiliarity of the person in the bed. I knew it was my mother because I knew it was my mother's bed and I knew my mother was currently confined to it. But if I'd walked past her on a hospital ward, I would have made no connection. I wouldn't have looked twice. Unless I was maybe marveling at how much suffering we're willing to allow at the end of a person's life. But still I'd be marveling at the life of a person I assumed was a stranger.

It was unbearable. Standing in her room, watching her suffer respiratory distress. Watching her not even know I was there. Watching myself hardly know it was her. It was utterly unbearable.

I stomped downstairs and faced off against the formidable Aunt Bitsy. She was in the kitchen, mixing up something that might have been cookies or might have been batter for a cake. Either way, it was clear Aunt Bitsy baked her way through sorrow.

"You said you would call me if she took a turn."

"She's still with us," Aunt Bitsy said.

"Does she even hear me?"

"Well, nobody really knows that. But she's no longer responding."

"And you don't call that taking a turn?"

"I meant I'd call you if you needed to come back right away if you were ever to see her again."

"You made me miss my chance to come back right away if I was ever to talk to her again."

"I don't know what you want from me," she said.

I probably shouldn't have told her. But it was a day of bad decision-making all the way around.

"I want you to be nice," I said. "I want you to be . . . normal. The way you see a thing like this makes no sense at all."

And you're hurting me with it, I added in my head. But I didn't say it out loud, because you don't show vulnerability around people like Aunt Bitsy. That would be stupid. That would be like walking up to a person you know wants to shoot you and saying "Here. Have some ammunition."

"Sure," she said. "Right. Everybody's out of step but Ru."

I shook my head and walked away. At least I have the good sense to know when something's getting me nowhere.

———

I found Gabriel out in the backyard. He was sitting cross-legged, his eyes slightly raised, watching something intently.

I sat down beside him.

"What are we looking at?"

"That squirrel," he said. And he pointed.

"I don't see him."

"It helps if you saw him run up the tree and then stop in that spot."

"I think I want to go home," I said.

That was met with a predictable silence. In my peripheral vision I could see him watching the side of my face.

"You *are* home," he said.

"Oh. Right."

"Did you mean my house?"

"Yeah."

"You called it home. That's weird."

"Yeah, I guess it is. Weird, I mean. But yeah. I did call it that. And I do want to go there now."

"But we just got here."

"But she's not responsive. She doesn't even know I'm here."

"You sure this is the right choice? You sure you won't regret it later?"

"I just feel like I have to go," I said. "Aunt Bitsy is being her usual hateful self and my mom can barely breathe and I just can't cope with any of this. I can't bear it, Gabriel. I just can't bear it."

My voice cracked like I was crying, but no tears happened. My tear ducts seemed to be out of order.

He put an arm around my shoulder.

"Okay," he said. "We'll go home."

We made it home in time for Friday dinner.

———

On Tuesday morning, my mother passed away. With no advance warning from Aunt Bitsy. I don't know if she had no warning herself or if she didn't bother to share it with me, because I was too angry to ask. I never wanted to talk to that woman again.

From that day forward, the fact that I hadn't stayed with my mother for that last weekend haunted me. From then on I longed for the days when my greatest regret was suggesting I would have been happier if my father had survived instead. That previous level of remorse and regret felt like a gentle heaven I had left behind. When I thought of those days, it felt like I was lifting and weighing that older regret, and it was a feather. It weighed nothing at all.

It wasn't as though Gabriel hadn't warned me.

Chapter Seven

How That Whole Amazing Chapter of Our Lives Got Started

Aunt Bitsy shared the news by telephone while I was at the university. But she didn't call *me*. She called the landline at Gabriel's mother's house—or home, as I had come to call it—and tasked Gabriel's mother with breaking it to me.

Poor Gabriel's mom wanted nothing to do with this, understandably, so she called Gabriel on his cell phone and asked him to do the unthinkable on the drive home.

But here's the weird part: I already knew.

I was sitting in class—Introduction to Astrophysics—listening to Ms. Stepanian lecture about exoplanets. I was reaching down to scratch an itch on the back of my calf. But someone was there, standing so close to my side that they were blocking the movement, and I felt almost like I was going to bump into the person if I kept reaching. I turned my head to look, but there was no one there. But it made my brain tingle, and I couldn't get over the realness of the feeling that someone was standing right by my shoulder. I can't explain or describe why it felt like my mom, but it did.

The whole experience was maybe a second in duration. Maybe less. But all day long I fairly buzzed from the shock of the thing.

So on the drive home, when Gabriel said, "I have some really bad news I have to tell you," I said, "My mother died. I know."

He didn't ask me how I knew. He was really good about only asking the questions that really mattered. The kinds of things I would want him to ask.

Instead he only said, "You seem . . . calm."

"Oh, it definitely hasn't hit me yet. It just feels like this totally fictional story that I'm watching play out on a movie screen. I'm not sure how long this stage lasts. A long time, I hope."

"That's interesting," he said. I thought he meant the fact that I had already known, or that it hadn't hit me yet. Or that I was watching it like a movie. But he didn't mean any of that. "You said 'died.' You used the word. You actually said it. You haven't used that word even once until just now."

"Yeah," I said. "Well. Turns out the words are not really the problem."

———

Gabriel came into my room after dinner that evening, which he didn't usually do. But these were not usual times. I was lying on my side on the bed, my upper half propped up on pillows, reading on my notebook computer.

"You okay?" he asked.

"Not so much, really. No."

"Is it better if I stay or leave you alone?"

"Stay is better."

He sat cross-legged on the rug near my bed, a respectful three or four feet away.

"What are you doing?" he asked.

"Reading stories about people who died of lung cancer. Not to be morbid. It sounds morbid but it isn't really like that. I was just having trouble wrapping my head around the speed of the thing. Like six weeks from diagnosis to death? It seems so impossibly weird, so I just wanted to see if it happened this fast for other people. And yeah. It has. I mean, it's not the average time, but it's not unheard of, either. I was reading comments on a cancer blog and this one lady said her husband felt just fine, it showed up on a chest X-ray during a routine yearly exam, and thirty days later she was planning his funeral."

"Is that making you feel any better?" he asked, his voice telegraphing that he didn't figure it could.

"A little bit. Not about the loss of her, exactly. But it's keeping my head from spinning because it all just seems too impossible to be true."

We didn't talk for a few seconds, and I closed my laptop.

Just then my cell phone rang. It was sitting on the bed beside me. If I had known it was Aunt Bitsy I wouldn't have picked up the call. But I purposely had never put her number into my contacts list, so it just came through as an unknown caller. And I answered it.

"Hello?"

Aunt Bitsy did not say hello in return.

"We need to discuss your move to Kentucky."

I felt her words like ice I had accidentally swallowed. I could feel its coldness drift down into my stomach.

"Leave me alone, Aunt Bitsy," I said. "I'm paid up here until the end of the month and I won't even discuss it with you before then."

She tried to say more. I could hear more words from her end of the line as I clicked off the call.

She called back immediately, but I only turned off the ringer on the phone and let it go to voice mail.

I looked at Gabriel and he looked at me.

"I'm not going to my aunt's in Kentucky," I said.

"What will you do?"

"Depends. Did you talk to your mom?"

"Yeah. It didn't go well."

"What if I got a job and paid her myself?"

"How can you get a job? You're thirteen. You'd need working papers, and a parent or guardian would have to sign off for you to get them."

"Wow. They get you coming and going, don't they? It's such a helpless feeling being a minor, especially when in most real ways you're actually not a kid and you can't get anybody to see that. But there has to be something. I could get a job tutoring students at the university. That could be more of an under-the-table thing, right?"

"It wouldn't change her mind," Gabriel said. I could tell by his voice and his face that he truly regretted having to be the bearer of this dismal news. "I'm sorry to have to say it, but it wouldn't. She's not your legal guardian. Your aunt is. If your aunt says you need to live with her in Kentucky, there's no way my mom is going to try to say otherwise."

"I'm not going to my aunt's in Kentucky," I said again.

"Is there any other plan?"

"I think it's best if we talk about that after bedtime. When your mom's asleep."

Most people don't like to be kept waiting that way. You know. For teased or promised information. But Gabriel was not most people. In the unlikely case I haven't already made that abundantly clear.

———

"I'm thinking I might run away," I said. Quietly, through the ventilation duct between our rooms.

"Where will you go? How will you survive on your own?"

"I'm not sure yet. But I'm smart, so I'm trusting myself to figure it out. What I'd really like is to stay in this area but sort of . . . go underground. Where no one knows where I am. Except you. Because there's really only one thing left in my life that I couldn't bear to lose. And that's you."

I waited in silence to see if he would say something directly in response to that, but I think it was just too unbearably emotional a moment.

"You'll be caught in a heartbeat if you show up at school," he said.

Nobody really likes unbearably emotional moments. Nobody I know, anyway. Not even Gabriel. It's just hard to know how to hit them head-on.

"Oh, I won't be going to school."

"Really? I thought it was important to you."

"I thought so too. But it turned out it was important to my mom. Without her driving me forward I just really don't know what I'm doing there. I mean, I'll go to college. At some point. But I managed to graduate high school at thirteen. Doesn't that at least earn me a gap year? Or a gap two years? I could take two years to have real-life experiences and still be three years ahead of my class age when I buckle down again."

He was quiet for a minute. Then again, I had just dumped a lot on him.

"I'm not sure how much life experience you'll get just hiding out near here so we can still be friends."

"Maybe you're right," I said. "I hate to think of going away without you, but maybe I should just make a college list and go for it."

"A college list? Why would you want to make a list of colleges?"

"No, not a list of colleges. A college list. Like people make a bucket list and it's all the things they want to do before they kick the bucket. This would be a list of all the things I want to see or do or experience or accomplish before I dive back into my higher education."

"Oh. I get it. A college list. That's a great idea if you could manage it."

We didn't talk for a long time.

Then he said the most wonderful, most life-changing thing anyone has ever said to me.

He said, "I could run away with you. And we could do your college list."

"But you love school. You were just finding yourself at school."

"My whole life has been school. Now I could go out and find myself in the actual world."

And that's how that whole amazing chapter of our lives got started.

Now do you understand why I loved Gabriel so much, and so soon?

———

I went to class the next day as though nothing had happened.

At the end of Introduction to Astrophysics I said goodbye to Ms. Stepanian.

Well, not literally goodbye. Not in so many words. I wasn't looking to tip my hand too completely.

I said, "I just wanted to thank you."

The rest of the students were all teeming for the door, and I thought it was weird that I was the only one who cared enough to approach the teacher after class.

"For what?" she asked, sounding less than fully connected to the conversation.

"Well. Kind of . . . everything. Taking my questions so seriously. Taking all the extra time to talk to me."

She was standing behind her desk, shuffling through some papers, but on that note she looked up from the papers and into my face.

"This sounds so final," she said. "Are you going someplace?"

Fortunately I had a good fallback for that.

"At the end of the month I have to go live with my terrible aunt in Kentucky."

"Oh, no. You won't be able to attend Wellington anymore? That's a miserable turn of events. Why is that happening?"

"Because my mom died."

It was the first I had said it out loud to anyone but Gabriel, and talking to him was almost as comfortable as talking to myself. I'll admit it had a frightening gravity out in the real world. Coming out of my mouth. Struggling there on the floor of the classroom. It carried far more weight than I had been giving it in my own brain.

"Oh, Ru," she said. "I'm so sorry. I had no idea. Are you okay?"

"I'm not sure. I'll tell you later, when the whole thing starts to feel real. If I'm still here, that is."

"You sure you're okay? You need somebody to talk to?"

"That's a nice offer," I said. "But I have my friend Gabriel."

I turned and started walking up the stairs toward the door because I had put something very real into the middle of that room and now I didn't want to be around it.

"You can call me here at the university if you need anything."

I waved a vague *Thank you* over my shoulder and then stepped out into the hall . . . where I nearly ran smack into my adviser, Rita Wilson.

"Ru," she said. "Just the person I was looking for. I'm so, so sorry to hear about your mother."

I stopped cold and just stood there, refusing to look at her.

"Who did you hear that from?"

"I just spoke with your aunt on the phone."

Another freezing slide of cold down my gullet as if I'd swallowed an ice cube whole. Aunt Bitsy had that effect on people.

"She called you?"

"Yes, she needed your address at the Gulbransons', so she can come pick you up. I asked why she didn't get it from you, but she said you're not picking up calls. Which I guess is understandable at a time like this. You didn't have to come to classes today, you know."

"Did you give her the address?"

"Not yet. I have to call her back. First I had to come talk to you and make sure you really do have an aunt named Bitsy Milford. I'm not in the habit of telling people where my students can be found unless I know for a fact who the person is who's asking."

"Thank you," I said, feeling that the ice cube had reached my slightly upset stomach. "You don't have to call her back. I'll call her and make an arrangement for her to pick me up."

"We'll miss you," she said, and I saw genuine regret on her face. Which felt odd. Other than Ms. Stepanian, I didn't know that anyone at the university had gotten particularly attached to me. "And again, my sincere condolences about your mother."

"I have to go," I said, and I skittered away.

And it was true. I did have to go. I had to quickly get someplace where people weren't talking about my mother's passing like it was a true thing that had really happened. You can't be too careful, you know. A thing like that could be contagious.

When I was well out of her earshot I called Gabriel on his cell phone.

"We have to go now," I said. "Not at the end of the month. We have to go today."

———

It was after ten at night when we stood in the foyer of his home with two big suitcases each. His mother had taken her sleeping pill at nine and was fast asleep.

He had left her a note on the kitchen table, but I hadn't asked him what it said. I was letting that be a private thing.

"Do you have a passport?" I asked.

"I do, actually," he said. "Because we have family in Vancouver. The other Vancouver. Not the one in Washington state. Why? Do you?"

"Yeah. I have one from when my dad took us to Mexico City. Did you bring yours?"

"I thought it was silly to bring it, but I did anyway."

"No, not silly. Perfect. Good."

Then we just stood still for a moment, each with a suitcase on the tile floor on either side of us. Just stood there, not leaving. The street-light on the corner spilled its glow through the glass insets of the front door, and we looked at each other in the dim light. I think the gravity and boldness of what we were doing had settled onto us.

"Are we off the rails here?" I asked.

"I think . . . ," he began, "yes. I think we probably are. Now let's hurry up and do this thing before we change our minds."

Chapter Eight

The Ghost in the Machine Giveth and the Ghost in the Machine Taketh Away

"The first thing we need to do," he said as we were driving out of the city, "is get a different car."

It was something we hadn't yet discussed, and I found it a little surprising. It did explain why he seemed to know where we were going when I hadn't even shared my college list yet.

"Because it's so yellow?"

"Because my mom knows the license number."

"Oh," I said. "Right."

We were driving over a bridge in the bright moonlight, and the way the moon shimmered on the water was a truly beautiful sight. It had been a long time since I'd been outdoors at night. It was a much wilder thing than the life I'd been living for so long.

"Is the car in her name?" I asked.

"No, it's in my name."

"Oh, you can do that? Legally?"

"Yeah, in California you can. My dad registered it in my name so she couldn't take it away."

"So how do we get a different car?"

"We go to my dad's shop in Santa Rosa. I'll leave my car here with him while we're gone and take one of his cars as a loaner. He won't mind. He's always looking for the chance to do something for me. And he has a lot of cars."

We drove in perfect silence for a while. And by "perfect silence" I don't just mean that nobody broke it at all. I mean it really felt perfect.

Then Gabriel said, "Did you even have time to make your list? Or are you going to be doing that on the road?"

"Oh, I made it."

"Where is it?"

"In my head."

"Oh. I thought you'd write it down."

"I don't forget anything," I said. "Ever. And besides, it's only three things."

"Okay," he said. "Go."

"One. I want to go to the darkest place in the entire country. The place with the darkest skies at night, I mean. I want to go to a place that makes Kelso Dunes in Mojave look like a shopping mall at night. Well, not literally. But if I could find a spot even a little bit darker, that would be great. As best I can figure from my research there are a lot of places. A lot of the more remote national parks are a one or two on the Bortle scale, which means they're nice and dark. But there's also a campground in Utah that I think is a better bet because it's really meant for astronomy. It has level concrete pads for telescopes and rules about things like campfires and flashlights. It doesn't get a whole bunch of use and what it does get is mostly real astronomy buffs, so the chance of someone ruining it for us is much lower."

"We could do that," he said. "That sounds like fun."

It struck me that my mom had more or less tasked him with teaching me to have fun, and that it was the last wish of a dying woman. I didn't remind him because I didn't for a moment think he'd forgotten.

"Two," I said. "See the aurora borealis."

"Where would we go to do that?"

"Maybe Alaska. Maybe Northern Canada."

"Which is why you asked me if I brought my passport."

"Right. Three. Meet an Atlantic puffin in person."

"Oh," he said. "That would be fun. But harder. Would we have to go to Iceland? That might be more money than we've got."

"They have them in Eastern Canada. Newfoundland. Places like that. There are islands in the Atlantic that are technically Maine where you can see nesting puffins. But since we'll be in Canada anyway, I think it's our better bet."

"Might still be more than we've got. You know. All that gas money."

"We could leave the car someplace and take a train across Canada."

"We'll do it," he said, "if we possibly can. We'll figure it out. But speaking of money, we'd better find branches of our banks and get our money out before we get too much closer to my dad's. Because we don't want to leave a trail of bread crumbs leading anybody to where we're headed. Also we want to get that money before your aunt even knows we're gone."

"Oh," I said. "Right."

Gabriel was smart in a different way than I was. And it's a good thing he was, too. I taught myself euclidean geometry when I was seven, but that doesn't mean I was the one who would be most likely to identify all the things that could possibly go wrong with our plan.

———

As luck would have it, we both had accounts at the same bank. It wasn't that remarkable a coincidence. It was a big bank.

It was early when we arrived, before banking hours, and we had to sleep in their parking lot for a time, but then we succeeded in walking out of there with our life savings to date. For me, $1,198.85 that I made tutoring. For Gabriel, $787.50 in birthday money from his dad that his mom forced him to save.

"We're lucky," he said as we were walking back to his very yellow car. "I think a lot of parents set it up in that custodial way, so they have to sign for their kids' withdrawals."

"I don't think it's luck," I said. "I think they trusted us and wanted to make us *feel* trusted."

He said nothing in reply, and I felt bad for what I'd said, because he might have been feeling guilty about letting his mother down. But I didn't ask, so I really don't know for a fact.

"How far to your dad's?"

"Maybe an hour," he said. "But I have to stop and use a gas-station bathroom."

We stopped in Petaluma, and he filled up the tank. Then he rummaged around in his suitcases in the back and disappeared into the men's room. And didn't come out for a really long time. Honestly, I was starting to get concerned.

After ten minutes or so the door to the men's room opened, and a young man I didn't recognize stepped out. I figured it was one of those restrooms with more than one stall, so two or three people can use it at the same time. I unlocked my car door because I was going to ask him if he'd seen Gabriel in there and if everything was okay. But by then he'd walked quite a bit closer to the car, and by then I could see that he *was* Gabriel.

He'd slicked his hair back with some kind of product, and since it lay close to his scalp it gave the impression of being clean-cut and short. He had removed all of his makeup. His fingernails were fingernail colored. He had changed into a pair of khakis and a plaid flannel shirt.

He looked like a model in a catalog for the outdoorsy man.

He got into the driver's seat and we drove away. North, toward Santa Rosa.

I didn't ask him why. Gabriel was really good about not asking stupid questions, and it seemed like the least I could do to return the favor. And, make no mistake, it *would* have been a stupid question.

Gabriel presents as himself until we're just about to see his father. Then he presents as someone else entirely. If I can do advanced trigonometry I can add two and two and get four.

After a few miles he volunteered some information, which was nice.

"He tries," he said. "He's pretty nice about it. He never made me feel bad for it or tried to change me. But he doesn't really understand it, and it embarrasses him a little. If we were going to his house it might be different. But I'm walking into his shop. He has eight guys working for him, and they're all auto mechanics."

"Got it," I said.

———

When Gabriel's father saw him, he said something that I thought was hurtful. But I know he didn't mean it to be. It's funny how often a compliment can cut a person right to the bone.

He said, "You look terrific, son."

I winced, though I'm not sure if I winced inwardly or right out in the world. Gabriel winced, but inwardly. Don't ask me how I knew, it being inward and all. I just knew Gabriel, and I could feel it.

In case you're not following, when you dress up as someone else entirely, it must hurt to be told that it's a terrific way to look.

Gabriel's father was a big bear of a man with hairy forearms and a shaggy beard.

We were standing just inside the doorway of his mechanics shop. There were cars and a big half-ton pickup sitting raised on lifts, and mechanics working underneath them. It was noisy, because they were using those pneumatic power tools that sound like a dentist's drill on steroids.

Gabriel said, "This is Ru. She's staying with me and Mom because she goes to Wellington."

His father reached his hand out to me, but it took me a few seconds to realize he wanted me to shake it. When I realized, I did. I thought it would be greasy, but it was warm and clean. I guessed grease was for the lower-level employees.

"This little slip of a thing goes to Wellington? Why, you look about twelve."

"Thirteen," I said. "But I'm freakishly smart."

"Can I talk to you in private, Dad?" Gabriel asked.

"Of course, son. Of course. Come right into my office."

They walked away and left me standing just inside the door of the noisy shop. There was a sign that said no customers were allowed in there, but I wasn't exactly a customer, and, anyway, I figured being there with Gabriel made me an exception to the rule.

When I was done reading the sign, I realized there was a counter and a window on my right with a cashier behind it. A woman who looked to be in her forties, with obviously bleached blond hair, was sitting back there. She was staring right at me, so I tried to smile. I'm bad at forced smiles, so I'm guessing it came out looking more like a grimace.

"That's a gift from God, you know," she said.

It was such a bizarre non sequitur that I began with the assumption that she was talking to someone on the phone using a Bluetooth setup that was undetectable from where I stood. But she was looking right into my face, and she seemed to be waiting for me to say something.

"What is?"

"That extra-special intelligence."

"Oh," I said. "That."

"You don't see it as a gift?"

"I'm not sure I believe in God," I said. "I mean, not a God who gives gifts, like Santa Claus. I believe there's an intelligence underlying the universe—what I once heard a quantum physicist call 'the ghost in the machine.' It's something that gives the almost scientific impression of being there, but they can't find it or quantify it, because it's unknowable. But I don't tend to call it God. I guess I could, but that gets into all the very complicated baggage left over from what other people mean when they use the word. But let's say, just for the sake of conversation, that I believed in a God who gives gifts. I think when God wants to torment you he gives you extra brain, and when he wants to bless you he gives you extra heart."

Somewhat predictably, she was staring at me as though I'd just stepped off a spaceship and asked to be taken to her leader.

"Well, I didn't follow a word of that," she said. "But that only proves how big a gift it was."

Gabriel stepped out of the office, opening his hand to show me a set of keys that were clearly not his. His old yellow Nissan had an old-fashioned ignition key. This was a more modern smart key.

"Okay," he said. "Come on. We're out of here."

———

A few miles down the road in our loaner Jeep SUV, I looked over at Gabriel, still looking like a male model from a sportsman's catalog.

"We should stop at a gas-station restroom," I said. "So you can undo all that."

"I figured you'd want to make miles," he said.

"I want to make miles with my friend Gabriel," I said. "I don't know who this guy is, but I miss the real you."

He gave me a smile that was the best one he'd offered me to date. He never took his eyes off the road, but I never doubted that the smile was for me.

———

"He didn't give you a hard time?" I asked, even more miles down the road. Shortly before our "restore Gabriel" rest stop. "I think the average dad would advise against running away with a much younger girl."

"I told him you were making a sarcastic joke about being thirteen. I said you're twenty-two, but you have a weird medical condition that makes you look like you're not aging. There really is such a thing. There was an actor who had it. And he played the role of a kid for all those years. But we'd better figure out what that's called."

Gabriel apparently had forgotten that I still know everything I've ever read or seen.

"Well, in his case it was because of a kidney disease called focal segmental glomerulosclerosis, and the medications he had to take for it. Also there's a very rare condition that's sort of the opposite of progeria, which is where kids age too rapidly. It doesn't come with a sharp adult mind, but I'd be really surprised if the people we talk to know that."

"We should just call it a rare condition and leave it at that. I think we're better off using that story all down the road. I'm eighteen and you're twenty-two. As soon as you open your mouth and they hear you speak it becomes a much more believable story than you being thirteen."

"Until we have to show our passports," I said.

Clouds passed through the sky of his eyes for the first time since we'd left home.

"Right," he said. "Until we have to show our passports."

———

When he came back into the Jeep as himself, I could feel the difference in him. It felt like he was breathing after holding his breath for hours.

"You know how to get where we're going?" he asked me.

"I do and I don't. We have some choices to make."

"Tell me which way to go just to get started."

"That's a little confusing," I said. "Figuring out the best way. If we try to go straight east we'll get forced farther north by the mountains and we'll end up in more northern Utah. Which we don't want. We want the southern edge. A route in between is hard because there aren't too many ways over the High Sierras. And what there is looks twisty and slow."

"We can't go over the Sierras," he said. "It's too late in the season. Snow could close the passes."

"See, I didn't know that."

"I've been to Yosemite. You have to carry tire chains at this time of year. Even when it's not snowing yet, you have to have them. That's one of the places you can cross over. The 120 through the high elevations of Yosemite, over Tioga Pass. But then if it snows, that's it. It's just closed for the season. No, I'd like to stick with some major highways."

I stared at my phone a bit longer before reporting my findings.

"Then we could take the 80, which would take us way too far north, or we could backtrack back to the I-5 South. Almost all the way to Bakersfield. Then the 58 East, and then we can pick up the I-15 and it'll be I-15 almost all the way through. That'll take us way too far south."

"This time of year I think we should choose the southern route."

"I worry it might be kind of a roundabout route, though. Either way."

"Doesn't matter. We're in no hurry."

He shifted the Jeep into drive and we headed off for adventure number one.

"We should stop and buy two sleeping bags," he said.

"Oh, good idea. We could put the rear seats down and sleep in the back of this thing."

"Except in the dark-sky campground, where I figured we'd want to sleep out under the stars."

It filled my mind with so much excitement that I could feel it tingle all the way down to my toes. For several minutes I only closed my eyes and imagined those wonderful nights. I didn't even tell him what a good idea that was until Coalinga, because it was so exciting it had usurped my ability to wrap that excitement up in words.

"Here's the thing about the puffins," he said.

"Okay. Tell me the thing about the puffins."

"They're out to sea all winter. They only come ashore from about mid-April through the summer. To hatch their eggs and raise the little ones."

"Pufflings," I said.

"Right. Pufflings."

"Oh," I said. "That's true. That's weird. It's weird because I knew that. And I never forget anything. But I don't think I forgot it exactly. I think I just wasn't putting the two things together. You know. Like what time of year this is, and what time of year they come in from being out to sea. Which was dumb. And I'm not usually dumb. So what do we do about that?"

"Stay out till then? We don't want to go home anytime soon, anyway. Do we? I'll be eighteen in a couple of months and then I don't have to go home if I don't want. You think your aunt will keep looking for you?"

I thought about that for a minute.

"That could go either way. She might keep trying to find me just because she likes to get her way. But she doesn't really like me, and I know she can't be thrilled about having me there. I think she told my mom she'd take me and now she has to perform the 'due diligence' thing on that, but if I take off and she can't find me, I expect she'd be relieved."

"I guess we'll find out," he said. "Whatever. All we know is: college list, here we come."

I didn't think much about my mom on the drive, because we were so far outside my regular routine. It was this wonderful vacation where my mind never expected to see her anyway. It was like the polar opposite of cleaning all her clothes out of her closet or walking into a room where she tended to be and finding it empty.

And that's how I achieved emotional survival for a really surprisingly long time.

Chapter Nine

Rusty Metal Kangaroo Pouches

We were sleeping in our sleeping bags in the back of the Jeep. Or trying to, anyway.

We were in a dirt lot in Baker, California, where people were allowed to park overnight. There were only a few other overnighters there, and they were mostly RVs and big rigs.

For what it's worth, we were across the street from what announced itself as the world's largest thermometer. True to its billing, it was very tall. Many stories, if it had been a building. The stars were brilliant above and behind it.

It was the gateway to Death Valley, this place. Death Valley also had good night skies, but I liked where we were going better. At least, as far as you can tell about a thing like that. You know. Before you arrive.

"He thinks you're my girlfriend," Gabriel said.

He sounded regretful, as though offering me some kind of amends for something.

"Who thinks I'm your girlfriend?"

"My father."

"Oh."

"He thinks I have a twenty-two-year-old girlfriend who looks thirteen. What a mess. Have you ever heard of such a thing? It's like something you'd see in a movie and just sort of roll your eyes. Like . . . yeah. Right. That happens all the time. Sure it does."

"Did you *tell* him I was your girlfriend?"

"No! Of course not. I wouldn't do that. I could just see that he had that idea. And I didn't say anything."

"That doesn't sound like a very big deal," I said.

"It felt like lying."

"I don't think it is, though."

"You sure?"

"Pretty sure," I said.

"So just let him think what he wants?"

"I think so," I said. "Yeah. I'm a big fan of letting people think what they want. It saves tons of time and aggravation, and it seems to make them happy."

———

In the morning I was brushing my teeth in the dirt, and Gabriel was talking to his mom on the phone. And that was when Errol came into the picture.

Okay, wait. That first sentence needs a lot of sorting out.

My teeth weren't in the dirt, and neither was my toothbrush. I was just standing there on that dirt lot, bent over at the waist, brushing my teeth. When I had to spit, it was just right down into the dirt. No sink involved. That's all I meant by that. Then I'd take a sip of water from a plastic bottle and swish it around, and again . . . right out into the dirt.

Also it's only marginally accurate to say that Gabriel was talking to his mom, because she seemed to be doing all the talking.

He really only said one word—"Mom"—a couple of times.

"Mom," he said, sort of in place of hello.

Then he had to hold the phone away from his ear because she was yelling at him. I couldn't hear what she was yelling because of the distance, but I could hear a general din from her end of the line.

"Mom," he said again, pulling the phone in closer and trying to get a word in edgewise.

It didn't work. He had to re-create some distance for his poor ear.

Meanwhile the guy who would later turn out to be Errol was stomping around kicking his car and swearing loudly at it, but I was only halfway focused on that, and even the half of me that noticed didn't find it all that relevant to our lives.

A few seconds later Gabriel clicked off the call. And I mean right in the middle of all that yelling. He walked over to where I was standing. I was done brushing my teeth, but I was still holding my toothbrush in one hand and the paste in the other, absent-mindedly watching Errol kick his car.

"Well," Gabriel said. "At least she knows we're alive, which was the overall point of the call. Let me get my toothbrush."

He rummaged around in one of his suitcases and then came back and held his toothbrush out toward me, and I put some paste on it and handed him the bottle of water.

"What's with that guy?" he asked quietly, indicating the future Errol with a flip of his chin. Well, you know what I mean. He was currently Errol, but we didn't know.

"No idea," I said.

And just at that moment, Future Errol stopped cursing and kicking. He sank down into the dirt and just sat there, his back to us. A second or two later we could see his back start to heave and shake.

"Is he laughing or crying?" Gabriel asked me.

"No way to see from here," I said. "But taking into account what came before it, I'd say laughing is a bad bet."

"I'd better go ask if he's okay."

He tried to hand me the toothbrush and water, but I said, "I'm going too."

Without any out-loud discussion of the thing, we walked around in a big arc so as not to seem to be sneaking up behind a stranger. When he saw us he looked up, and he was definitely crying. He swiped tears away with the outside of one hairy forearm, as though they were a secret he still had time to keep.

"You okay?" Gabriel asked.

"Not really," he said. "But thanks for asking."

He looked to be in his forties, with a potbelly and lots of dark hair everywhere but on his head. Well. There was *some* hair on his head. But probably not as much as he would have wanted, given more choice in the matter.

"Anything we can do?" Gabriel asked.

"No," Future Errol said. "I don't think so, but thanks. I'm just screwed. My car broke down, and now I'm going to miss my nana's funeral."

"There must be some way to get there," I said. "There are buses and trains and Ubers and stuff like that."

"No trains from here. I mean, not close enough that I could get to the train station without a car. One bus a day and it left. I called. Too far to Uber. I have to get all the way to Las Vegas."

Gabriel and I looked at each other.

It was a thing we could say or not say, and we both knew it. We didn't have much in the way of time. I mean, you have to answer the guy. And once we said it—if we said it—there was likely no taking it back. Even if we lived to regret the decision.

I nodded to Gabriel very slightly.

I figured *not* doing a thing is what one usually lives to regret.

"We have to go right through Las Vegas," Gabriel said. "We could give you a ride."

———

"I want to give you my gas money," Errol said.

We were rolling along through the California desert, and we had just passed a sign for Mojave National Preserve. That had made me think of my dad, so I was trying very hard not to miss him.

The situation with my mom was pushed much deeper and much more firmly into the background. So much so that I couldn't even feel it lurking back there at the time.

"You don't have to do that," Gabriel said.

"But I want to. I would've spent it anyway if I'd driven there on my own."

"At least save enough to get back to your car somehow," I said. "After the funeral."

"My brother will drive me," he said. "Or . . . if he can't do it I'll hit up one of my cousins."

And, with that, he dropped quite a bit of cash over into the front seat.

I picked it up without counting.

"You sure?" I asked.

"Unless you've got money coming out of your ears," he said.

"No," Gabriel said, "we really don't."

"I figured. You guys look so young."

We didn't really care to answer that, so the moment plunged us into silence.

Two or three miles later Errol said, "Really. Are you guys even old enough to be going so far on your own?"

"We're older than we look," Gabriel said. "I'm seventeen—almost eighteen—and Ru is twenty-two."

I thought that was interesting, because the plan was to tell everyone he was eighteen to my twenty-two. I didn't know if he had done that on purpose or if it was a mistake brought on by force of habit.

"Oh, come on," Errol said.

"No, really," I said.

"Is that a joke? You're like . . . twelve."

"I have a medical condition. It makes me look like I'm not aging."

I caught a glimpse of his face in the rearview mirror and he looked positively horrified.

"Oh, my gosh," he said. "I'm so sorry. I'm so stupid."

"You're not stupid," I said. "I get it that I don't look twenty-two. It's not like I didn't know."

"But why didn't I just keep my mouth shut and take your word for it? I'm so stupid."

"You're not stupid," I said.

"You have no idea how stupid I am."

We drove for a good five or ten minutes in silence.

Then Errol said, "I'm really ashamed to even admit this, but I have to tell you a secret."

It jolted both of us. I could feel it in my gut. I could see it on Gabriel's face. Like, this is the moment when the stranger you allowed into your car tells you he's a serial killer or a cannibal or something.

We didn't answer because, I guess, we weren't that anxious to hear how big a mistake we'd made.

"I think I broke my foot," he said.

When he said it, I remembered that he had more or less hopped to our car when he got in. Oddly, I hadn't paid much attention at the time.

"Is that the secret?" I asked.

"Yeah."

"That's not really the kind of thing people tend to keep secret."

"Yeah, well, I guess that's because most people didn't break their foot kicking their own damn car. And that's how stupid I am."

"You need to go to the hospital?" Gabriel asked.

"No. I need to go to my nana's funeral. I'll worry about the foot after that."

———

Gabriel had his phone on vibrate, and it buzzed off and on through the southwestern corner of Nevada.

"Your mom?" I said on about the fifth call.

He nodded.

I guess we thought Errol wasn't paying any attention. We were wrong.

"Here's a piece of unsolicited advice," Errol said. "If you don't want someone to know where you are, the phone is a problem."

Gabriel looked confused, bordering on worried. But I didn't think Errol could see that from his seat in the back.

"Why would you think I don't want her to know where I am?"

"Well, you said you're seventeen."

"Right," Gabriel said. "I guess I did say that, didn't I?"

From the tone of his voice I gathered it had been accidental.

"That gives her a lot of power over you," Errol said.

"I can just . . . not pick up."

"Wrong. Rookie mistake. Common mistake, but still. I used to do a lot of wilderness hiking when I was younger. I'd go alone, because I didn't know anybody who hiked the way I did. Even my friends who liked to hike thought I was beyond the pale. I was living with my nana at the time, and I'd leave her some information she could use if I wasn't back by nightfall. One of the things you leave with somebody for safety is your cell phone number and your cellular provider. Because with that, if you're technically a missing person, the provider can ping your phone and get a location on it. Usually that works even if you don't have enough reception to make a call. Even if you have location services turned off. So . . . I hate to say it, but if you really want to get lost, you're going to have to ditch the phones."

I looked at Gabriel, and he looked at me. At least, for as long as it's safe to do when you're driving.

Then we rolled through the Nevada desert for a long time, both of our brows furrowed down, thinking what life would be without a phone. And occasionally speaking elements of the disaster out loud.

"Maps," Gabriel said.

"Emergency phone calls."

"Using the internet to find out stuff like whether the campground takes reservations."

"Take it from me," Errol said. "I'm a lot older than you guys. When I was growing up, nobody had a cell phone. And we managed."

Gabriel and I exchanged another look.

"Maybe we should just hurry up and do this fast," I said. "Before we have too much time to think about it."

We both powered our windows down at the same time. The morning desert wind came roaring through, and it was crisp and clean. It battered our faces and blew our hair around.

"Wait!" Errol said, shouting to be heard over the wind.

"What?" I shouted back.

"Don't just throw them away. They're worth money."

Gabriel and I looked at each other again. Then we powered up the windows. The silence was stunning, and quite welcome.

"What were you thinking?" Gabriel asked, half turning to address the rear-seat area.

"If you want to permanently get rid of them you should wipe them completely and then sell them. Take them to a pawnshop or something. But I would think you'll want them when the trip is over, or when you turn eighteen, or whatever. So I meant stash them somewhere you can find them again on the way back. Or mail them home. Or mail them *somewhere*. That way you don't lose everything you had on there."

We drove in silence for a time. Probably we were all lost in thought. I know I was.

"We owe you one," I said to Errol. "You probably just saved our big trip."

"Well, you saved mine," he said. "So now we're even."

———

Somewhere along the I-15 between Baker, California, and Las Vegas, Nevada, we stopped at an old abandoned property that had obviously been a roadside diner at one time. It was currently mostly dry-rotted wood and rusted metal. In the long-dead dirt yard sat the decrepit remains of big metal sculptures of animals. And I do mean big. I think at one time they were meant for kids to climb around on. It would have been unwise to use them that way by the time we came along. There was an elephant, a bear, a dinosaur, and a kangaroo—which messed with my sense of order, since they could not possibly all have existed at the same time. But I guess in Metal World, anything is possible.

The kangaroo was farthest from the entrance. We had to hike for a bit to get to it.

Its pouch was caved in, as though someone had taken a baseball bat to it for fun. Odd what some people mistake for fun. Still, there was room to get a hand in there.

Gabriel had put our phones in a plastic bag and then wrapped them in a T-shirt. I watched, feeling a bit forlorn, as he stuck his hand down in that pouch with the phones and then pulled it free without them.

"Bye-bye, twenty-first century," I said.

We walked back toward the Jeep together.

"Next time we pass a mile marker," he said, "memorize the number."

"That's a weird way to put it."

"Why is it weird?"

"Because I don't need to memorize it. I look at it, and then it's in there forever."

"Oh," he said. "Right. I forgot."

"But I never do."

"Right. You never do."

We arrived at the Jeep then, and climbed in. And drove on.

We found out later that we could have just kept the phones powered off, but, you know. Live and learn.

"Another unsolicited piece of advice," Errol said.

I thought he was going to share an additional observation about the logistics of staying lost, but he had moved more into the feelings realm. My least favorite place.

"Okay," Gabriel said.

"Make your peace with her somewhere down the road. Right now maybe you two can't see eye to eye. That happens. But later, when you're not a minor, and she has no control over your life, try to put things back together with her. My nana and I used to be so close. I even lived with her through most of my twenties. Then I got it in my head to change my name to Errol and move to Hollywood and have a career as an actor. She thought it was a terrible idea, so we kind of broke off touch after that. I was always going to go back to Las Vegas and see her. You know. Later. When I was an actor. When I was successful. Now I work as a temp and I'm on the way to her funeral. Hopefully that says everything that needs saying."

"Yeah," Gabriel said, and he sounded a little bit depressed. "Thanks. It pretty much does."

Chapter Ten

Clouds Are Clouds, Which Is Not Always the Good News

We were driving through a residential neighborhood in Las Vegas, or a Las Vegas suburb. I'm not sure which. We were following Errol's directions, which were handy to have, since we had no phones.

I hate to admit my own ignorance, but I had never pictured Las Vegas having residential neighborhoods. I mean, I knew people lived there, or else who would be staffing all those hotels and casinos? But I still pictured Vegas as being the Las Vegas Strip, and it seemed odd to realize so many people were living quiet lives here, raising families, probably not involved with any of the flash and neon and gambling at all. It's just one of those things that you'd know if you thought about it, but you don't think about it, so you don't know.

"That's my nana's house," Errol said.

But we weren't looking at him when he said it, so it was impossible to know which house.

Gabriel started to pull over, but Errol corrected him. Loudly, and fast.

"No, don't stop! We're not going to her house. We have to go to the synagogue."

"Oh, it's actually starting," Gabriel said.

"Start*ed*. I've missed half an hour of it. But at least I didn't miss it all, thanks to you guys. It's just another seven blocks down and to the right. It's walking distance. If you have two unbroken feet, that is."

We rode in silence for several blocks.

Then Errol said, "Turn here."

We made a right, and the synagogue was impossible to miss.

It was made from some kind of white stone, and looked as though it had been built in the '60s to be very modern by '60s standards. The roof was set at a sweeping angle, and there were tall, vertical sections of stained-glass windows. But they were not representational, as they say in the art world. They were more abstract. Long, uneven, stylized triangles.

There were many cars in its parking lot. Many. Nana had been popular.

Gabriel swung a U-turn in the street and pulled up as close as possible to the door.

"Can you get in okay?" he asked Errol.

"Yeah. I'll hop. Thanks for everything, guys."

I turned around and looked him dead in the eyes.

"I'm sorry you lost someone who was important to you," I said. "I know how much that sucks."

"You lost a grandparent?"

"I lost all four of them if you count my grandfather being put in a nursing home and not even knowing me. And then both parents."

"Holy crap," he said, and for a minute no one spoke. Then he added, "I hope you at least have some siblings or cousins or something."

"I have my brother here," I said, patting Gabriel's forearm.

"Oh," Errol said. "Good."

And that was how Gabriel and I became brother and sister, at least to all we met along the road. It was emotionally true, and a good way to put to rest the idea that we were boyfriend and girlfriend while at the same time explaining how we could be so devoted to each other and so close.

Isn't it weird how people will question any bond that doesn't hinge on romance? I think that's weird.

"Thanks again for everything," Errol said.

He got out and slammed the Jeep's rear door, and we watched him hop to the door of the synagogue, swing it open, and hop inside. He had taken off one shoe, and it dangled from his hand. Probably because his broken foot was swelling.

After he disappeared we just sat a minute.

Then Gabriel said, "I started to tell him I think his nana would have wanted to see him, successful actor or not. But then I realized that would only make him feel bad."

"I don't think it's that he thought she wouldn't want to see him. I think it was about *him*, not her. You know. His pride."

"That's sad."

"It is."

He swung a U-turn again, and we set about trying to reverse our directions back to the interstate.

Within just a few blocks we got turned around and lost.

"Read me the route to the I-15," he said. "Okay?"

"Read it from what?"

"Oh," he said. "Right. No phones."

We drove in silence for a block or two, and I watched his brow furrow down.

In time we saw an older woman walking a very clean white minia- ture poodle, and Gabriel pulled over. Pulled level with her. It seemed to make her nervous. She hurried on, dragging the poor dog by its collar, and Gabriel had to put on the gas again.

I powered down my window.

"Can you tell us how to get to the I-15?" I asked.

She stopped, and seemed to halfway relax.

"First of all, turn around," she said. "You're going the wrong way. Then you go down to the fourth stoplight and make a left. From there you can't miss it."

"Thanks," I said.

We drove on.

It was a busier street than the ones we'd been on before, and I knew Gabriel wouldn't want to make a U-turn. He made a left into a driveway, carefully backed out into one of the traffic lanes, and our life went on.

"I guess that's how they did it when Errol was growing up," I said.

"Guess so."

Having been reminded of Errol, I pulled his money out of my jeans pockets and counted it.

"He gave us over two hundred dollars," I said.

"Wow. Nice."

"Maybe we should give more rides to more people."

"I don't know," he said. "Sounds risky. I mean, if someone is just standing by the side of the road with his thumb out . . . what do we know about that person? I was thinking it would be better if I figured out ways to work a little. Stop in a place for a few days. Bus tables or pick crops. Then drive on."

"Are we really that bad off for money? I thought it was holding up pretty well."

"Now, yeah. Sure. It's holding up. We're just driving from California to Utah. But after that we head for Alaska or Northern Canada, and that's a whole other deal."

"We'll work it out," I said.

"I believe you're right," he said. "I believe we will."

———

We were driving through the Moapa Valley when Gabriel first commented on the clouds. At least, that was where I gathered we were, based on road signs.

The clouds were sweeping and dramatic. Really pretty breathtaking. They seemed to have been painted on in layers. Blue sky with feathery white clouds above, then darker cumulous between us and that scene. Then a whiter layer that looked almost like fog, hovering at a low altitude.

"Those clouds are so beautiful," he said.

"Yeah, but they're clouds."

"Well, that was never in question. Meaning . . . ?"

"Clouds obscure the night sky."

"Oh. Right. I wonder how long before they blow through."

I reached for my pocket to get my phone. To look up weather in our current location. When the pocket came up empty, I questioned how long it would be before an empty pocket came as no surprise.

"Hard to know," I said.

We were eating in a diner somewhere in Utah. Maybe less than thirty miles from our destination, but without a phone I couldn't have said for sure. We were splitting a grilled cheese sandwich with water as our beverage because, without any discussion, we had dropped into extreme cost-cutting measures.

There were a bunch of astronomers, or at least astronomy buffs, sitting at the next booth over.

How did I know they were astronomy guys? Partly from the bits and pieces I caught of their conversation. But I would have known anyway, because one of them had brought his equipment into the restaurant, and it was all strewn around on the floor where the waitress had to be careful not to trip over it. There were a couple of carrying cases for telescopes in that pile, and they had the names Tele Vue and Takahashi printed on them.

Just as I was thinking all that, another astronomy buff came in and joined them. He was tall and skinny with a friendly face. No real age I could pin down. Could have been an old-looking twenties or a young-looking forties.

He stopped dead when he saw all the equipment strewn around.

"Dave," he said. "What'd you bring all this in for?"

"Because I had it in the back of my pickup," Dave said. Or at least he must have been Dave, because he answered. "I wasn't about to leave my scopes unlocked out in the parking lot. Or my brand-new mount for that matter."

The new guy carefully navigated his way into the booth.

The three guys who had been there all along were eating big plates of ribs. They sure did look better than our little halves of grilled cheese sandwich, but what can you do?

"You need a camper shell," New Guy said to Dave.

"So you keep telling me," Dave said.

The two other guys were too busy eating ribs to join in the conversation.

I leaned over closer to their booth, thinking it would be nice to know somebody there when we got to this dark-sky campsite.

"You guys going up to the Cosmos Campground?" I asked.

Four sets of eyes turned to me.

"No, we're just coming back from there," Dave said. "You're not going up there now, are you?"

"We are," I said. "Yeah. Why?"

I glanced at Gabriel, who looked worried. They all glanced at Gabriel. They all stared just a little too long, as people tend to do with Gabriel. Then they shifted their eyes away, as if suddenly aware of their own accidental rudeness.

New Guy answered.

"There's a storm blowing in," he said.

"Dangerous storm?" Gabriel asked.

"Well, I wouldn't go that far. But it'll ruin your viewing opportunities."

"How long do you think we'd need to camp up there to ride it out?" I asked.

"Hopefully just tonight. It could be partly cloudy tomorrow night, but you might get lucky and get some viewing in. Just make sure your equipment is locked up in the car tonight and staying dry."

Gabriel and I glanced at each other, a little uneasily.

"We don't have any equipment," I said.

"Oh," Dave said.

Nobody said anything more for an awkward length of time.

I was worrying about how they must have had us pegged as hopeless and stupid, which was odd, because I normally don't care much what people think.

"We were just going to bring our eyes," I said. "You can enjoy the night sky with just your eyes, right?"

It was unexpected, their reaction to that. The two who had been eating ribs stopped eating, their hands frozen in the air. They all looked up, or at least off into the distance, staring at nothing. Their eyes seemed to grow soft.

"Not only *can* you," New Guy said, "but it's seriously underrated, in my opinion. Unaided-eye astronomy. That's a beautiful thing right there."

"It's how we all got started," Dave said.

Then hands moved again. Beef ribs approached teeth once more.

"You'll be surprised what you can see from up there," New Guy said. "If the weather ever clears. M45. That's the Pleiades."

"I know what they all are by their catalog numbers," I said.

"Oh." He sounded more than a little surprised. "You might even make out a little nebulosity around M42. And you can see the core of M31 without even binoculars. Because it's so dark. If you get a good night, that is. Do you have an astronomy app on your phone?"

"No," I said. "We don't even have our phones."

"Oh. Star map?"

"I have a star map in my head," I said. "I've memorized it all."

Having an eidetic memory is not exactly the same as memorizing something, but it's the easiest way to communicate it to people.

He looked a little green around the gills when I said that. He probably didn't believe me, and he had probably just decided he was in a conversation with an unreliable narrator. And now he wanted out of that conversation.

"Well, good luck up there," he said.

And we all withdrew our attention back to our own tables.

Just as they were packing up and leaving, we overheard some conversation regarding whether it was worth taking the uneaten ribs with them. But nobody had a cooler, from what we could gather.

They must have seen us staring at the leftovers and drooling, because Dave said, "You guys want these?"

"Yes, please," Gabriel and I both said, almost exactly at once.

So that's how we ended up going to the Cosmos Campground on a full stomach. We had vanishingly few creature comforts up there, but we had a few gas-station snacks and our full stomachs, and that was something for which we could be grateful.

———

When we got up there it was pitch-dark and raining hard, and there was no one else there. Literally. No one. Just us, our Jeep, the howling wind, and a lot of water coming down from the sky.

Car camping in the pouring rain sounds simpler than it actually is. You figure you can stay in the car and stay dry. But you have to get out to go to the bathroom. Then you end up back in the car soaked, and there's not enough room in there to change your clothes.

We ended up in wet clothes, with wet hair, in our sleeping bags in the back of the Jeep. I didn't even take off my shoes.

We just lay there, trying not to shiver. It was a cold storm, and the wind slapped the rain against our windows and made us jump. It rocked the Jeep on its suspension, and it howled all around us. And we were utterly alone.

"I'm used to feeling like I can make a phone call in case of emergency," I said.

"We probably wouldn't get reception all the way out here anyway."

"Oh. Right."

We lay in silence for a time.

Then he asked, "Are you scared?"

"Are *you*?"

"Pretty much," he said. "Yeah."

"Then I guess it's okay to say I am too."

"Was I wrong to bring you out here? I feel like maybe I drove us into trouble. Are you sorry we did this?"

"No!" I said. It came out so loud that I think it startled us both. "No, it's good to be scared."

"How do you figure?"

"It's like . . . a life. It's wilder than anything I've ever done before. And riskier. And it feels like being alive."

"You were alive before we came out here," he said.

"Not really. I mean, technically. Yeah. But my whole life was mental. It was all on the inside. There was no risk, so there was no fear. No, this is good. This is living. Actually living a life that's really happening outside your brain. Besides, it won't rain forever."

"No," he said. "It can't."

After that we didn't talk for so long that I thought he might have fallen asleep.

"Gabriel," I said. Just quietly enough that he could sleep through it if need be.

"What?" he said. And it was obvious he'd been awake.

"What did you decide you wanted to be?"

"Career-wise?"

We had to speak up to be heard over the howling wind and the rain it slapped against the Jeep's windows.

"Yeah. How come I never asked you that?"

"I don't know. Maybe because it's not the most important thing?"

"But I feel really selfish," I said. "Like we've mostly been talking about me."

"Well, not all along," he said. "I think it used to be pretty balanced. You know. Before your mother died."

When I heard him say it, I actually felt like something had hit me in the stomach. Like, an actual, physical something, though I couldn't quite describe what. It would be inaccurate, or at least exaggerated, to say I'd forgotten. And yet it felt like something close to that. I had buried it so deeply that it was a shock to be reminded.

That killed all conversation for a surprising length of time.

"Was I wrong to bring that up?" he asked after a whole bunch of silence.

"No, it's okay. It's the truth. So what did you decide to be?"

"I haven't decided yet," he said.

"What?"

It came out so loud and so vehement that it made him jump. Actually it even made me jump, and I was the one who said it.

"Do you think that's bad?" he asked.

"No, I think it's amazing. What a luxury! I'm just surprised the world let you get away with it."

Then we fell silent again. And, even though I would have told you it was close to an impossibility, in time I did drop off to sleep.

Chapter Eleven

Shhhh—Don't Disturb the Universe

I woke in the night but, in my phoneless situation, I didn't know what time. There was no rain drumming on the roof of the Jeep or slapping against its windows. The wind had died completely.

I lay in silence for a time, letting my eyes adjust to the darkness. When I looked out the window I saw stars!

There were still big areas of deep cumulous clouds, but they had begun to break up and move away. And the stars I could see between them were amazing. Better than the ones I'd seen when I was camping with my dad in Mojave. Or at least better than I remembered them.

I pressed my face to the hatch-like back window of the Jeep. The glass was freezing cold but I really didn't care.

It woke Gabriel.

"What's happening?" he asked in a sleepy mumble that didn't sound fully conscious.

"The stars are out," I said.

He sat up as best he could in that cramped space. Then we abandoned our nice warm sleeping bags, got out, and stood out in the cold night air.

And we stared. And stared. And stared.

"What time is it?" he asked. Then, before I could even answer, he said, "Oh, that's right. Sorry. We don't know."

"It's between three and three thirty."

"Are you just making that up?"

"Not at all."

"Enlighten me."

"I know what time all these stars and planets and constellations rise and what time they set. And what time they transit across the meridian. So it's not hard to estimate."

"So you memorized not only the star map, but all its rise and set times?"

"'Memorized' is not quite the right word."

We were speaking quietly, almost in a whisper. As if there were someone nearby we might disturb. But there was only the brilliant, brilliant universe, so I guess that's what we were being careful not to disturb. That and ourselves.

We stared in silence for a few minutes.

Then Gabriel asked, "What's that really bright star?"

"The reddish one right there?"

I was pointing, of course.

"Yeah. It looks like a jewel."

"That's not a star. That's Mars."

"Oh. Mars. That's embarrassing."

"Why is it embarrassing?"

"I should know that."

"Well, if you're not interested, you're not interested. It's not really a failing."

"I'm interested *now*. In the city they're not so exciting."

More silent staring.

Then he asked, "That really bright one just down from the Orion constellation. I know Orion. But is that another planet?"

"No, that's a star. It's just an unusually bright star. That's Sirius."

After that, talking just became less and less the thing to do. We didn't discuss it, but I think we could both feel it. I could feel my teeth chattering and I could hear his. We were trembling in the cold, but we made no move to go in. We just stared.

The clouds cleared entirely, and it was just us and every star or planet that had risen above the horizon, minus the area blocked by the Jeep.

I watched so intently that I was actually marginally aware of their movement across the sky. Except of course they were not moving. We were moving. A lot of people have trouble absorbing the idea that the Earth is spinning while the stars, for all intents and purposes, stay where they are. But I knew.

In time I could see light at the eastern edge of the horizon, and all but the brightest stars began to fade. We climbed back in but first we left the tailgate and back window open. I figured Gabriel had dropped back asleep, because we had been quiet for so long. But when it got light enough I sat up and looked over at him, and his eyes were wide open. He had just been staring with me.

I thought it was really nice to be able to observe out there with someone who could let a dark night sky be amazing, without having to constantly comment on how amazing it is.

He looked over and saw me sitting up.

"I feel like I'm a different size now," he said. "My whole life feels resized."

"Smaller, right?"

"But not in a bad way," he said.

———

Avery showed up a little before noon.

He was maybe fifty, with well-worn clothes, and hair and a beard I can only describe as raggedy. But he had a very open smile.

He waved broadly at us as he stepped out of his little van. It wasn't exactly a camper. It was just a van. But it had curtains in the windows, so I got the impression he had turned it into a camper in a sort of impromptu way.

He started hauling equipment out onto the concrete pad of his campsite.

He had one of those portable piers that you can put together one piece at a time to hold up your tracking mount. The mount was so big and heavy I could see him strain with the weight of carrying it. And we were still a fair distance apart.

When I saw him carrying the scope, I knew I had to go over.

"I think that's a solar scope," I said to Gabriel.

"How can you tell?"

"It has that logo on it. From a solar-scope manufacturer I know. At least it looks like it does, from here. I'm going to go ask him."

We both walked over, and he greeted us with that very open smile I described earlier. He told us his name was Avery, and stuck out his hand. And we each told him our names as we shook it.

"You kids out here all by yourself?" he asked.

We were getting used to that, and would be much more used to it as the trip wore on.

"We're older than we look," I said.

"You'd almost have to be."

"Is that a solar scope?" I asked. But I was just making polite conversation, because I could see now that it obviously was. The brand name, Lunt, was very clear.

"It is," he said. "One hundred millimeter. Double-stacked. Hydrogen-alpha blocking filter. Any of that make sense to you?"

Gabriel said, "No," and I said, "All of it," at exactly the same time.

Then Gabriel asked, "Is there some benefit to coming out to a dark-sky site to view the sun during the day?"

"Actually, I'm not viewing. I'm imaging. But anyway, to answer your question, no. Not really. Artificial lighting doesn't wash out the sun, and the exposure times are in the milliseconds anyway. The reason I bring my solar scope out here is to give me something to do until it gets dark. You two have any equipment?"

"No sir," Gabriel said.

"Really, don't call me 'sir.' Please. Makes me feel old. Avery is fine."

"We don't," I said. "The plan was just to lie on our backs in sleeping bags all night."

"Ahhh," he said, drawing the word out some. "That's a nice experience. But then it rained all night last night."

"Right," I said.

"And tonight the ground will be too wet."

"True."

"I have a tarp you could use under your bags."

"Ooh," Gabriel said. "That would be nice. Thank you."

"Well, let me go ahead and finish setting up, and then we'll chat some more."

And with that he disappeared back into the van.

"Okay," Gabriel said. "Tell me what all that stuff about the scope meant."

"A hundred millimeters is the diameter of the aperture. Double-stacked means he's using two etalons." He looked confused, so I added, "An etalon is a kind of interference filter you use when you want a super narrow bandpass." That caused him to look even more confused. "And hydrogen alpha is a wavelength of light."

"Sure," he said. "Whatever."

I made a mental note to try to speak in more accessible and less scientific terms. Which, when I thought of it, I realized I could have done years earlier. With everybody.

By then Avery was back outside again. He was carrying a laptop computer and what looked like a fabric hood for it—to keep the glare of sunlight off the screen. He had a couple of cables draped over one arm and a heavy-looking battery pack, about the size of a suitcase, hanging by its handle from the other hand.

"Nice to see young people taking an interest in astronomy," he said. "I wish I were still young. I used to love to spend a night out in a sleeping bag under the stars. Now it's too hard on my old bones. But I miss it. There's something very pure about observing that way. Now I hardly ever observe. I see everything on a computer screen, or in the raw images. It's all automated. You know. Using capture software and all that. I set it up and go to bed in the van, and it takes care of itself until something transits or sets and I have to move the scope. I have to wake up then, but even that I can do from my laptop inside the van. I have software to control the mount."

"You should sit outside under the stars while the images are being taken," I said. "Even though you don't really need to."

"Awful cold," he said.

For a while he said no more. Just worked on his setup. He had his phone out, open to the compass app, and he was aligning the mount so it pointed true north.

"Maybe I should, though," he said out of nowhere.

"You should. We should all sit up tonight under the stars. It's too important to miss." He didn't answer, so I added, "How important is it that your mount be aligned just right for solar? I mean, I know how important it is with night photography. But the solar exposures are milliseconds . . ."

"Not overly important," he said. "It just helps to get it well enough aligned that I can take thirty seconds of video to stack. Also that way the sun is still in the frame while I'm focusing or whatever. But it's not really going to be properly aligned until the polar star comes out tonight."

We watched him in silence for a few minutes more. He was booting up his laptop and probably opening some programs, but that's all guesswork on my part, because both the computer and his head were inside that hood that kept glare off the screen.

"Are we bugging you by hanging around like this?" Gabriel asked.

Avery's head popped out.

"Not at all," he said. "Let me just get the sun framed and focused and I'll do a little pressure tuning, and then you can see what it looks like on the live view in the capture software."

He pulled the dust cap off the scope, punched a few buttons on the keypad, and his mount gradually slewed the scope toward the sun.

Then he disappeared under the hood again.

"The tuning is perfect," he said from under there. "Almost got it focused."

"You can focus from the computer? You have some kind of after-market autofocuser on there?"

"I do." His head popped out again. "Come take a look," he said.

I motioned for Gabriel to go first. He hesitated briefly, but then his curiosity got the best of him, and he stuck his head under the hood.

"Whoooaaahhh," I heard him say, and the word just seemed to go on forever. "That's our sun?"

"That's our sun," Avery said.

"You can see, like . . . little flames shooting off the edges."

"Prominences," Avery said. "Actually burning plasma. But it's very active. Especially right now. And they may look little from where we stand, but you could probably fit multiple Earths in the bigger ones."

Gabriel's head emerged.

"Ru, you have to see this."

I stuck my head under the hood.

Avery had opened an image-capture program called SharpCap, and the solar disk was perfectly centered in its live view window. The detail was amazing. I could see the individual bits of granularity, and three active regions with multiple sunspots in each. He had the exposure turned up just enough that I could see a brilliant ring of prominences at the sun's limbs. Or edges, as regular people call them.

I pulled my head out into the light.

"Those images are going to be amazing," I said.

"Hope so. Come by later and I'll show you what I get."

"It's nice that you guys understand," Avery said. "My wife doesn't understand."

We were all three sitting about halfway between our campsite and his, under a brilliantly clear night sky. Avery sat in a camp chair, and Gabriel and I were cross-legged on our sleeping bags on the ground, with the borrowed tarp underneath to keep them dry.

Gabriel and I were snacking on peanuts and beef jerky, but really it was more than a snack. It was our dinner, because it was the best of what food we had left.

I could see a few tiny red lights off in the distance that marked Avery's equipment. One on his guide camera. One on the mount. A softer but larger red light on the battery pack that powered it all. He was using a DSLR camera on his scope, and, now and then—or every three minutes, to be exact—I could hear the shutter click closed and then open again. It was a soft sound from the distance, but I was aware of it.

"You should take your wife out someplace really dark like this," I said. "Let her see for herself."

"She won't go. She did once. Back when we were newlyweds. She wasn't that impressed. She just kind of said, 'Yeah, yeah. Very nice. Lots of stars. They twinkle. Very pretty. But then when you've seen them you've seen them. And then what?'"

"But she's seen the images you take, right?"

He had shown us a brief slideshow on his phone. The Flame and Horsehead Nebulae. The Andromeda Galaxy. The Helix Nebula. The Sombrero and Triangulum Galaxies—Avery was clearly a big fan of galaxies. A few other things.

"Yeah," he said. "Sure. And she thinks they're good and all. But the equipment is expensive. And it takes me away from home at night because we live in a Bortle eight zone. Right in the bright, light city. Sometimes I buy things that I don't even tell her about. I know I shouldn't, but I feel like I need to justify everything I buy. Between you and me, I have scopes she's never seen. And even not knowing the whole of it, she thinks it's too much. She thinks it's an addiction, and that makes it unhealthy."

"It's not an addiction," I said. "It's a passion."

"Well, I'm glad you understand the difference," he said, "because she doesn't. She keeps comparing me to her brother, who's a surfer. He's been a surfer all his life, but now he's close to sixty, and he gets hurt a lot more. He keeps tweaking his back. His doctor tells him to stay out of the water for a few months to let it heal, but when the waves are really good, he doesn't. And then he reinjures it."

"She must see that nobody gets injured in astronomy," Gabriel said.

"Yeah, I tried that. She pointed to financial injuries."

"Oh," Gabriel said.

"I don't know, guys. I love her. I don't mean to make it sound like I don't. But we're just so different in what we care about, and sometimes I wonder if that's okay. But *you* understand." Avery seemed to be addressing me with that last sentence. I could see his head turned toward me in the starlight. It was so dark and clear out there that the stars actually cast some light on the scene. I think he had figured out that Gabriel was much newer to the whole astronomy scene, and not as deeply committed. "Right?"

"I do," I said. "It's different from other passions because it redefines your world. It actually changes what you think the world around you *is*. It shifts your perspective. It adds these absolutely mind-blowing realities into your awareness that most of us go through our whole lives without even acknowledging. I think of it being like if you'd lived inside a house your entire life. Never gone outside. Or even like if you'd lived in a basement. If you'd never seen natural light, and then all of a sudden you were taken outside to see the sun, the sky, the clouds. Mountains, rivers, forests. The ocean. The desert. It changes everything. It changes *you*. It adds something to the inside of you, to your spirit, that was never there before, and then you don't ever want to go back in that basement again."

We were all quiet for a time.

Then Avery said, "Yeah. Now I think I finally believe you. You're a lot older than you look."

Chapter Twelve

Any Minute Now, AKA in a Hundred Thousand Years

Gabriel and I spent the rest of the night in our own campsite, on our backs under the stars. Since there was nobody else in the whole campground besides Avery, we moved the Jeep away from where we slept, so it didn't obstruct any part of our view. We had a 360-degree night-sky view.

It was amazing.

It was like being in a fishbowl. It didn't even feel flat. I was aware of the curve of it, the dome over our heads. It was like the dome of a planetarium, except it was clear and cold . . . and absolutely real.

"Tell me what that man in the diner said we could see," Gabriel said. "Point it out to me. I don't remember what he said. It was all letters and numbers anyway. But I know you remember."

We were doing that thing again. Speaking in a near whisper, as though there were someone nearby who might be disturbed. Chalk it up to awe, I guess.

"M45, the Pleiades. It's that little tight cluster of stars a few degrees to the right of Mars."

"I saw that!" he said. He sounded excited, which was nice to hear. "I wondered what that was."

"He said we might be able to see a little bit of nebulosity around M42. That's the Orion Nebula. You know where that is, right? In Orion's sword?"

"Hanging from the belt, right there," he said. And pointed to the three iconic stars that formed Orion's Belt. Alnitak, Alnilam, and Mintaka.

"Right. So the sword hangs down from the lowest star, Alnitak, and right around the middle of that sword, there's a bright spot that looks like a star. But it's not a star. I mean, there are stars in and around it. But it's a very bright nebula."

We observed in silence for a minute or two. There was something intense about our staring, as though it involved concentration.

"I'm not sure about nebulosity," he said. "Which, by the way, I had no idea was a word until just now. But I can kind of tell it's not just a star. It's not a sharp point of light the way a star would be. And it looks a little bit shimmery."

"For unaided-eye observing, that's good. And he also said we might see the bright core of M31. That's the Andromeda Galaxy."

"Oh, I've heard of that."

"So that's on its way down to set in the west-northwest right about now. Jupiter is near the horizon on the south side of west. So . . . it should be right about . . . there."

He followed my pointing finger.

"I think I see it," he said. "Does it look like kind of a soft, fuzzy, oval-ish ball of glow?"

"That's it. We can see it better than any other galaxy because it's closer. It's headed our way. In fact, it's about to come crashing right through us."

"What? Why doesn't anybody else know about this?"

"Oh, everybody knows it."

"Everybody knows that another galaxy is about to slam into us and end life as we know it?"

"In about a billion years," I said.

I heard him laugh lightly to himself. Nervously. Or just on the return trip from nervousness.

"I should have mentioned," I said, "that 'about to' in astronomical terms is usually at least a billion years or so. When they say a planet like Betelgeuse is about to go supernova any minute now, 'any minute now' usually translates into around a hundred thousand years or more. Also the 'end life as we know it' isn't quite right. We think of these massive galaxies as solid objects, but there's such an unimaginable amount of space in between the matter. There likely wouldn't be perceptible changes in any one person's lifetime—assuming there's a person anywhere around here in a billion years, which is a big assumption."

Gabriel was quiet for a long time.

Then he said, "That's mind-boggling to try to imagine."

"All of space is mind-boggling to try to imagine. That's why I love it so much. It makes you stretch your mind. People don't stretch their minds enough. That's why so many of them are narrow-minded."

Another long string of silent moments. Absolute peace.

Then he said, "We did it, Ru. We really did it. We crossed something off your college list."

"Thanks to you," I said.

"Are we staying tomorrow night?"

"I don't think so. We're almost out of food. But that's not really why. It's because we really can cross this one off as a success."

———

In the morning we stopped to give Avery his tarp back on our way out.

"Oh, you're not staying?" he asked. He sounded disappointed.

"No," I said. "We have to drive on. We have to go see if we can catch the aurora borealis."

"Where?"

"Not sure yet."

112

"I know a great place. I spent two weeks there once, imaging. The lights put on a show nearly every night. That was mostly luck, of course. I'm not saying they'll do that all the time. But it's really consistent up there compared to most other places."

I looked at Gabriel and he looked at me.

We had already made up our minds that we weren't going to try to go to Alaska. That would involve more than one border crossing each way. We were not at all sure our trip would survive even one.

"Where's that?" I asked.

"The Northwest Territories. Canada. I was in Paulatuk, but anywhere in the Territories will do it. It's a long way from here, but it's pretty much due north from where we stand right now. So it's probably closer than any other place you could go to see the lights."

"That sounds promising," Gabriel said. "Thanks."

He reached out the folded tarp to Avery, but Avery waved it away.

"If you're going to be doing more camping along the way, then you need to keep it," he said. "Think of me when you spread it out at night, and send me mental pictures of the aurora so I can see it vicariously in my head."

We moved toward the Jeep, but then I stopped. I stared into Avery's face for a time. It was clear he didn't know why.

"Tell your wife it's what makes you *you*," I said. "Tell her the man she married, the man she fell in love with and who fell in love with her, can't possibly be separated from the stars at night. Tell her they make you happy, and the happier you are, the more you can make her happy."

He just stared back at me for a beat or two. Then he cracked a quirky little smile.

"Think that'll work?"

"No idea," I said. "Probably not. You know how hard it is to change people. But it won't make things any worse."

Then we waved a few times, and Gabriel and I got back on the road.

———

"I think we might get arrested at the border," Gabriel said.

We were driving north, heading for Canada, even though it was still several states away. We were eating cheap gas-station hot dogs with no regard for the fact that it was barely seven o'clock in the morning.

"I'm sorry to be a downer," he said. "But we've been pretending we're not underage, and that only works until you show someone your passport. I'm not even sure it's legal for minors to cross the border unaccompanied by an adult. And even if it's legal, they're going to have questions. And if we've been reported missing, then that's the end of everything."

"I've been thinking about that," I said.

"Have you come up with anything?"

"I think so. Remember when I said we should give more people rides for gas money? Well. If we can find somebody who needs a ride into Canada, then we're not unaccompanied. We'll look like a family."

"We won't have the same name."

"If it's a woman, I doubt anyone will bat an eye. Women have different last names from their children all the time. My mom and I didn't have the same last name." It jolted me. The word, as I said it. The M word. It jolted me like walking into a room and expecting to see her there. And then suddenly remembering. I put it away again as best I could. "And lots of moms have children with different last names than each other, because they had different fathers."

"Oh," he said. "That's true. But where do we find somebody like that?"

"I haven't figured that part out yet. But I don't really think it's a thing you figure out. I think we just have to be in the right place at the right time. I think we just hang out near the border and meet as many people as we can. I always figured that was the secret to being in the right place at the right time."

"Meeting lots of people?"

"Well, in this case. But more generally, being in a lot of places at a lot of times."

"Could take a while."

"But it's not like we're in any hurry," I said.

———

We were a few dozen miles over the state line into Idaho when I started asking questions.

We had stopped for gas, and Gabriel had called his mother on a pay phone. I waited in the car in case he wanted privacy.

"How'd that go?" I asked when he got back.

But that isn't what I meant by questions.

"She wasn't there. I left a message."

"Is that good or bad?"

"I think good," he said. "But it's hard to say for sure."

We got back on the road again, and I asked him, "Why did I spend all that time trying to learn about the stars from books or in a classroom? If I loved the stars so much, why didn't I just go sit out under the stars? I realize you already pointed out this exact same thing to me, and I'm not trying to act like it's a new idea or like I thought of it. But at the time I wasn't really feeling it, and now I just sort of *get* it, in a way I didn't get it before. It's like if there was this paradise on earth, but there was also a slideshow presentation on it, and I had my choice, and I chose the slides. Why would I do that?"

"I think everybody does that," he said. "To some extent, at least. Or at one time or another."

"But *why*?"

"Well, that last one is beyond me," he said. "But I do think it's good that you're asking the question."

Then, a few miles outside of Idaho Falls, I said, "I have another question."

"Okay," Gabriel said.

"You know I didn't really get along with my mom, right?"

"I got that impression."

115

"We got on each other's nerves. I spent as much time apart from her as I possibly could. It was like heaven to get off by myself."

Then I fell silent, and we watched ten or fifteen miles go by.

"Still waiting for the question," he said.

Too bad. I was regretting having started that line of discussion, and hoping he'd let it drop.

I didn't answer straight away.

"There's a question in there somewhere, right?"

I took a deep breath and pushed it out with the exhale.

"Why doesn't that help me now?"

"Oh," he said, sounding a little deflated. As though he were feeling the thing on my behalf. "I actually have this theory about mothers. But I think I should wait and tell it to you when you're ready to let the whole thing in."

"That would not be now."

"I didn't think so."

"I'm sorry I'm asking all these questions," I said.

"I don't mind. I just wish I had better answers."

"Your answers are good. Better than mine. All these years thinking I'm so smart, but only about stuff that isn't very useful when you're trying to have a life. It's like I know all this stuff but all of a sudden none of it seems very important."

Then we didn't talk much more until almost the Canadian border. I think the world was getting heavier. Weighting us down. I think the gravity of both of our lives descended in that moment, and everything felt very real. Both the good things and the bad things. Just very, very real.

Chapter Thirteen

How to Max Out Your Tips at a Truck-Stop Diner

You're doing great, girls. Better than I thought you would, and I don't mean that in a critical way at all. It's me. I'm going into a lot of detail. You're showing remarkable patience under the circumstances.

Still, give me some credit, too. It's only two bathroom breaks and one lunch later, and I've almost got us to Canada.

There's a little town twelve miles south of the Canadian border in Montana. Not much of a town. The kind of place you hear people call a "wide spot in the road." A few hundred people live there. But there was a diner there—hopefully still is—that we'd heard was popular with long-haul truckers. That's always a good sign. Trust a trucker to know where to eat. Make a mental note of that.

When we got into their parking lot, four big rigs were pulling out at pretty much exactly the same time. We figured it was a coincidence. We figured wrong.

When we got to the door, Virgil was just stepping out. Virgil was the man who owned the diner, though of course Gabriel and I didn't know that, or his name, at the time.

He was a short, muscular man in his sixties with a full head of gray hair and the bushiest eyebrows I could ever remember seeing. Wait, strike that. Inaccurate statement. The bushiest I had ever seen. It's not like I might ever have seen something and then forgotten it.

He was just turning the "open" sign to "closed" on his way out the door.

"Oh, no," Gabriel said. "You're closed?"

Virgil looked Gabriel up and down the way people of older generations tended to do. As though they had to come to some sort of understanding of him before the conversation could resume.

We hadn't been eating enough, and we'd been looking forward to this place ever since a woman in a gas station had told us about it early that morning. We had both already lost so much weight that we had taken to hitching up our pants frequently as we walked.

"I'm sorry," Virgil said. "Family emergency. I have a cook, but what good does that do when you have no waiter and no busboy?"

"Wait," I said. "Your waiter and busboy both had a family emergency at exactly the same time?"

He sighed. I could tell he hadn't really meant to stop and talk.

"My waitress is my daughter. The busboy is my son. And my mother—their grandmother—just took a bad turn."

It hit me hard, like a sucker punch to the gut. That expression, and the feeling it created. The memory of Aunt Bitsy promising she would tell me if one of those bad turns appeared over the horizon, and then failing in that promise.

I did something that surprised . . . well, everybody. Myself included. I dove in and embraced him.

I could feel his shock, and his resistance, but I didn't let go.

"I'm so sorry about your mother," I said.

He softened up some then.

"Ru's mother just passed away," Gabriel said.

A rather brittle moment passed in silence, and then Virgil embraced me in return. A moment later we stepped back and glanced at each other with a shared measure of embarrassment and regret.

"We were really looking forward to eating here," I said. "We heard good things."

"Well, believe me, it hurts me more than it hurts you. This place is one hundred percent of my livelihood. When I hang out that 'closed' sign, income grinds to a halt. If we have to be away for a week or two . . . wow. That's really gonna hurt."

Gabriel saw an opening I never would have seen. You could have given me a hundred years and I wouldn't have seen it. This is one of many reasons why I say Gabriel is smarter than I am in some really important ways.

"But you wouldn't have to close if you had a waitress and a busboy," he said.

"But I don't," Virgil said.

"Sure you do," Gabriel said. "They're standing right in front of you."

Virgil narrowed his eyes at us for what felt like a long time.

"You two seem awful young," he said.

"We're both older than we look. I'm a little bit older than I look and she's a whole lot older than she looks."

"Any experience?"

"No, but we're quick learners."

More silence, furrowed brow and narrowed eyes. He looked pretty skeptical, so I was sure he was about to turn us down flat.

When his stupor broke he said, "Hang on. Don't go away."

He left us standing there in the cold morning air and stepped back inside his diner.

He was gone for several minutes.

Gabriel and I shifted from foot to foot in the cold. Glancing at each other here and there.

"Interesting idea," I said.

"It probably won't work."

"No. Probably not. But it was still impressive that you thought of it."

A minute later Virgil popped back out.

"Freddy says he's willing to give it a shot. Freddy is my cook. He'll be your boss while we're gone. Just learn from him and do what he tells you. If it doesn't work out he'll fire you and hang out the 'closed' sign, and we haven't lost much. If it works, when I get back I'll pay you eight dollars an hour, plus of course you'll have your tips."

And that was how two underage teens ended up practically running the table area of a truck-stop diner near the Canadian border for eleven days.

Life has this way of letting these perfect events drop into their perfect slots at just the right moment. But there's a catch to that kind of living. You have to be doing it right.

Watching Gabriel always amounted to learning a lot for me.

———

Speaking of tips, do you want to know how to earn killer tips at a truck-stop diner? Well, no. Probably you don't. But maybe you will someday.

Tell people honestly that you have no idea what you're doing.

I didn't make this up. I learned it from Freddy the cook.

Freddy was tall but stooped, with hair buzzed very close to his pale scalp. I made him to be fifty, but he could have been older. He looked tired enough to have been older.

The place was empty for about ten minutes, because the existing customers had been told Virgil was closing up shop. While we waited for someone new, Freddy gave us a crash course. Putting on a hair net and apron. Where to hang the orders. Keeping syrup and ketchup and hot sauce stocked on the tables. Writing up a check to present to diners after their meals.

It seemed basic enough, but then that's easy to say when there are no customers.

"I don't have to write down the orders on a pad," I said. "I have an eidetic memory."

"A what?"

"It's like a photographic memory, except that's a misnomer."

"A what?" Freddy asked again.

"A misnomer. The wrong name for a thing."

"Oh. Got it. You really are older than you look, aren't you? Well, sorry, but you *do* have to write the orders on a pad, because I don't have one of those memories, and I need to refer back to the order while I'm cooking."

"Oh. Okay, fine. I'll write it down, then."

He showed Gabriel the stack of plastic tubs to use to bus tables, and how to properly load the industrial dishwasher. It wasn't anything like the ones people have in their kitchens at home.

Then he sat me down and gave me the talk about waitressing.

"Everybody is in a hurry," he said. "Nobody wants their waitress costing them any time. But here's the thing. People will get mad if they think you don't care, not if they think you don't know. So you go up to every table and you say, 'Hi. I'm Ru. I'll be your waitress today. But I really don't know a darned thing about waitressing. It's my first day. And I haven't really had any training, either. I'm filling in because Virgil's mother is in a bad way, and I didn't want him to have to close his doors. So your food might be a little slow today, but I'm hoping you'll like that better than just finding a "closed" sign on the door. If you could be a little extra patient with me, I sure would appreciate it.' That way they know you're honest, and you're doing your best. And you'll rake in the tips, because everybody loves someone who's doing her best."

The bell on the door jingled, and Freddy looked up.

"You're on," he said. "Good luck."

I realized I was nervous, which I'm usually not. Then again, I'm not usually faced with a task that can't be solved by analytical thinking.

It went just fine, but that's because there was only one table.

The lunch rush would bring me to tears. Actual, literal tears.

———

I have a great deal of respect for those who wait tables, and I hope you'll follow in my footsteps on that score as your life goes on. It's a tough, thankless job, and to this very day I tip well and speak to the waitstaff with respect. Once you know, you know, and it never wears off.

All the customers were nice enough, especially after I explained my newness in almost the exact words Freddy had given me. It wasn't that anyone was short with me or said anything mean. There was just this moment when everything was happening all at once.

Freddy had just rung the bell that indicated an order was up. A guy at a corner table was holding up his mug for a refill. Another diner was writing in the air with an invisible pen as a semi-universal signal to ask for his check. And all this happened as I was headed behind the counter to find a booster seat for a traveling couple's toddler.

I just froze for a second. My body gave signals to move in four directions at once. That being impossible, the signals just canceled each other out and broke my nervous system the way too much amperage will fry a circuit board and render it inoperable. At least in my case, though, the damage was not permanent. It just felt that way at the time.

I stood there a few seconds too long and then started to cry. That thing I hadn't done for so many years but that seemed to be making a resurgence.

If I'm being honest, they weren't really tears of frustration or over-whelm, though certainly those factors played in. I think in truth I was crying because I realized I was no longer a child. I was an adult with a job. I had no mommy to go home to even if I'd wanted to. Even though I had Gabriel, he was busy busing tables and washing dishes. I was alone the way everyone is alone when they die, even if they're surrounded by family and friends. I was in a place in my life where I had to function as an adult and no one could help me.

I haven't forgotten that I said my childhood ended the day I was taken to kindergarten. Of course I didn't forget. I don't forget any-thing. But that was a different level of the thing. On kindergarten day I realized I was like the adults and unlike the children . . . on the inside.

But on the outside I got to keep living like a child. Being supported. Attending to my schoolwork. Living at home.

Now I was suddenly a waitress in a truck-stop diner.

A weeping one.

Remember when Freddy said I'd rake in the tips because everybody loves someone who's doing her best? Well, take a tip from me. If you really want to rake in tips, break down in tears in front of your customers. I didn't do it purposely or cynically, and I'm not suggesting you should either. But let me tell you. People respond to that.

The guy who wanted his check waved away the request, as if he were suddenly in no hurry after all. The couple with the toddler got their own booster seat, and the guy with the raised mug got his own coffee refill.

As I moved back into picking up the order and delivering it to its correct table, three different diners quietly came up to me, patted me on the forearm or the shoulder, and slipped money into my apron pocket.

I didn't look until after closing time.

They were all twenties.

———

We closed after lunch at two.

Freddy explained the whole cleanup and closing routine.

"But before we do all that," he said, "you two must be hungry."

We were starving. We had been mildly hungry when we'd stumbled in that morning. By the time he brought it up, our stomachs were in a state of crisis.

"Do we get to eat here for free?" Gabriel asked. He sounded as though the very idea was too good to be true.

"Two meals per full shift," he said. "And you missed your first one. Not steak and eggs, but anything else on the menu. You in the mood for breakfast or lunch?"

"Breakfast," we both said. Almost exactly at once.

"Anything special in mind?"

"Just a lot of food," I said.

He cooked us scrambled eggs, bacon, sausage, hash browns, pancakes, and toast.

We had not eaten like that for a very long time. You don't appreciate a big meal until you've been getting by on almost nothing for a while.

We sighed while we ate. We ignored the stretched signals from our stomachs and just kept stuffing them. We felt the pressures of the day, of our trip and our lives, simply slide away. It's funny how bleak the world looks on an empty stomach, and how benign that same view can appear after a big meal.

———

We all three stepped out of the diner at three, Freddy locking the door behind us.

That was when we realized we had time on our hands.

We briefly considered a motel room. We reached into our pockets for our phones to check the local rates. Then we wondered out loud whether we would ever learn to stop doing that.

We counted our tips for the day, knowing they were unusually high, and decided that if we rented a motel room at night we would more or less only break even in the long run. Which was not what we were after. It was a long drive to the Northwest Territories, and we needed gas money.

We drove to the nearest open business, which was a twenty-four-hour gas station, and bought a deck of cards.

We lay on our sides in the back of the Jeep, our hips pressing hard into the floor, up on one elbow, and played gin until it was too dark to see the cards.

It was mid-autumn, and night fell early. With nothing much else to do, we crawled into our sleeping bags in the cold and tried to get some sleep.

———

We woke to someone knocking on our back window.

I gasped. Gabriel sat up so fast he banged his head on the Jeep's roof.

My first thought was that some kind of state police had come to tell us we couldn't sleep here. But lots of truckers were sleeping in that same lot. We could hear a hum of something like generators or refrigeration units coming from their big rigs.

"Who is it?" Gabriel asked, sounding panicky. "What do you want?"

"It's Freddy," Freddy said.

We both breathed at once. I could feel myself exhaling like a sigh, and I could hear Gabriel do the exact same thing at the same time.

We opened out one of the back doors.

"No," Freddy said. "No, no, no, no, no, no."

"Are we not supposed to sleep here?" Gabriel asked.

"No," he said again.

"All those truckers are doing it," I said.

"That's different. They have bunk warmers and portable cab heaters. They know what they're doing and they won't freeze to death. You will. I kept telling my wife you two were smart enough to get a room or something but she made me come by and check. Now I'm glad she did. Pack up your stuff. You're coming back to my house."

Chapter Fourteen

Life, if You're Doing It Right

Freddy's house was the first place I thought we might have a problem with Gabriel's way of presenting himself. But maybe that's not fair to Freddy's family, because we'd gotten looks before. It was more like . . . until that moment we'd been passing through and could simply walk away from those moments at will.

But now it was seven forty-five in the evening and we were seated at the dinner table with Freddy, his much younger wife, Bessie, and two miniature Freddies. That is, two boys, about thirteen to fifteen, with the same lanky frame and buzz-cut hair.

And we were committed to being there for the night.

I remember thinking, *Here we are in Montana, with men who won't even let their hair grow half an inch.* I might have seen this coming.

We were eating chili and corn bread, and I remember I leaned over to Gabriel and whispered in his ear, "Toto, I don't think we're in California anymore."

Meanwhile the wife kept sneaking glances, but she wasn't being as discreet as she probably thought she was. The boys would quickly look, then look down at their plates, then snicker.

I thought it was odd that they would have so strong a reaction, seeing as Gabriel hadn't reapplied any makeup since our days camping, and it was all pretty faded. If I were just meeting him, I'm not sure I'd even notice. Then again, I don't live in Montana and buzz my hair.

One of the boys let out a braying laugh that seemed to burst out against his will.

His mother leaned over and cuffed him on the back of the neck.

"Ow!" he shouted, and rubbed the spot.

It did seem to knock the mirth right out of him.

He looked up at Gabriel, his eyes hurt, as if Gabriel were the source of all corporal punishment.

"Why do you wear makeup and nail polish?" he asked, his voice whiny.

"Marshall!" his father barked.

"What? I didn't laugh. I just *asked*. What, now I can't even *ask*?"

"If you boys can't be civil," Freddy's wife said, "you can just stand up from the table right now and go to bed without the rest of your supper."

"I don't see what's so uncivil about *asking*," Marshall whined.

"You just don't ask personal questions when someone is a guest. Now these nice folks are from California, and things are a little different there. And besides, I'm sure he has his reasons."

That actually bothered me more than the teenage nonsense.

"He doesn't need a *reason*," I said. "It's not about—"

But then Gabriel caught my eye and I let the sentence dangle where I had hung it.

Gabriel and I had hit a real stride in our friendship by then, and it was easy to talk to each other without ever opening our mouths. What he had said to me with his eyes in that moment was *It's easier for me if you just let it slide.*

And I took him at his word on that, because he knew more than I did about how it felt to be him.

The older boy, the one who was not Marshall, said, "You need a reason where *we* come from." More or less under his breath, but also just loudly enough that everyone could hear.

Freddy slammed his open right palm down onto the dinner table. Everything sitting on the table rattled. Everybody seated at the table jumped.

"That's quite enough out of you boys!" he shouted. His volume rattled me a little, too, like the dishes. And I could tell it made Gabriel uneasy. "These two young people are honest and hardworking and you better decide what's more important to you—eating your dinner or keeping up this disrespect—because you sure as hell can't have both."

The room fell deathly silent, and stayed that way for a long time. Gabriel and I shoveled in food, though I had lost my appetite and sensed the same might be true of him.

After two or three minutes of silence, the younger boy looked straight at me.

"How old are you?" he asked.

"Marshall . . . ," Freddy said in a deep, warning tone.

"What? What's wrong with that? I just asked how old she was."

"She's older than she looks and just leave it at that."

"Well, *obviously*," Marshall said. "You can tell when she opens her mouth and talks that she's not a kid. I just wondered *how much* older than she looks."

"I'm twenty-two," I said.

Marshall got that same look he'd had when his mother hit him. Just totally knocked off-balance and lost.

"But *how*?"

"I have a medical condition," I said. "It makes me look like I'm not aging."

"What's it called?"

I opened my mouth to tell him the lie Gabriel and I had decided on, but his mother cut me off.

"That's quite enough of this," she said. "We're going to talk about something else entirely. Where are you two young people headed after this?"

"We're going to Canada," Gabriel said.

Freddy chimed in. "Oh, beautiful country. You'll like it up there. What part?"

"We're going to the Northwest Territories," he said. "We want to try to see the aurora borealis."

Freddy and his wife exchanged a look. It made me edgy, because I had no idea what it meant.

"You know who they should talk to," Freddy said to his wife.

"I was just thinking that exact same thing," she said back. She sounded squirmy with excitement.

Then they both said a name at almost exactly the same moment.

"Gladys!"

"Now why would you want to go and wish Gladys on them?" the older boy said.

"She's not so bad," Freddy said.

"She's a nut."

"She's just . . . cantankerous. Is all. But she was born and raised in Yellowknife and she still has family there. Talks about it all the time. She's been wanting to get back there for a visit for years but she refuses to fly, and it's an awful long drive for an eighty-year-old woman to take all on her own. It's a long way to there. Probably better than twelve hundred miles. One person traveling alone would have to drive for days to get up there."

Gabriel and I exchanged a glance.

Remember what I said about things falling into place if you're doing life correctly? I think we both sensed that moment had come.

———

We were shown to bed in what I could only assume was the boys' room. Twin beds with Star Wars sheets and posters of football and soccer stars on the walls.

"Oh, no," I said. "Did we put the boys out of their room?"

"They'll be fine in the basement," Freddy said. "There's a heater."

Gabriel spoke up. "I just figure this might make them like me even less."

"They don't dislike you," Freddy said. "They're just used to things a certain way and it made them forget their manners. But they won't forget again after tonight. I'll see to that. You two need anything more? Bessie put towels and washcloths in the bathroom for you. And there are drinking glasses in the bathroom if you're thirsty. The tap water is good in these parts. Anything else?"

"No, we're good, Freddy," I said. "Thank you. This is really nice."

He turned to leave the room, but I stopped him.

"Just one thing, though. How do we find this Gladys person?"

"Oh, you won't have to find her. She'll find you. She works weekdays over at the Chevron station, but she comes in every Saturday and Sunday morning for pancakes. Seven a.m. You could set your clock by old Gladys. Just pancakes. No eggs, no coffee. Not even a glass of water. Just a short stack of pancakes with real maple syrup. So you'll be seeing her soon enough, and you can tell her your plans. I'm sure she'll have some advice for you regarding the Northwest Territories. But be careful. She might end up wanting to ride up there with you, and I don't know how you'll feel about that."

Gabriel and I exchanged glances. We both knew how we felt about that. Even if she was a little bit . . . cantankerous, as Freddy had put it . . . even if she was a nut, as one of the boys had said . . . we needed to meet her. We couldn't pretend an eighty-year-old woman was our mother at the border, but there was nothing so out of the ordinary about teens taking their grandmother home for a visit.

And she had family there. And it was clear to us now that we couldn't sleep in the Jeep without freezing to death.

I looked back at Freddy again, who was hovering by the door. Maybe just in case there was something else we needed or wanted to say.

"Does she have lots of long white hair with feathers braided into it?" I asked him.

He looked more than a little surprised.

"Now how did you know that?"

"You said she works at the Chevron station. We bought a deck of cards from her this afternoon."

And that, girls, as I said earlier, is life. Provided you're doing it right.

———

True to Freddy's version of events, Gladys showed up on Saturday morning at straight-up seven o'clock. She wanted absolutely nothing to do with me when we first met.

I walked up to her table, and she peered at me with narrowed eyes. The gaze looked almost threatening.

She was a tiny old woman, very thin. She simply gave the impression of occupying very little space in the world. But she had a truly impressive head of long, straight white hair. It seemed to cover almost as much area as the rest of her combined.

Her skin was weathered as if by years of sun. Tanned, leathery. Creased.

As I got closer, I was nearly overwhelmed by the stench of stale cigarette smoke.

"Who the hell are you?" she asked.

She sounded like a young actor portraying a witch in a school play.

"My name is Ru," I said. "I'm filling in for the family while they're off tending to their family emergency."

"Oh," she said. "Yeah. Heard about that."

I wanted to ask her why she'd even questioned me, then. If she knew the family was away. But you quickly learn not to say or do anything to suppress tips. You're always welcome to speak your mind as a waitress, if you're prepared to find a quarter on the table when the patron leaves. If that.

Besides, we were hoping this woman could get us across the border.

I opened my mouth to speak, but she cut me off.

"I been comin' in here every Saturday and Sunday morning for twenty-two years. Since those kids who work here now were kids. And I got to say, I'm not real big on change. I like things that stay the same. It's a comfort to me. Why, if you was one of them, I wouldn't even have to tell you what I want for my breakfast. You'd just know."

"Short stack," I said. "With real maple syrup. And nothing else. No eggs, no coffee. Not even a glass of water. Just the pancakes."

She narrowed her eyes at me again. They were gray, those eyes. A very distinct, unusual shade of gray.

"Now how'd you know that?"

"Freddy the cook told me."

"Why were you even talkin' about me with Freddy?"

"He asked where we were headed after we finish up here. I told him we were headed up to the Northwest Territories in Canada . . ."

That was when she suddenly wanted something to do with me.

Those unusual gray eyes grew from narrow to wide. Very wide. Very fast. Everything changed in that moment. Now Gladys looked at me as though she'd just rediscovered a beloved long-lost friend.

"You goin' all the way up there?" Her voice was thick with wonder.

"Yes ma'am."

"When?"

"As soon as Virgil and his family can get back. Might be a couple of weeks or might be sooner."

I watched her face as I spoke. Watched a cloud cross her gray eyes, causing her to deflate again. Causing that atmosphere of wonder to crash.

"Oh," she said. "You're prob'ly flyin'. Everybody flies."

"No, we're driving up there in our Jeep."

"Hey," she said. Her voice and mood were straining now. Almost desperate. "Hey," she said again. She reached out one tiny, clawlike hand and grabbed my sleeve, tugging me closer. "You got room for one more in that Jeep o' yours? I know you don't know me or nothin'.

But I'd pay for all the gas. Where you stayin' in the meantime? I got a guest room."

In my peripheral vision I saw Gabriel busing a table in the far corner of the dining area. I asked him to come over with my eyes and a slight gesture of my head.

He showed up in practically no time.

Because we'd been in a real house the night before, he had reapplied his makeup and nail polish. A bit more subtly than if we'd been in Coastal California. But it was fresh.

"This is Gladys," I said.

She narrowed her eyes at him, too.

"You two goin' through Yellowknife?" she asked.

"We can," Gabriel said. "We can go wherever the situation takes us."

"I'll pay all the gas, like I told your friend here. I won't smoke in the car and I'll keep my damn mouth shut. I got a guest room, and I'll put you up till we go. You stayin' in a motel now? You could be savin' that money instead."

"We're at Freddy's," Gabriel said. "But it's not really all that comfortable there for me. He has two teenage boys, and they're not . . . you know . . . accepting."

Gladys looked him up and down again, but without the narrowed eyes. She took in his face, especially, and his painted fingernails, which were black that day.

He waited while she completed that silent assessment.

"If that's less of a problem for *you*, that is," he added.

Her gaze popped back up to his eyes.

"Honey," she said, "I was born and raised in Yellowknife. I'm a US citizen now, and at the time that seemed like a good idea. Nothin' against the US, but I been wantin' nothin' more than home for as long as I can remember. I'm eighty-one years old, and every year goes by it gets worse, the wantin' to be home. So listen to me good, and believe what I say to you. I don't give a rat's patootie if you wear gardenias in your hair and dance the hula with a rose in your teeth. You get me back to Yellowknife and you're A-okay by me."

———

When we told Freddy we were going to stay with Gladys for the remainder of our time in town, he looked mortified. At first I wasn't sure why.

"I guess I don't blame you," he said.

"It's nothing about your family," I said.

That was when I figured out why.

Gabriel was in the back, loading the big industrial dishwasher. I had drawn the short straw, figuratively speaking, and agreed to talk to our current host.

"It's everything about my family, and I'm sorry."

He was scraping the griddle with this big, flat metal spatula. Long, even sweeps that reflected years of practice. The sound had grown oddly familiar to me in a very short time.

"We just figured she has a guest room, and that way your boys can have their bedroom back."

Also we needed to bond with Gladys as much as possible. She was our ticket over the border. We had no idea how hard it would be to find another person who wanted to go, since this one had dropped into our laps without effort. And we needed to get our stories straight before answering any questions for a border guard. We had to know we could count on her to rubber-stamp our cover story.

But of course I didn't tell Freddy all that.

Meanwhile his hands kept scraping but his eyes looked far away. Soft, and a little sad.

"I got nothing against anyone," he said.

"I know that."

"Anyone who's honest and halfway decent," he added. "And I tried to raise my kids the same way. And I thought I did. But I didn't do anything special to try to stretch their minds to be more open. I just sort of thought the way *I* was would end up being what *they* were."

"Not necessarily," I said. "Kids are themselves. Take it from me. No one in my family is unusually intelligent except me. Kids just pop out into the world as their own people. But also, they're getting a lot of pressure right now, your boys. They're in school with a bunch of other boys, and they're all trying to figure out what it means to be a man these days."

"I was hoping they'd model themselves after me," Freddy said.

"They probably will. In the long run. But right now they're being bombarded by these wild messages of what a man is in this country. In music and movies and on TV. And most of them are really bad messages. Really toxic and twisted. I'm sure they're good boys, but they're young and impressionable and it's easy to get confused. And if you get it wrong, peer groups of kids are so brutal. Nobody wants to fall onto the wrong side of *that*. So maybe cut them a little slack."

Freddy's hands paused in their task. For the first time since we'd begun speaking that afternoon.

"You got a lot of wisdom for twenty-two," he said.

"I don't know about that. I just look around the world and I don't forget what I see."

"I'll tell the wife you're leaving."

"Thanks," I said, and moved toward the hanging aprons to put mine away.

"I heard from Virgil," he called after me. "His mother died."

I paused, my hand in the air, holding up that apron. I could feel those words reverberate through me, as though I were a thin sheet of metal that could shudder back and forth in the wind. Except this was a different kind of wind.

"That's too bad," I said over my shoulder when things had steadied some.

"He'll be gone a while, making all the arrangements. Cleaning out her house and closing all her accounts and such. But his kids are coming back right after the memorial. Then we'll have a waitress and a busser again. And you two can get on with your trip."

"When's the memorial?"

"They haven't scheduled it yet. I'll keep you posted. I told him you and Gabriel are doing a great job. He said to say he owes you a debt of gratitude, and he authorized me to pay you cash under the table the day you leave. Ten dollars an hour, not the eight he promised you. He's that grateful."

"Wow," I said, and hung up the apron. We would lock the doors in just a matter of minutes. I was nursing a feeling of warm satisfaction that was unfamiliar to me. "That's really nice. Thanks."

"Well, you were nice to him. You taking Gladys with you?"

"Yeah. We are."

"Good. That's good. That's real nice to hear. I keep worrying she's gonna die without seeing Yellowknife again. She wants to reconnect with home. That was nice of you, to take her. She's a little different, but she's harmless."

"She offered to pay for gas," I said. "So we all win."

But of course only Gabriel and I knew—only Gabriel and I would ever know—just how big a win it really was.

Chapter Fifteen

Kids Today, Am I Right?

We saw very little of Gladys in the days before we resumed our journey. We got to her house after three. She worked two to ten.

On the rare times we did bump into her, she was strangely solicitous. Not that we really knew her well enough to know what was strange for her, but she had never done anything to give us the impression that she tended to bend over backward to be polite to people. As best we could gather, she'd never done anything to give anybody that impression.

The first day she got up at four thirty to make coffee for us before our shift at the diner, even though we knew she couldn't possibly have gotten to bed before eleven.

"You comfortable in that room?" she asked us. More than once. "Warm enough? Need any towels or washcloths? More blankets?"

We tried to dismiss the questions by assuring her that we were enjoying our stay, but it never seemed to put her mind at ease.

It was Gabriel who finally broke through the wall of indirect communication and said something real.

"We're going to take you with us, Gladys. You have our word on that. We're not going to change our minds."

That just sat there on her kitchen table for a moment, like something wounded.

Gladys's house was absolutely brimming. It's hard to say brimming with what, because nothing fell neatly into categories. There were bones and shells, beads and quilts. Quartz crystals and other lapidary items. Garden gnomes and pink lawn flamingos inside the house. A vase full of peacock feathers. Needlepoint art on the walls. Walking sticks with woven straps leaning in the corners. Wood carvings and china knick-knacks covering all available surfaces. And souvenir ashtray after souvenir ashtray after souvenir ashtray, all overflowing with cigarette butts, smoked right down to the filter.

It felt hard to move around. Technically we fit, but somehow we felt squeezed out. Sometimes it was even hard to breathe, but not so much because of the smoke. It was more a vague feeling that all the *things* had displaced too much of the air.

"Well, I guess that's a load off my mind," she said, her voice sounding like a sigh. "I guess I figured since you don't know me and what have you, I'd be easy enough to leave behind."

"The gas money will really help," I said.

But, once again, it was Gabriel who cut through the white noise of chitchat and hit bone.

"Would you have any problem saying you're our grandmother when we cross the border?"

"That's a good way to go," she said. "You're bein' smart. I thought of it. If anybody knows crossin' that border, it's yours truly. Always paint 'em as simple a picture as possible. Nothin' to get their curiosity goin'. In fact, I'll take the wheel for that part of the trip, and you let me do most of the talkin'. Whoever's on duty'll ask us where we're headed. I'll answer that. He'll ask you each a simple question, like 'Where were you born?' Even though he can read it for himself off your passports. That's 'cause they like to hear your voice. See if you have an accent, if you sound relaxed or scared. Stuff like that. They wave people through all day long. Nine times outta ten they won't ask you no more than just that. So you just sit there in the passenger seats and leave it to me. I know that border like it was my livin' room. If anybody can get us over, it's me. Of course a border guard is always a wild card. But I'm your best bet for no problems."

I didn't know if that little speech meant she knew we had potential problems. I also didn't ask.

———

The evening before we left, we had to go back to the diner to pick up our pay. Freddy didn't have it at the end of the shift because he'd been working too, and he had to go to the bank and get cash.

I left Gabriel in the driver's seat to run the engine and the heater while I ducked in, because it's just easier for the passenger to jump out.

Freddy had let himself back into the place and was sitting on a stool in the kitchen, waiting for me.

"You know, we're all gonna miss you around here," he said.

"That's nice to hear."

"Stop in and say hi on the way back through if you're going this way. If you do, your meal's on us."

"Thanks," I said. "Maybe we will."

He pulled a thick envelope out of his pocket and handed it to me.

"You can count it if you want," he said. "But it's all there."

"I trust you."

"It added up to a lot. I'm not sure if you ever stopped to figure out what it would add up to."

"Not really," I said. "But I could do it now. It's easy math. Ten dollars an hour times a ten-hour shift. For two people. That's two hundred dollars a day for the two of us. For eleven days is twenty-two hundred dollars."

"And that's what's in the envelope."

"Between that and our tips," I said, "and the money we already had that we hadn't put in the gas tank yet, we're leaving Montana in better financial shape than we left California."

"Good," Freddy said. "You worked hard and you deserve it. You have a good trip. Take care of yourself, and take care of Gladys. She's more fragile and delicate than she'd have you believe."

I stepped out into the cold, dusky afternoon.

There was a man there, leaning his back against the outside wall of the diner, rubbing his hands briskly and blowing into them to keep them warm. He was maybe in his late twenties, or maybe thirty, with a big fur hat with earflaps. I was startled, because he seemed like a thing out of place, and I was carrying so much cash.

I wondered if Freddy could see us from inside. Just in case. I knew Gabriel was watching. But Gabriel didn't have a phone.

I looked at the stranger and he looked at me.

"Thanks for helping out while we were gone," he said.

"Oh. You're Virgil's son."

"I am."

"I'm really sorry about your grandmother."

He averted his gaze. Turned his head slightly away. I heard a sound come out of him I couldn't interpret. A kind of snort.

"I know you're headed up to Canada," he said. "So you probably couldn't tell anybody this if you wanted to. But I'm going to say it anyway. Please don't quote me on what I'm about to say. She wasn't really all that nice. I didn't like her very much."

"That doesn't help, though. When somebody dies. You want it to, and you think it will, but then it doesn't. Or at least, not as much as you might hope."

"That may well be true," he said. "Hasn't really sunk in yet."

"I get that."

I turned to go back to the Jeep, but he had more to say, so he called it after me.

"Everybody liked you two," he said.

I stopped. Turned. I was ridiculously flattered. Probably because I hadn't seen such a thing coming.

"Really?"

"Yeah, really. Everybody said you were both really friendly and nice and worked hard, and in a lot of ways you didn't even seem like you were from California at all."

That last part caught me off guard, and I snorted out a rude burst of laughter.

"That's very magnanimous of them," I said.

"Yeah, I thought so." But it was clear he was enjoying the joke with me. "Safe trip," he said.

"Thanks."

I climbed back into the Jeep with Gabriel, and it was freezing in there. He had the driver's side window down, so that when I opened the door this blast of icy wind roared through.

I closed the door and he powered up the window, and we headed for Gladys's house again, teeth chattering.

"What did you have the window down for?"

"I wanted to hear what that guy said to you. I was a little worried, because you were carrying so much cash."

"You heard it all?"

"Yup. I did. Everybody liked us. I've got to tell you, I did not see that coming."

———

When we woke up in the morning and stumbled out of our twin guest beds, Gladys was sitting by her front door. Just sitting there, staring at it.

I suppose we were lucky she wasn't staring at us in our sleep. She was obviously trying to will the trip to start with the sheer force of her mind.

In front of her on the floor sat two of the most amazingly large suitcases you can imagine. Just imagine the biggest ones you think you've ever seen, and then double that.

"How did you even lift these?" I asked her.

"Didn't. Packed 'em right here. You two are young and can fling 'em in the car for me. I mean . . . please. Please and thank you."

"This might present a problem," Gabriel said. "You asked us if we had room for you, and we said yes. But this is like you and then two more yous."

"Gotta have my stuff," she said. "You got that big space in the back."

"Our sleeping area," he said.

"You won't be sleepin' in your car up there. Talked to my brother, and the cold set in early this year. Late fall and it feels like January, and you'd wake up froze to death if you tried to sleep there. No, we got two choices. Drive straight through, tradin' off drivers, or stop in a motel every night. If we do that second one it'll take us maybe three days to get up there."

"So, like I said," Gabriel began, "our sleeping area."

"We got the side of the back seat that I'm not usin'."

"Which is where we stack our own suitcases. And then when we put the back seats down to sleep we have to move them up front. This is definitely a space problem."

"You promised I could go!" Gladys rose to her feet as she spoke, her voice rising and hardening. "You gave your word!"

"You're going," he said. "Just let me think." He opened her front door and stared at our Jeep parked in her driveway. As if it might have suggestions. "We could tie them to the roof rack if you have some rope."

"I got better'n rope. I got the nylon tie-down straps I used to use when I hauled hay in my truck. They're in the garage. I'll go get 'em."

And with that she bustled out of the room.

Gabriel and I exchanged half-amused, half-exasperated glances.

"Maybe we should have asked her how long she plans to be gone," I said.

He opened his mouth to answer, but Gladys was back, and talking a mile a minute.

"Now these here're the best tie-down straps you can get. They have these little winches on 'em. That takes up the slack, and then they can't back off again. None of that loosenin' up as you drive down the road. And speakin' of the road, come on now. I've been waitin' for years upon years upon years. I want to *go*."

———

"Gimme your passports," she said.

"Why?" we both asked at once.

I knew neither one of us was thrilled with the idea of showing them to her. We hadn't exactly advertised to her that we were both minors.

"Because he'll ask for all of 'em, and I'm at the window, and I need to hand 'em all over."

Gladys was driving, as she had requested. And the border-crossing station was frighteningly clear up ahead.

We handed them to her, hoping she wouldn't take her eyes off the road to study them. For two reasons.

Up ahead we saw stop signs, and a green roof over an area with little shelters like tollbooths. There were two lanes going through it, but a series of orange cones had funneled them into one. I could see the words "Customs and Immigration" and the word "Canada" in much larger letters. I could see a Canadian flag drooping in the still and windless morning. All the signs were in English and French, even though Quebec was a very long way away from that place.

There were four cars waiting in front of us.

Gladys pulled up behind them and shifted into "park."

She looked over at me in the passenger seat, then over her shoulder at Gabriel in the back. She made a disapproving clucking noise with her tongue.

"Want to know the biggest two reasons people get pulled over and searched?" she asked us. She didn't wait to hear if we wanted to know. "Number one, sass. You don't sass these guys. They got power over you.

They got all the power. When I was in high school a friend of mine sassed a border guard. Guy pulled him outta line and had his men take the driver's door off my boy's car and break it down into tiny little pieces. I don't mean *broke it* broke it. I mean broke it down into all its parts. Took off the handles and mirror, took out the window, took off the liner thing from inside it. And then—get this—the guy told my friend he was under no legal obligation to put it back together. He did put it back together. But first he put the fear of God into that boy. So you be nothin' but polite. Which I know you will be. I'm not worried about that. I'm worried about reason number two. People who look nervous."

Gabriel and I caught each other's eyes.

It was almost funny, or might have been at a different time and place. We both sought the other out thinking we had no idea what she was talking about, because we didn't look nervous. And then we saw how right she was.

"Now you're gettin' it," Gladys said. "Breathe deep and start believin' your own cover story. Back to the old country with Grandma."

We moved forward.

Gabriel and I looked up to see only one car in front of us.

"Whoa," he said, and he sounded scared. "That was fast."

"Told you. They wave people through all day long. Oh. Names. If you're my grandkids I should know your names. But just like it's on your passport. Gabriel and . . . is Ru short for somethin'?"

"Rumaki," I said.

"Isn't that some kind of appetizer?"

"Don't get me started," I said.

And then, just like that, the car in front of us drove off. And we pulled up.

The border guard was a man. Not tall, but broad shouldered. Short haircut under an official-looking hat. His face looked hard. Well, maybe hard is not the right word. It was . . . inscrutable. Blank and closed and impossible to read. He would have made a great poker player, except nobody would ever invite him to their games because he was intimidating.

He draped one forearm onto the roof of the Jeep and looked at each one of us carefully.

"Passports," he said.

But before he had even finished the word, Gladys had handed them over.

He examined them and spoke at the same time.

"Final destination?"

"Yellowknife, NWT," Gladys said.

"Purpose of your visit?"

"We got family up there. This here's my older girl's boy, Gabriel, and my middle girl's girl, Ru. I been tryin' to get 'em up to Yellowknife all their lives to see where our people come from. But kids today. They got no sense of history. Know what I mean?"

The guard glanced up at her, but I still couldn't read his face.

"Whatever you say, ma'am. Place of birth?"

"Yellowknife, NWT. But I'm a naturalized US citizen."

"How long do you plan to be in Canada?"

"Maybe two weeks," Gladys said.

He stuck his head most of the way through the window and looked me right in the face. Gladys had to lean back into the headrest to get out of his way.

Reason number two. People who look nervous.

Gladys's words echoed in my head, and they were the last thing I needed to hear. There's no better way to look nervous than to have someone tell you not to look nervous.

"Place of birth?" he barked at me.

"Garden Grove, California."

I thought my voice sounded a little squeaky, but I honestly think it was one of those things that was more obvious to me than anybody else. I was sure hoping so.

He turned his iron gaze onto Gabriel.

"Place of birth?"

"Santa Rosa, California."

The guard folded the passport booklets closed again. All three together, like Russian nesting dolls but all the same size.

A beat seemed to go by when nobody breathed.

He held the three passports out to Gladys.

"You folks have a nice trip," he said.

Gladys rolled up the window, and we drove on.

"And *that*," she said proudly. "Is how. It's. Done."

Chapter Sixteen

Throw Me a Lifeline Named Gladys Through the Blowing Snow

I'd like to tell you we saw lots of Canada on the drive up. We certainly drove through lots of Canada. But Gabriel and I had been forced to take the night shift.

We slept through Calgary and Edmonton while Gladys drove, trying to turn our days and nights around. Just as well, I suppose, as we didn't drive all the way to Canada just to see cities. Cities all look alike to me.

After the first day, when we got farther north, things got wilder and more deserted.

What we saw on the night shift was a lot of snow illuminated by headlights. My deepest impressions came from moments like owls swooping through the light beams, and large animals like elk or deer or caribou dashing across the road in front of us, forcing Gabriel to brake quickly but gently to avoid skids. I could feel the slight fishtail of our rear tires on the icy highway.

It occurred to me more than once that any kind of accident out here, even skidding off the road and into a snowbank, could easily equal death. Judging by the look on Gabriel's face, I'm sure he felt the weight of that truth as well. Maybe more so, as he was the one currently in charge of preventing it.

In that moment he seemed a mere seventeen to me, though usually he didn't. Stranger still, I felt thirteen years old.

It's a big, cold, scary world in Northern Canada for two so young.

Once we stopped to let a big elk with a gigantic rack of horns cross in front of us. Or maybe it was a caribou. I've never really been sure. Next thing we knew there was another. And then another. And then a hundred. And then two hundred.

We just sat there staring with our mouths agape, hoping nobody would hit us from behind. But there were darned few motorists out on that road at night. It filled me with a slight, tingly sense of danger, and made me wonder if they knew something we didn't.

Meanwhile Gladys snored like a buzz saw in one of our sleeping bags in the back. Oh how that woman could snore!

And then at the very end of the elk parade trailed one lone coyote, padding along. Tracking the herd.

When we started up again, I talked to Gabriel, because I wanted to be sure he'd stay awake. We had shifted our nights and days, sleep-wise, much too rapidly. It would have been easy for him to doze off on the road.

"You nice and awake?" I asked.

"Like anybody could sleep through Gladys's snoring. Have you ever heard a sound like that in your life?"

"Never. You know, I think she's pretty smart. Maybe more clever than we might've given her credit for. Did you notice she told that border guard we were the kids of two of her daughters? She made it sound like she was one of those chatty sorts who always says too much. But meanwhile she planted it in his head that there was a good reason why none of us have the same last name. Her daughters would have married names, and that would make us cousins, not siblings."

"Which means she looked at our passports."

"I guess she must have. Since we never told her our last names."

"Then she probably knows how young we are."

"Maybe so. But she got us into Canada."

"Smart and bold," he said. "We got lucky. Now let's just hope when all this is over we can get back."

———

As we wound farther north there were some little dots of towns along the way, but they were both small and far between.

When the sky grew light, and we stopped to trade drivers and use the bathroom, the only bathroom was frozen tundra dotted with skinny, snow-laden trees.

We stood beside the Jeep, bundled in our best jackets—which would clearly not be good enough for where we were headed—and waited for Gladys to reappear from over the snowy rise where she had gone to do her business. We jumped up and down, hugged and slapped our own arms. Watched our breath fill the air as frozen clouds.

"It's. So. Flipping. *Cold!*" I said through chattering teeth.

"You can say that twice."

"It's hard to talk when your lips are numb."

"We'd better get used to it," he said.

Seconds later Gladys appeared from over the rise. She hadn't bothered to put on her huge, fur-trimmed parka and was wearing only a sweater.

"So frickin' *beautiful!*" she called to us. "It's like the dead of winter! I tell ya, I missed this kinda cold. I just love this weather!"

"We noticed the cold too," Gabriel said as he headed out to find a spot. "But probably not for the same reasons."

———

Gladys woke us by yelling loudly from the front seat.

"Hey! Hey, you guys! You must be hungry, right?"

We sat halfway up. I rubbed my eyes. Gabriel just blinked a lot. The sun was hovering not too far above the horizon outside the windows.

"What time is it?" Gabriel asked.

"Ten thirty. And I figured we'd best get us some breakfast quick before the diners stop servin' it. We're almost in Fort Providence. We'll eat and gas up there, and then it's less than four hours into Yellowknife. You can go back to sleep and I'll wake you when we're at my brother's house."

We sat up as best we could in that vertically small space. Well, actually it was small in every direction.

"How can it be ten thirty?" Gabriel said. "The sun's barely up."

I said, "It's our latitude."

Gladys said, "Welcome to late in the year in the Northwest Territories."

The two sentences came out more or less at the same time, but he seemed to get the idea.

"Oh, right," he said. Then: "Yeah, food would be good."

It was a serious understatement. We were more than twenty hours out of Montana, and all we'd had to eat were a few peanuts and a small piece of beef jerky.

"Great!" she said. Or, actually, shouted. She seemed inordinately happy. "Because I used to like to eat in that diner, and I can't believe all these years later it's still there."

She pulled into the parking lot and parked as close to the door as possible. We struggled into our jackets and knitted caps and stepped out into a world that was purely white. The ground was white. The sky was white. Snow drifted across the tarmac in the howling wind, making the air appear white.

Only the dark wood of the diner stood out as nonwhite. Other than our Jeep, it was the only perspective in sight.

We raced for the door, slipping and sliding on the ice.

Inside it was aggressively warm. It just hit us in the face like an oven. We quickly peeled off our jackets and hung them on one of the many hooks by the door.

Gladys looked them over, feeling the weight of their down filling in her arthritis-bent fingers, and clucked her tongue in that way she did when she did not approve.

"We'll have to get you better'n this," she said.

We looked around for a table and then sat down.

The place had freestanding fireplaces placed at intervals through the dining area, with warm roaring wood fires going in each one. They had long chimneys that vented up through the ceiling. The walls were done in very thin horizontal slats of wood paneling, which seemed an odd match with the loud black-and-white linoleum tile floor. In the way of windows, there were not many. Just two little snow-crusted lookouts the size of square portholes. Maybe people came in here to forget the whiteness of the world outside, or maybe a lot of glass made it too hard to keep the place warm.

In any case, we'd had only a few minutes outside the Jeep so far, and what we'd had was made abjectly miserable by the weather, so we were comfortable and happy in that moment.

A waitress appeared immediately to hand us menus. She was an Asian woman in her forties. She turned over the coffee mugs that were sitting upside down on the table, flipped them upright. Tried to pour.

Gladys blocked hers with one tiny claw of a hand and almost got it scalded in the process.

"Don't need that," she said. "Don't need your menu, either. I'll take a short stack of pancakes and nothin' else. I mean, maple syrup. Of course. That goes without sayin'. But beyond that, nothin' else. Don't know what these two want."

"We need some time to decide," Gabriel said, opening his menu. "No coffee for us either."

The hot drink sounded good, though in general we drank very little coffee. But I think he had it in his head that we'd get back to sleep while Gladys drove us into Yellowknife.

The waitress turned to leave but Gladys stopped her.

"Hey," she said. "Hey. You there. Waitress. Don't hurry off so fast. Wilbur still own this place?"

The woman's eyes grew wide.

"Wilbur McMahon?"

"That's the guy."

"Oh goodness no. Wilbur's been dead going on twenty years now."

"Of what?"

"Congestive heart failure."

"Oh," Gladys said. "I know how that goes."

Not for the first time since we'd know her, Gladys's tone put me in mind of a punctured tire. She got high on happiness when she got happy. But she also deflated fast.

"Damn it all to hell," she said as the waitress hurried away. "See? Everythin' changes. I hate that."

"I'm sorry you lost your friend," Gabriel said, his eyes still glued to the menu.

"He wasn't my friend," Gladys said, her voice hard. Inhospitable. "I didn't lose no friend. He was just the owner of this place. What I lost is the way things used to be." Neither one of us answered, so she added, "Dutch treat. We each pay our own way. I said I'd pick up the gas but I didn't commit to no more than that."

"Fair enough," I said.

While we waited for the waitress to come back I stared out that tiny window into the blinding, frightening white landscape. I think it was the first time that our location struck me as a different world—the first time I felt we had left our own world and traveled to one entirely foreign and new. And my overriding emotion surrounding this new world was fear.

Had we ever meant to be this adventurous? Was it really the plan to travel someplace so close to uninhabitable that we could die simply by being exposed to it?

It struck me that if we hadn't had Gladys with us, I'd find all of this truly terrifying. That made Gladys our very odd lifeline. And that was an unnerving feeling, to say the least.

———

We were halfway back to the Jeep when Gabriel grabbed me by the elbow and pointed. I stopped cold and looked where he was looking. But a gust of wind blew a swirling devil of snow up from the parking lot, and all I could see was white.

"Give it a minute," he said.

A few seconds later there was a gap between gusts, and I saw them. Sitting in a drift of snow at the edge of the parking lot were six or seven huge, shaggy brown animals. A lot of people would have called them buffalo, but they were bison. There's no shortage of confusion between the two, and the names have unfortunately been used interchangeably, but basically if it's in North America it's a bison.

They were curled up so calmly, staring off into nothing, and the air between us was still so white that I wasn't positive if I was seeing them or not. They might have been a vision of bison. They might even have been a mural of bison painted on the side of a building that was otherwise obscured to us.

But then one big male turned his head and looked right at us.

A second later the space between us had gone white again.

"Look," I said to Gladys.

"What?"

"Over there."

"What? You mean over by the bison?"

Neither one of us answered. She didn't appear to be kidding, and we were both a bit on the flabbergasted side.

"Oh, you *meant* the bison. I get it. 'Oh, Gladys. Look! Bison!' That's like me comin' to your land in California and sayin' 'Look, look! Guys! Seagulls! Ain't that just the most amazin' thing you ever seen in this world?'"

She snorted derisively, and we all piled into the Jeep. Gabriel and I stretched out in our sleeping bags in the back, hoping to get a little more sleep. Actually, make that a lot more.

But sleep did not come easily.

"Are we north of the Arctic Circle yet?" he asked her as we drove.

"We are not," Gladys said, "and we ain't gonna be."

"Yellowknife is not above the Arctic Circle?"

He sounded genuinely surprised. I think we both were.

"No it ain't. It's the southern part of the NWT. It ain't the Arctic Ocean. It ain't the Queen Elizabeth Islands. Now *that's* a whole different world up there. I wouldn't send you up to those islands, and I wouldn't recommend you go. Not just anybody can survive up in those parts. But if you really want to go north of the Arctic Circle I could send you up to Inuvik. I got me some kin up there."

"What do you mean 'send us'?" I asked, what with having so recently identified her as my lifeline in this scary new world and all. "You wouldn't go up there with us?"

"Oh hell no."

"Is it that bad up there?"

"It's nice up there. It's pretty. Colder, though."

"Is it a scarier drive than the one we just did?" Gabriel asked.

"It ain't no drive at all," Gladys said. "It ain't no drive because there ain't no road."

"There's no road going into Inuvik?"

"Well, there is, actually," she said, swerving to avoid a fox that Gabriel and I were just barely able to see disappearing into the woods. "But not from here. There's the Dempster Highway that goes right through Inuvik and then all the way up to Tuktoyaktuk. Now that's right on the Arctic Ocean, Tuktoyaktuk. That's the north for real. But it don't start in the NWT, that road. It starts in the Yukon. There's ice roads in the winter, but they ain't for the faint of heart, and they won't be open now anyway. This's just an unusually cold fall. Takes time for those lakes and rivers to freeze solid."

"So how do you get there?" I asked, already halfway sure I did not want to go.

"Floatplane," she said. "Lots of floatplane business in those parts. It's how everybody gets everywhere. It's a way of life."

Once again, Gabriel was the one who cut through to what mattered.

"So that's why you would send us there instead of going there with us. Because it involves flying in a plane."

"Bingo," Gladys said. "I ain't never got in one of those contraptions my whole life and don't think for a minute I'd be startin' now. I said it was a way of life in the NWT. I never said it was no way of life for *this* old gal."

Chapter Seventeen

Ill-Fitting Boots and a Lot of Yelling

We woke later that afternoon to lots of commotion and shouting. It turned out it was happy shouting, but it took us a minute to put two and two together on that score.

We sat up as best we could in the back of the Jeep and noted that it was not moving. Outside the window we saw a row of stark, modern-looking homes, and shapes of bundled-up people who appeared to be jumping up and down.

We opened a back door and stumbled out into the freezing afternoon. Before I could even reach in for my jacket, a big man grabbed me up into a bear hug and started jumping up and down with me too.

"This here's my brother, Darryl," Gladys screeched in her "high on happiness" voice.

"Sorry," Darryl said, still crushing me in a hug. "I know you don't know me from a hole in the ground, but you fetched me home my big sister and that makes you just like kin to me."

He let me go, and grabbed up Gabriel into the same hug. I watched Gabriel's face for a second or two. He looked equal parts embarrassed and pleased. It's hard to know how to react to a thing like that, but he did his best.

I reached again for my jacket, but before my fingers could snag it I was swept into another strangely enthusiastic hug by a stranger. A woman this time.

"I'm Evelyn," she said. "Darryl's wife." Her voice was projected at such a volume as to hurt my eardrum. "You are so, so welcome in our home! I can't believe Gladys finally made it back here!"

Meanwhile, not only were Darryl and Gladys still shouting excitedly at each other, but it seemed as though the whole neighborhood was shouting about something. To this day, I still believe Yellowknife is the loudest place I've ever been.

"Get your jackets," Darryl shouted. "We'll get you inside and warm you up. And then we'll go down to the pub and have us a decent supper. On me."

Gabriel and I reached into the back of the Jeep and pulled out our jackets. Darryl took one look at them and shook his head, his brow furrowed down.

"Never mind," he said. "Just leave 'em. Those'll never do. Come inside and we'll get you some real parkas."

We followed them into their odd house. It looked like some kind of prefabricated building in a bright, unusual orange. It had a short set of metal steps leading up to its clashing blue front door, with riser surfaces that felt like grating under our feet, probably so they couldn't get too slippery with the ice.

Inside, the house reminded me a lot of Gladys's. The only real difference was that it was overstuffed with items that had a more modern feel. But it was packed with decorations and carvings and pictures and hangings from floor to ceiling. Woven blankets hung on most of the walls. I couldn't even tell you the color of the walls; they were that completely covered.

I figured it ran in the family.

We were invited to have a seat on one of two couches near a roaring fire in a cast-iron woodstove.

"I'll make us some hot cider," Evelyn said.

And she disappeared into the kitchen.

We looked at Darryl, sitting beside his sister on the other couch, and he grinned back at us. I honestly think he had the biggest grin of anyone I've ever met. It seemed to take up his whole face and continue in his eyes. He wore a spotty beard and wire-rimmed glasses, and looked much younger than Gladys. *Much* younger. It was hard to imagine him being much over sixty. But the greatest mismatch was their size. Sitting next to each other, they looked like an advertisement for the smallest and largest person in the Northwest Territories.

"You two don't look related," I said.

"Yeah," Gabriel said. "I was just wondering if it was okay to say that. I would never have guessed you two were brother and sister."

"Half brother and sister," Darryl said. "We have the same mom. But our dads looked nothin' alike and there's twenty-one years of age between us. Here. Wait right here. I'm gonna get you some decent parkas before you die. You need decent parkas in the NWT. We got us an early winter goin' on."

He hoisted his great bulk to his feet and dug around in the closet by the front door for a few beats.

"We got these ones we save for when the kids come visit. They never show up wearing proper stuff ever, and they were born here, so you'd think they'd know."

"They still come?" Gladys asked, her voice louder than necessary.

"No, they don't hardly come," Darryl shouted back.

He pulled his head out of the closet and brought us two parkas, both in a deep navy blue. And let me tell you, these were the serious stuff. These were the kind of thing you'd expect to see on some intrepid soul dogsledding through the Yukon. They had fur-lined hoods and sleeves that drew as tightly closed as you wanted at the wrist. The sheer bulk of them was amazing. Unlike anything I'd ever worn.

"Look in the pockets," he said. "In there you got your gloves and your toques and your balaclavas and your scarves. That oughta set you up pretty good. Oh, but boots. We gotta get you some boots. I don't see as the ones I got for the kids'll fit ya."

So far we knew the meanings of the words "gloves," "scarves," and "boots," but nothing much beyond that. But we would quickly learn.

———

It was after sunset when we all made our way down to the pub. On foot.

We hadn't been expecting to go on foot. We figured people drove everywhere in this climate. But we were in Rome, as the old saying goes. Not literally, but I think you know what I mean.

So we clomped along in our borrowed boots, the ones Darryl had already said wouldn't fit us. And he'd been right. We were wearing three pairs of borrowed socks underneath, amazingly thick wool socks, but the boots still shifted around awkwardly every time we took a step. At least, I know mine did. Judging by the clumsiness of Gabriel's gait, I could see he was no more comfortable.

The boots had good traction as winter wear goes, but we still had to be careful not to slip on the ice and hard-packed snow.

Our faces were covered with the balaclavas, which were something akin to a ski mask. Our hands were both gloved and shoved deeply into the parkas' huge pockets. Our hoods were up and tied tightly under our chins.

And the cold still felt unbearable.

"So you guys walk places when you could drive," I said.

My lips were so numb that the words came out fuzzy and slurred, as if I were drunk.

"Yeah," Darryl said. "It takes like ten minutes to walk to the pub. It takes half an hour to warm up the engine on the truck and scrape all the ice off the windshield."

After that we walked in silence for a time. But really, to be more specific, I mean *we* were silent. I do not mean we enjoyed silence as we walked. As I think I mentioned before, everybody seemed to shout at everybody in Yellowknife. People seemed to congregate on street corners, shouting. Some seemed like genuine altercations. Others might just have been happy excitement. In many cases it was hard to tell.

"Why do people make so much noise here?" Gabriel asked as we clumped along.

Darryl said, "Why? Not sure what you mean by 'why.' Are the people all quiet where you come from?"

"Quieter than this," Gabriel said.

"They're just enthusiastic," Darryl said.

Evelyn jumped in to correct him.

"Not all of 'em are just enthusiastic, honey. Some of 'em are drunk."

"Well, yeah. All right. Maybe. But you can be drunk and enthusiastic at the same time, can'tcha?"

Nobody answered the question. We just clumped along.

It was our first real look at Yellowknife, but it was already pretty dark. But I could see it was more of a city than I had expected. It seemed to be built on rocks over a massive lake, now thinly, partially frozen near the shorelines. It had a downtown, with multistory office buildings creating a skyline. It was not the bare frozen tundra or the tiny remote towns we had driven through to get here. It was not wild or quaint. It was just a small but very real city.

"How many people live here?" I asked.

"Around forty-four thousand," Darryl said.

"Really," Gabriel said, sounding surprised. "That's a bigger city than we expected."

"Oh, the *city*," Darryl said. "You meant Yellowknife. How many people live in Yellowknife. About twenty thousand. When I said forty-four, I was talking about the NWT as a whole."

Both Gabriel and I stopped walking for a minute, then had to awkwardly hurry to catch up.

"Wait," Gabriel said. "The entire Northwest Territories only have forty-four thousand people?"

"Give or take," Darryl said.

"But it's so big."

"Over a million square kilometers."

We clumped along in silence again. I saw a pub at the end of the block with neon-lighted signs for different brands of beer. I was hoping that was our destination. I'd had more than enough of stumbling along in ill-fitting boots in subzero temperatures.

It struck me as unfortunate that we had traveled to a place so sparsely populated, yet ended up in a city that housed nearly half the population of more than a million square kilometers.

Maybe taking a floatplane to Inuvik would not be such a bad idea after all.

I looked at the sky, hoping we would be lucky enough to see the aurora borealis from right where we stood on a city street. But it was overcast, and I saw not even one solitary star.

———

"Get the fish," Darryl shouted to be heard over the other patrons. "You have to get the fish in Yellowknife. Comes straight out of the lake, and it's fresh. Best you've ever had, I guarantee ya."

We were sitting in a dimly lighted pub at a natural wood table that seemed to have inches of shiny, clear coating. The walls were covered with pictures of lake pike struggling on lines, caribou, and bald eagles.

"Even when the lake is frozen?" I asked.

"It's not yet. Not really. But oh yeah. Always. People ice fish in the dead of winter and supply the restaurants. There's always great fish in the NWT. But it's seasonal. So you just tell 'em you want the fish and they bring you whatever featured fish dish they got right now."

Gabriel and I both nodded. We would both have the fish. When in Rome, like I said before.

"What brings you young people all the way up here?" Evelyn asked us.

"We wanted to see the aurora," I said.

"Sure, that's what I figured. That's why most people come."

"Can you see them from right here in the city?" Gabriel asked.

"Oh yeah. Lotta nights you can. Maybe not quite as strong and clear and often as if you was all the way up on the Arctic Ocean, but they're good here."

We were still all raising our voices to be heard above the din.

"I was thinkin' I might send 'em up to Gerry in Inuvik," Gladys shouted. "But that don't come cheap, and I don't know if they want to spend that much money."

"What're you talkin' about?" Darryl said. "Gerry'll give you a free-bie. All you gotta do is ask."

"They're not kin, though."

"Yeah they are. They brought you home, so they are."

"Gerry makes so much on that cabin, though. It's income."

"Not a cabin. It's a yurt."

"I thought it was a cabin."

"No, it's a yurt. Actually it's kinda like a geodesic dome. See, if you'd get on a plane once in your life you'd know these things."

"Don't start with me, Darryl."

Meanwhile no one was asking us if we wanted to go to Inuvik. But I think by then we both sort of . . . did. I think we felt as though we hadn't come all this way to see the aurora over a city skyline of down-town office buildings.

"It's the offseason," he said. "The yurt might just be sittin' there empty. At least ask."

"I could ask," Gladys said. "Yeah. They'd still have to pay their own floatplane pilot."

"How much would that cost?" Gabriel asked, straining to be heard.

"Ain't cheap," Darryl said. "Might be five, six hundred a person each way. Think about it."

"What's the population up there?" I asked, because that felt like it cut to the heart of whether I wanted to go despite the admittedly daunting expense.

Suddenly it felt like my goal was a wilderness experience. It was terrifying—so much so that I wasn't positive I wanted it. And yet it tugged at me. Called to me. We'd come so far, and it had begun to seem like the thing we'd come for. It didn't feel right to turn around and go home without it.

"Population of Inuvik? Maybe three thousand or a little more. But that's just where Gerry's based. The yurt is out on the tundra between Inuvik and Tuktoyaktuk. And the population there is zero. Unless you count wolves. And your chances of seein' the lights there are as good as just about any place in the world. We might be able to get you a discount pilot. Sometimes they just need the work and they'll cut you a deal. And also, maybe this doesn't go without sayin' . . . I was talkin' Canadian dollars. Convert that to USD and it's a better deal, if that's what you got on you. Anyway, I know it's a lot of money, and if you don't got it you don't got it. But if you got it, think about it."

From that moment forward I could think about nothing else.

———

We were given beds of inflatable air mattresses in front of the woodstove at Darryl and Evelyn's house. We lay in the warmth, our bellies full of fresh-caught northern whitefish and french fries that were referred to in Canada as "chips."

We already knew we wouldn't get much sleep. We'd slept most of the day while Gladys drove, and besides, there was this *idea*.

"Kind of scary to think about," I whispered to Gabriel. "But exciting. Do you know how to convert Canadian dollars to USD?"

"I would if I had my phone," he said. "It might eat up so much of our money that we wouldn't have gas money to get home."

"I thought Gladys would pay gas money home."

"That's what she says. But I think we need to be prepared in case she runs out of money or falls out on us in some other way. We don't really know her that well."

"Okay. Then first we need to figure gas money home and set it aside. But then, if they can get us a bargain flight . . . what do you think?"

"Sounds like a very, very adventurous thing to do."

"Is that a good thing or a bad thing?"

"Yes," he said. "I think that's exactly what it is."

Chapter Eighteen

The Day We Floated over a World of Swiss Cheese

In the morning we bundled up and Evelyn took us to see the Pilots' Monument while Darryl went off to work for the day. Gladys did not come along, and for the moment I didn't spend much time wondering why not.

The monument was on top of a rock outcropping so high that we had to climb four or five flights of wooden stairs to stand on top of it. The locals rather predictably called it "The Rock." There was a wooden viewing platform at the top, but to see the plaque for "The Rock," or the monument itself honoring the bush pilots who'd settled the town, you stepped off the platform and just walked around on this snowy, icy, rocky hilltop. And there were no railings or anything like that. I'm not suggesting we were ever standing right at the edge of a four-story drop-off, but what with all the slipperiness, it did give one pause.

The lookout spot was a definite "must" for tourists, but the point of going up there—as best I could figure—was not the monument itself. It was the bird's-eye view of the city. We looked down over homes and shops and warehouses, and a lake that was one of the ten largest in the world. We marveled at the islands half-frozen into its milky surface as the wind scrubbed our faces and stung our eyes.

The ice on the lake was so far only a thin film at the shallowest edges of the water, nearest land, but I might've mentioned that before.

"Why did Gladys stay home?" Gabriel asked our hostess. "Did she just figure she's seen the monument enough for one lifetime?"

"Oh, she can't be coming up all those stairs," Evelyn said. "She's not a well woman." Then she just stared at our faces for a moment, apparently reading our surprise. "You didn't know that? I just figured you knew. Bad ticker. Congestive heart failure."

Gabriel and I caught each other's eyes, and in that moment we shared something we hadn't even known: that we knew Gladys enough to care about her. I hadn't known it, anyway.

"Really?" Gabriel said. "I'm surprised. I know she's at least eighty, but she works full-time at home in Montana."

"Yeah, she sits on a stool behind a counter and rings people up. Not much choice. Her Social Security checks are pretty skimpy and she couldn't make it without that job."

"She didn't tell us any of that," I said.

"Well, I can't say as I'm surprised. I mean, that's Gladys. You know darned well how she is."

"Is that why she didn't try to drive up here on her own?"

"That and a lot of other reasons. She acts tough but she's really scared a lot. She wouldn't take that drive by herself, and she's probably smart not to. I mean, there's no telling what might happen, medically speaking. And if you're out on the deserted stretches of that road all by your lonesome—"

Her cell phone rang before she could finish the sentence.

"Oh, this is Darryl," she said. "I got to pick this up."

We waited in silence while she listened on the line. She caught our eyes, one of us at a time, and grinned like she knew something good, and like it delighted her that we didn't know it yet.

"Oh, they'll be excited. At least I think they will be. That or scared. Lemme go tell 'em and we'll see just how adventurous they really turn out to be."

She slid the phone back into her pocket and addressed us excitedly.

"He called, and Gerry says the yurt's not booked till all the way in mid-November. You can use it as long as you like, provided you don't bump into those dates. But you weren't gonna want to stay that long anyway, I wouldn't think. It's free, so it's a little bare bones. There'll be bottled water to drink and all the food you can eat if you don't mind dehydrated backpacker food. Sometimes they do fancier meals, but that's for the paying guests. And here's another bit of good news. Darryl called around to some of the floatplane pilots, and he found a couple who'd go as low as four hundred per person each way."

"Canadian?" I asked though frozen lips.

"Right. Canadian."

"You know how to convert that?"

"I think I could do it on my phone here. Lemme bring up the browser. Let's see. Canadian dollars to USD. Here we go. Four hundred Canadian dollars is . . . a little under three hundred USD."

I looked at Gabriel and he looked at me, our eyes narrowed against the frigid wind.

"Let's do it, Gabriel," I said. "For one time in our lives let's have a real, genuine adventure."

He nodded once, seeming almost breathless. He didn't speak, but maybe he couldn't speak. It was hard to tell.

In any case, we were doing it. It was real.

There was something in the back of my mind that pushed me off that nice safe cliff into a frozen and absolutely deserted adventureland. I know it sounds strange to say I think it was in Gabriel's mind, too, because how was I to know what was in Gabriel's mind? Still, we knew each other well by then, and I'm going to make the statement anyway, even though I can't back it up with proof. I think we were both thinking it.

It was not reasonable to believe we'd be free forever.

Maybe Gabriel would be. He'd be eighteen in just a matter of weeks and could do as he pleased. I had nearly five years to go dodging the hell that was my aunt Bitsy's house in Kentucky. I knew I could dodge it for a time. I had proven that. But five years is a long time. It had been many days since I'd consciously thought about that place where the world expected me to live. Still, it was in there somewhere. I felt it at the back of my mind, and it felt like darkness. Like the end of everything.

It felt almost like death, except death is over faster.

And I think the reason we got so brave and adventurous is because within every living soul is the instinct to live—really *live*—before you die.

———

Our flight was scheduled for pretty early the following morning, so of course we lay awake that night wanting to sleep but failing miserably.

I watched the fire flicker, and without even looking over to the next mattress I knew Gabriel was awake too.

"You know what's weird?" I asked him.

"No. What's weird?"

"It's been so long since I thought of myself as a smart person."

"You're just as smart as you ever were."

"Right, I know that. But I used to *think* of myself as a smart person. All the time. I never stopped seeing it that way. It's like it never left my aware-ness. I moved through the world as a smart person. I always felt like a smart person. And now we're on this amazing adventure and I turned around and looked back and realized I've just been thinking of myself as a person."

"Ohhhh," he said, drawing the word out long. "You meant that in a good way."

"Absolutely. I had no idea that didn't come through all along."

———

We were not the only passengers on our flight to Inuvik. There were two other people, a man and his fourteen- or fifteen-year-old son. Also there were two canoes, right inside the cabin with us, but I don't suppose they count as passengers.

The man was maybe forty, and looked rugged and outdoorsy, but he also looked scared.

We were sitting waiting for the pilot to finish some paperwork and fiddle with his controls. There was no closed cockpit—we were all more or less in the same area.

"You okay?" I asked the man flying with his son.

For some reason, since losing my mom, I had become highly tuned to people who were not okay.

"Yeah," he said. And he sounded surprised. "Why do you ask?"

"You just looked worried."

"Oh." For a minute he said nothing more, and I thought maybe he never would. Then he went ahead and spilled it. "It's just that we planned this fishing trip so long ago, and it wasn't supposed to be this cold. Usually around this time of year it's around freezing but not much below."

Meanwhile his son was staring into his face, as though trying to will a change of mood for both of them.

"It's gonna be okay, Dad," he said.

"Your son's right," the pilot said. We all jumped, because his voice was amplified. He was wearing a headset with a mic hovering in front of his lips, and his voice echoed through the cabin. "Those fishing cabins are pretty safe. They give you lots of wood to burn, and they're sealed off from the elements. I've been flying people out to those islands for decades, sometimes in the dead of winter. I've flown guys out to stay in cabins right on a frozen lake, where they ice fish day and night. We haven't lost one to hypothermia yet. I mean, the ones who made proper use of the shelter. The ones that freeze to death are the ones that get lost or injured outdoors and have no one to see they're in trouble, and no sat phone."

"We have a sat phone," the father said.

Which was a little bit like saying they had a toque or a balaclava, in that it was a language we didn't currently speak.

"You'll be fine. People fish out here when it's minus forty. They make it back."

"Thanks," the guy said.

The pilot stepped out and untied the ropes that secured the plane to the dock. He jumped onto one of the floats as it drifted away from the dock, climbed back in, and fastened his seat belt. He started the motor, and the propeller spun. Almost weakly at first, but then with more sureness. We began to taxi out across the water.

The propeller played that strange trick, that optical illusion, in which it seemed suddenly to rotate in the opposite direction. As we picked up speed it began spinning so fast that it seemed to disappear, leaving only a round shadow in the air just ahead of the nose of the plane.

"I wonder if that's minus forty Celsius?" Gabriel asked me quietly. "Or Fahrenheit?"

"At minus forty they're the same," I said.

It seemed as though the man and his son had overcome their fear of the weather and passed it on to us.

I looked out my window and watched the wake the floats made on the water as we gained speed. I felt surprisingly close to the lake, as if I were looking out a car window and down onto the road. Well, that's a slight exaggeration. But the lake did not appear far removed from where we sat.

Then suddenly the wake was gone, and I knew we must be airborne.

For the longest time the plane glided above the lake at an alarmingly low altitude. If there had been trees, I felt as though we might have run smack into one. But of course there were no trees. There was an island up ahead, but we gained sufficient altitude before we got there.

Then we sailed out over the Mackenzie River, and I suddenly understood why you couldn't get there from here if not by air.

As if reading my mind the pilot spoke, startling us again.

"People always wonder why there are so few roads up here," he said in his amplified voice. "Then they get up in the sky and they don't wonder anymore. The delta's like Swiss cheese and every hole is a lake. Some of the lakes are so tiny they don't even have names. But can you imagine trying to build a road over this? You'd have to put in a bridge every couple of miles or zigzag between lakes, but even if you did that the road would flood out in the spring thaw."

By that time we had flown a fair distance from Yellowknife. I think I could still have seen it if I'd turned around, but I didn't turn around.

In front of us I saw a few little shacks on the shore of lake- or riverside communities. But they grew rarer as we flew along, still at a bizarrely low altitude. Soon all that was left was an expanse of snow and snowy trees, broken by Swiss-cheese holes filled with water that reflected the clouds and the blue of the sky.

And from our seats on that little floatplane, it seemed to go on forever.

"How cold do you think it'll get where we are tonight?" Gabriel asked the pilot. "We'll be about halfway between Inuvik and Tuktoyaktuk." He might have mangled the name of that town. I'm guessing tourists generally do. But he gave it his best. "I know you said it could get to be minus forty, but it won't get that cold tonight, right?"

"Well, of course, the farther north you go . . . ," he said, leaving us to intuit the fairly obvious end of that sentence. "But no, it won't be minus forty. Forecast low in Inuvik is supposed to be minus twenty-five. That's around minus thirteen if you think in Fahrenheit. High tomorrow might go all the way up to Fahrenheit one degree."

We were silent for a time, just watching the watery, snowy wilderness slide by under the plane.

"Degree," I said after a time. "Singular. Remember when we lived in a place where degrees were always plural?"

The father and son travelers must have been more comfortable by then, because they laughed.

Nobody spoke for maybe twenty minutes. Maybe forty-five. Time had begun to warp strangely and it was hard to judge.

"We just crossed the Arctic Circle," the pilot said, startling us yet again. "In case that interests you."

Needless to say, it did.

———

By the time we landed at Inuvik, we were the only ones on the plane. The pilot had already made a stop to let the other two passengers and their canoes deplane on a remote island.

As we taxied over water to the docks, I think I felt more fear than I had at any other time on the trip. More than I'd felt in that dark-sky campground, huddled in the Jeep while the wind whipped rain against its windows and rocked us on its suspension. More than I did as we fishtailed on the ice while wild beasts galloped across snowy roads in front of us. Because we were now in a very frigid, very remote place alone, without even the Jeep for shelter. The pilot's job was just to drop us, not to take care of us after that.

And we had simply been given the scant and sketchy instructions "Someone will meet you there."

We said nothing to each other, Gabriel and I. But I glanced over at his face and I knew he felt it too.

And then, suddenly, we saw a man standing by the dock.

He was wearing a fur hat and massive fur gloves that made his hands look bigger than his head, and a bright red parka. He had a bushy beard, and was blowing clouds of steamy breath out into the freezing morning. In both his furry hands he held a sign. It was like a chalk-board, but in a frame. The frame was printed with the words "Northern Lights Tours." On the chalkboard portion, in a wild scrawl of uppercase letters, were chalked the words "GLADYS'S FRIENDS."

I could hear both Gabriel and myself release a long breath at the same time.

We waited while the pilot tied up to the dock. Then we stepped out and waited in the gray and frigid half-light morning while he off-loaded our suitcases. We carried them onto land and approached this man, who looked possibly aboriginal at closer range. He offered us an enormous, friendly grin. It rivaled even Darryl's grin. One of his front teeth was made of some kind of silver metal.

"Welcome to the Northwest Territories!" he fairly bellowed.

We thought he would be the chatty type, but it turned out those five words would be the bulk of his conversation.

"So you're Gerry?" Gabriel asked.

He let out a laugh in such a sharp burst that it made us jump. He shook his head, still grinning.

Then he picked up our bags and carried them to a slate-blue utility vehicle with huge, knobby tires studded with chains.

We climbed in and drove through the streets of Inuvik in silence.

It was all just a little overwhelming.

It was a definite town, Inuvik. It was not the wilderness . . . yet. But it was quaint and small compared to Yellowknife. The houses all seemed to have the same shape, and I was especially struck by the brightness and variety of their colors. Now and then I saw a duplex, or a triplex, or a quadruplex, with each section painted its own distinct color.

Because the town was small, it was only a matter of two minutes or so before we pulled up and parked in front of a tiny storefront office. Over the door was a sign that read "Northern Lights Tours."

"Gerry is inside?" Gabriel asked.

"Yup," the man said.

And that was it. The sixth and final word from him.

We piled out into the frozen morning and carried our bags inside.

It was a miniature version of an office, and very warm. It contained exactly one desk, and in fact had room for exactly one. Behind that one desk sat a woman of about fifty. She had blazing red hair and a serious expression. Fierce, almost. She looked up at us and we almost took a step back, faced with the fierceness of that gaze.

"We're looking for Gerry," I said.

"And you found her," she barked back. "You must be Gladys's friends."

"We are," we both said at once.

"Why, you're just children."

"We're older than we look," we both said at once.

We'd been doing that a lot lately. More and more as the trip wore on. It was something like people who finish each other's sentences, except we both started and finished together. Which is nicer if you ask me.

"Okay, then," Gerry said. "Well, let's not waste any time. Let me just get my coat and we'll go."

Chapter Nineteen

The Thing You Said You Wanted Until the Moment You Got It

For what I'd estimate to be forty-five minutes we drove the Dempster Highway nearly due north. Gerry's vehicle was similar to the one driven by the man who'd met us at the docks. Huge, knobby tires. High clearance. Tire chains.

The road was one lane in each direction, and not exactly plowed. Instead it just had double tracks that other people's tires had driven into the snow. The sky was white from the horizon up, the way it had been in Fort Providence with Gladys, and the wind howled.

The minute I thought of Gladys, Gerry seemed to read my mind.

"It was nice of you to bring Gladys up here," she said, seeming less fierce. "We were starting to think she was going to die without getting back."

"It was good for us, too," Gabriel said. "I would have been awful scared driving up here without someone who knew the area."

"Well, people do it all the time, but don't get me wrong. That doesn't mean it never turns out to be a mistake."

Meanwhile I was more focused on her second sentence about Gladys.

"You said something about Gladys dying. Is that something you think might happen soon?"

"Who knows?" Gerry said, her bare hands gripping the steering wheel tightly. We had to talk over the wind of the heater, its fan blasting on high, and the wind battering the vehicle from outside. "Nobody ever knows when they're gonna die. Maybe she'll live for years. Maybe months. More likely months. But who can say? I don't blame her for not wanting to drive up here alone, what with her heart condition and all, but why that stubborn woman won't get on a plane is beyond me and everybody else who knows her. I guess she's scared to fly, but you'd think she'd bite the bullet and do it anyway. I guess she's scared of a lot of things, but she'd never tell you, so it's hard to say. There was even some talk of somebody driving down and getting her, but that's quite a round trip. Even if you could go straight through with hardly a single break, it still wouldn't fit into a weekend. And we're working people. But we were considering it. Thank goodness you saved us all that trouble."

Right around the time she finished that little speech we arrived at something I think must have been a road, though only in the loosest sense of the word. Its intersection with the highway was marked by a couple of reflectors on long poles. Beyond that we could see a row of long, thin, flexible-looking plastic sticks spaced at intervals, disappearing off into the distance, their tops marked with reflective tape. They swayed slightly in the fierce wind. Their height was a dizzying indication of how deep the snow must get in those parts.

It was clear that no one had driven the road since the last snows.

Gerry made a left and we headed west over unadorned tundra.

"Not sure how much anybody told you about the place. I hope they warned you about some things."

I felt my stomach tighten. I glanced over at Gabriel. He had that look in his eyes again. The one we'd had while taxiing toward the docks. You know. Before we saw there really was someone there to meet us.

"Like what?" I said.

"Like the fact that I'm not doing any fancy meal service."

"Oh, yeah," Gabriel said, sounding relieved. "They did tell us that."

"You won't starve. I have a whole trunk full of dehydrated food. You'll have to heat water on the woodstove to bring it back to life. It'll keep you going. But people get tired of dehydrated food after a while. How long did you figure on staying?"

"Oh," we both said at once.

Then I said, "We're not really sure. Is it okay if we're not really sure? Part of it depends on the aurora, and if we see it right away, as opposed to if we have to wait a few nights. But I guess we were thinking . . . well, we haven't really talked much about it, but maybe three or four days?"

Gerry cracked a slight smile that looked a little bit sarcastic as we bumped along overland.

"We'll see," she said.

"We can stay less than that if you need us to," Gabriel said.

"Oh, I don't need you to come in sooner. Place is not booked for weeks. It's just that everybody says they're gonna stay for days and then thirty hours later they call me on the satellite phone and say they want to come in."

I remembered the pilot and the other passengers talking about a "sat phone." I hadn't understood at the time, but now I figured I did.

"We don't have a satellite phone," Gabriel said.

"Yeah you do. I always leave people with one in case of emergency. And in case they want to come back in early. And they almost always want to come back in early."

"Why?" I asked. "What goes wrong?"

"Nothing goes wrong. Nothing happens at all. They're just not prepared to be in a place that remote. They think they're prepared but they're not. They think they want it but they don't really know what they're getting themselves into. This is genuine wilderness where we're going. Unless you're an expert at winter navigation there's nothing much to do but be alone with yourself and your own thoughts. That's not as much fun as people tend to think it will be. Sounds romantic and noble until you try it. Some people like it, but they're definitely the exception to the rule. You two might be the exception, who knows. But most people call and ask to come back in early. I guess it's spooky to people to be the only humans on eighty square kilometers of nothing. They always say the same thing. 'There's nothing out here!' And I don't say it, because I got a business to run, but I think, *Duh. Isn't that what you asked me for? Isn't that exactly what you said you wanted until the moment you got it?*"

The reference to the eighty square kilometers brought up my next question.

"How far off the highway is this place?"

She glanced down at the odometer.

"We've come about nineteen kilometers and we've got another twenty to go."

After that nobody said much. We just bounced along into more nothing than we'd even known existed in the world.

———

When we first saw the cabin—though more accurately the person who called it a geodesic dome was correct   it was a huge relief. It was a genuinely welcome sight. It was gratifying just to see it because it was *something*. She'd said there was nothing out here, but there was this. And it was something.

It was made of natural-looking, snow-dusted wood with lots of windows. Not just at eye level but overhead as well. Whole sections of its geodesic pattern were inset with windows instead of solid wood. There was a wrought-iron chimney jutting from the roof, and, next to the chimney, at the very apex of the dome, a sort of platform. A railed platform with a couple of snowed-in outdoor chairs. The path to get up there was thus far unclear.

"This is beautiful!" I blurted out.

Gerry laughed. "Not sure I'd go that far. It's bare bones in a lot of ways."

Gabriel said, "I think what Ru means is that it's everything a person needs to be okay in a place like this."

"That it is," Gerry said. "In this great wilderness of nothing man-made, it's something. It's an oasis of something. Come on. I'll show you around."

We clomped toward the door of the place, through snow up to our calves. We were still making do with those ill-fitting boots, because we hadn't had time to find anything better. Also we hadn't wanted to cut any more deeply into our gas money for something we'd likely never use again.

Gerry unlocked the door and we stepped inside, looking up and around.

It was a big place, at least for a cabin in the woods. It looked as though it could sleep eight or more. The ceiling was a good twenty feet high in the very center, which gave it a spacious, airy feeling.

It was just as cold inside as it had been on the walk from the truck.

"You'll have to keep a fire going for heat," Gerry said, pointing with a sweeping motion to a cast-iron woodstove on one side of the big room. "But it's a big stove for a small space and you'll be toasty. This place'll get toasty warm in no time."

Next to it was a stack of stove wood that extended almost to the ceiling. It might even be more accurate to call it a wall of wood. On the other side of the stove we saw baskets of stick-size kindling and some of those commercial fireplace logs that are wrapped in paper packaging and not really made of actual wood.

Gerry must have seen me looking.

"If you're not good at fires and you can't keep one going, you can burn those," she said. "But they're expensive. So try. Please. But if it's between using those or turning into human popsicles, do what you need to do. But the stove wood is dry, and there's plenty of kindling, and there's a box of fatwood sticks to use as starters. So even if you're not used to making fires you should do okay.

"That's the crate full of all kinds of dehydrated meals," she said, pointing. "Help yourself to as much as you can eat. There's pour-over coffee and tea and hot chocolate. There's pots and bottled water in that pantry cabinet. You'll have to heat it on the woodstove. No hot water, so no showers. Maybe another reason people come back early. There's solar, but all it does is run a couple of electric lights and not too much more. The bathroom is a composting toilet through that little door. It's actually a shed outside, but it adjoins, so you don't have to walk outside at three in the morning when it's twenty-five below. If the door is closed it'll be cold in there. If the door is open you might not like the smell. Your call. People make their own decisions. But it's sanitary. Directions are on the wall. Directions for most things are on the wall."

She walked toward a second door in the back of the dome, a second portal to the outdoors, and we instinctively followed her.

"If you stay in, I don't worry about you," she said. "But you might get tired of that. If you go out, some important things you need to know: If you get lost, your chances of dying go way up. This is your sat phone."

She handed it to Gabriel, and we both stared at it as if it might be about to say something. It looked like a cell phone from back in the old days when they were too big to fit in your pocket. Not that I had ever seen such a thing in real life.

"All you've got to do is extend the antenna and turn it on. But don't turn it on inside. Don't turn it on close to the dome, or close to trees. It needs a clear, unobstructed view of the sky. And here's the catch. Here's the mistake people tend to make. They think they can turn it on under the trees or right outside the door and then walk to a better area. But once it searches for a satellite and finds an obstruction, it won't ever connect. If that happens, you have to turn it off for fifteen minutes and then do it all over again. Not too much fun in an emergency. So first find your good area and then hit the power button."

She reached out toward the phone and pointed to a raised black disk on the right side of its top.

"This is a little cover that pulls off," she said. She flipped it open, and under it was a red button. "This is your SOS button. It's programmed to call me, but only use that in an emergency. I'll call the rescue team right away and the phone will help us track your location. But that's only if you're in trouble. If you just want to come in, dial my number and tell me so. The red button is for more life-or-death stuff."

She handed me a business card, because Gabriel seemed transfixed, staring at the phone. The card had the name of her business and the name Geraldine Walker, with an address and phone number in Inuvik.

"Keep the cover on that button so you don't press it by accident," she added, her voice fierce, the way it had sounded when we first met her. "Nobody likes that. And that's the mild version of how we feel about an accidental SOS. Now. Put the phone in a nice deep pocket of your parka and zip it or snap it up so you can't possibly lose it, and then let's talk more about going outside. Never go out without your sat phone, and have it someplace secure, like I said. If you reach in your pocket and it's not there, good luck finding where you dropped it in a foot of snow over a few square kilometers of land, especially if more snow is falling and filling in the hole."

She took two steps forward to a metal cabinet by the back door and lifted up on the latch to open it, swinging the door wide with a long squeak. Inside we saw two rifles, half a dozen pairs of snowshoes, and a gargantuan can of bear spray.

"Some people feel comfortable with guns," she said. "Others not so much. I *suggest* you bring one if you go out, but I *insist* you bring the bear spray. This place is wild, and full of animals, and it's not a petting zoo. They don't all want to meet you. Some are more scared of you than vice versa. Others might be feeling territorial. Then there are the ones that think you look delicious."

"Like what kind of animals?" Gabriel asked, his voice a bit thin. "Do you have polar bears here?"

"Yes and no," she said. "I mean, we do. But we're just a handful of kilometers from the Arctic Ocean, and they're more likely to want to hang out there than here. Then again, *because* we're just a handful of kilometers from the Arctic Ocean—well, the Beaufort Sea, but that's more or less the Arctic Ocean, it's part of it—it can happen. If they're there, they can just as well be here. It's not such a long walk. Meanwhile you got your grizzly bears, black bears, musk ox, wolves, moose. Don't underestimate the moose. They'll stomp you to death quick as look at you. Oh, and don't get too freaked out if you look through a window and see eyes looking back in at you. Wildlife can get curious, especially if you have any electric lights on. They don't see a lot of that."

We opened the back door and stepped out into the vast expanse of snow.

"As you can see, we got a path marked if you want to take a hike." She indicated a row of the tall reflector sticks spaced maybe thirty feet apart. "It goes to the closest lake. But I wouldn't go off the path if I were you. If you're not on this marked trail, I'd keep the cabin in plain view. Some people have good electronic GPS devices and they feel pretty confident because of them, but even those can let you down. They freeze, or stop getting a signal. You think it'll be easy to retrace your steps but then you turn around and there's nothing but white as far as the eye can see. People go off trail thinking they can follow their tracks back but then the snow starts to fly and the tracks disappear. Then we gotta come out and rescue you, which we find aggravating if it was preventable. And if I'm being honest, most disasters are. Preventable, I mean. Ninety-nine percent of what goes wrong out here is user error."

She led us around the side of the building, where we saw ladderlike railed stairs that led up to the roof.

"If the northern lights are going real good and you're feeling brave you can go up to that little viewing platform. The wind'll scour you real good up there if it's blowing, and you'll have to knock snow off the chairs, but it's the best seat in the house. Three-hundred-sixty-degree view of the sky. You can lie in bed and watch through the windows if you're not feeling so adventurous, but it's not quite the same. The warmer you keep it inside the less likely the snow will build up on the windows. But there'll likely be some snow, and they might fog over some. If you do go up there, a word to the wise. Bring some folded blankets to put on those metal chairs before you sit down. Your butt will thank you for it."

She turned and stepped back inside, and we followed her in.

As she closed the door behind us she said, "What do you think, young'uns? You up for this?"

"I don't know if we're up for it or not," Gabriel said, "but we're definitely doing it."

"Great. That's the spirit. I'll be back for you in four days, or when you call me and tell me you've had enough. Whichever comes first. Good luck and try to have some fun. It's not like you get to do a thing like this every day."

And without any further fanfare, she turned and let herself out.

Gabriel and I stood very still in the middle of that big, arching room in the freezing cold, listening to the sound of her vehicle's engine fading away.

After that there was nothing to listen to except the wind.

Chapter Twenty

Glances with Wolves

Gabriel and I made a fire in the woodstove as our first task, and huddled in front of it in the hopes of being able to take off our coats. After half an hour of that we decided if we were going to freeze we might as well be outside.

We struggled to strap snowshoes onto our ill-fitting boots, and I zipped the sat phone securely into the pocket of my parka. We put on our balaclavas, our toques, our hoods, our scarves, our gloves.

I had fallen in love with my scarf—which was striped lengthwise in bright primary colors—though I couldn't have explained quite why. All the outerwear served a good purpose, but the scarf made me happy.

Gabriel grabbed one of the rifles, which struck me as brave. Then he grabbed the bear spray with his free hand.

We stepped out onto the snow.

It might sound weird to say "onto" the snow instead of "into" it. Believe me, it was a much weirder thing to do than to say. Neither one of us California kids had ever worn snowshoes before, and we both just perched there on top of its surface, waiting for that inevitable act of gravity that never came.

We squinted our eyes against whipping snow, the wind biting what little skin we had left exposed. Eyelids and lips, mostly. The very edges of nostrils.

We took a few steps in the direction the trail was leading us, but it was startlingly awkward. In addition to the ill-fitting boots, we now had something like small boats strapped to our feet. We had to swing them up very high to take a step, and we couldn't put our feet normally close together.

But we struggled to the top of a rise, where we discovered that while in the dome we'd been nestled in a shallow little valley that offered partial protection from the wind. Until we caught the full force of it we could not have imagined that we had ever been protected.

We couldn't see. We couldn't keep our eyes open. Even when we managed to look out through slitted eyes there was nothing to view. Just white. The sky was as white as the ground, which was as white as the air in front of us. And the strange thing is, it wasn't snowing. Every now and then we'd enjoy a second or two between gusts, and in those rare moments the sky was a steely light blue. The wind was simply whipping up the snow until it was everywhere, as if it were falling.

It was like a sandstorm, but with snow.

Meanwhile I was guessing we had come maybe two hundred yards. Maybe not even that.

Without having to say a word to each other, we turned back. We had already lost sight of the dome because we had lost sight of our own extended hands. As instructed, we had not left the trail that was marked by reflector sticks. We just couldn't see the sticks.

We followed our own barely visible tracks back.

We tumbled back inside, stripping away snowshoes and scarves and gloves and balaclavas and toques. Everything but our parkas.

The fire had gone out.

"I think I see now why people want to call Gerry and come back in early," I said.

"But we're not going back early," he said. "Right?"

"Oh hell no. I said I see. I didn't say I agreed."

———

We sat in front of fire number two for more than an hour before we got warm enough to strip off our massive parkas.

The wind howled outside and battered the windows with snow. It made a constant ticking sound. There was literally nothing out there to see. With a dozen windows onto the wilderness, there was nothing out there except white.

We had a pot of water going on the stove in hopes of rehydrating some lunch. But it was heating very slowly.

Meanwhile we were playing cards. We had brought the deck we got in Montana, and we had already played almost twenty hands of gin.

Gabriel looked up at me over his hand of cards.

"Ever think these cards might be magic?" he asked out of nowhere.

I raised one eyebrow at him.

"Magic, you say?"

"Well, not magic. Not *magic* magic. More like . . . scientific magic. If such a thing exists. It's sort of my own concept, and it's not something anybody else might say. I'm not explaining it very well, am I? It's like . . . you know I'm not religious exactly. But if you really pay good attention to life and the universe you'll see all kinds of patterns. Things falling together just the way I figure they were meant to. It reminds me of those fancy patterns of dominoes you'd set up when you were a kid. And then at the very end you'd touch one, and it would knock over the next one and the momentum would keep going just the way you planned it."

"I never did that when I was a kid," I said. "I was too busy teaching myself Latin and euclidean geometry."

"You know what I mean, though."

"So how are these cards like the dominoes?"

"I just feel like we were supposed to be here. Like we're right where we're supposed to be. And to get here we had to meet Gladys. This deck of cards feels like magic because we bought it from Gladys and didn't even know it, because the universe was already pushing us over so we could bump into the next domino, which was her. Again, not like the silly sort of magic that doesn't exist, but like the kind of everyday magic the universe is so famous for. I mean, if you're really paying attention."

For a few beats I just smiled at him and didn't even try to answer. I was just feeling happy.

"What?" he said. "Do you think that's silly? Why are you looking at me like that?"

"I just missed you is all."

His face softened into a half smile. I think he was feeling happy too. And these things don't go without saying. In our lives there had been only a sprinkling of that kind of joy, like salt on an otherwise bland meal.

"I don't know what you're talking about," he said. "I've been right here with you the whole time."

"But what you just said, about the cards and the universe and the magic. That was such a Gabriel thing to say. You used to say Gabriel things to me all the time. But since we've been traveling, not so much."

"I've been a little scared," he said.

"Well, sure. Sure you have. I've been scared too. Who wouldn't be?"

"But maybe a little extra," he said, "because I felt like I had to be in charge."

"I get it," I said. "And thank you. For driving and being in charge. I could never have done any of this without you."

"I wouldn't be out here without you either," he said.

"So maybe the universe wanted us to meet. Maybe we're the first two in a long row of its dominoes. In a big fancy pattern much nicer than anything a kid would put together."

"Be interesting to see where we end up when the last one falls," he said.

Over our rehydrated dinner, I looked up from my metal cup of stew and right into his eyes.

"What?" he said.

"Go ahead and tell me that thing about mothers."

"What thing about mothers?"

"You said you had a theory about mothers, back when we were driving alone. But we both figured that wasn't the right time to talk about it."

"And you're pretty confident this is?"

"I'm going to give it a try," I said.

"Well. Okay. Here's my theory. I figure, we used to be part of our mother's body. I mean, we did. I don't just figure we did. That part is a given, but this next part is what I figure. She breathed for us, and pumped blood through us. And there's only one person in the entire world we can say that about. So we're less separate from our mothers than anybody else on the planet. We're not literally one body with them anymore, but I think we carry this really instinctive subconscious memory of the time when we were. Until we could breathe on our own there was no surviving without her. And even when we came out into the world we would have died without her care. Actually somebody else could have cared for us at that point, but we didn't know it. We just knew *she* did. So when we lose our mother, it's different. It's just different from any other loss. And it isn't all about what a great relationship it was. It isn't necessarily a loss of all these wonderful things you shared. It's not only with the best mother-child bonds. It's all of them. If it was great, you miss that. If it was troublesome, you suddenly realize the door has been slammed on it ever being any better way. So no matter what it was, it's really hard to lose. Anyway, that's my observation from watching both my parents lose their mothers."

"It's a good observation," I said.

"You still don't sound too emotional about the whole thing."

"It's still not all the way in."

I ate three or four bites of stew, which was decent but not the same as fresh.

"Do you feel like you lost *your* mom?" I asked. "Because we left so suddenly and you're cut off from her?"

"No, not at all. I'll see her again."

He didn't say straight out that he was painting a contrast to my situation. Then again, he didn't need to. I would not see my mother again.

Just for a split second it almost got all the way in.

I was careful not to let it.

———

It got dark early, and we went to bed that night thinking we might never see the aurora borealis because we might never see the sky.

But then I woke up in the night, and the fire had died down, and it was cold.

I looked over at Gabriel in his own little twin bed under a pile of blankets and quilts. He was fast asleep.

I got up, shrugged on my parka, and turned on a little lamp by the woodstove—one of the very few things in our new environment that was in any way powered.

I fed sticks of kindling into the stove, onto the existing embers, and blew on them until they glowed. When a few flames burst up around them, I tossed a piece of stove wood on top and waited until I was sure it would catch. Then I threw in a few more.

When I felt confident about my fire, I stood up and found myself facing two of the windows. One was high, to take in the sky. The other was below it, nearer the ground. In the high window I saw brilliant stars. The wind had died and the sky was perfectly clear. In the lower window I saw a pair of glowing eyes staring in at me.

At first it was a jolt, but my alarm soon morphed into fascination.

I stood frozen for a long time, wanting to observe both views at once, but more transfixed by the eyes. I couldn't see any more of the animal because the lamplight was reflecting in the window. I reached over very slowly and turned it off. Then I carefully reached over and closed the door of the stove to keep that light at bay.

Then I waited for my eyes to adjust.

Ever so gradually, like the way my mom used to describe waiting for a Polaroid picture to develop itself, a wolf materialized in the darkness outside the window. He had a dark coat, nearly black, and I could barely decipher his outline against the still snow. His eyes were wide. Wild. Curious. Not predatory. Just interested and more than a little bit cautious.

I looked at him for a long time and he looked back.

I remember thinking to myself, *How did I get here? How did all this happen?* Or maybe I just felt it. It was there, but maybe not in words.

Then I decided I needed to wake Gabriel so he could see the wolf.

I moved over toward his bed as slowly as possible—no sudden moves—and shook his shoulder.

"You have to see this," I said, and pointed.

He sat up and looked out the window.

"Oh wow," he said. "Look at that sky."

"Yeah, It's beautiful, but I meant the wolf."

"What wolf?"

I turned to look, but there was nothing outside that lower window.

"Oh," I said. "Too bad. I wanted you to see the wolf."

"But the lights," he said. "You woke me up to see the lights, right?"

I raised my eyes to the higher window. Like a wide road arching up from the horizon, the sky was adorned with a positively massive band of green light.

We walked to the window and stood shoulder to shoulder, looking up.

It wasn't moving enough for its movement to be noticeable. I mean, it moved. We stared for a few minutes, and after those few minutes the green light covered more—and a different part—of the sky. But it was so gradual you almost didn't notice it while it was happening.

"I always see videos of the lights jumping all over the place," he said. "Flying around the sky. I wonder now if those were time-lapse."

"Maybe," I said. "But from what I've read, sometimes they're more steady and other times they dance."

"Now we can always say we saw them. But maybe if we stay a few more nights we can see them dance."

We watched in silence for a long time. Ten minutes, twenty. Time is so meaningless at a moment like that.

"Should we go outside and climb up to that roof platform?" he asked.

"I don't know," I said. "There's a wolf out there."

"You sure you didn't dream the wolf?"

"Positive. There was a wolf."

So we stood inside and watched until the last of the green faded, though I could not have told you how long a time that was.

While I was watching, I sent a mental image to our friend Avery, from the dark-sky campground, so he could enjoy it vicariously. When he asked me to do that he probably thought I'd forget, but I don't forget anything.

———

Speaking of things one might have dreamed . . . just as I was about to drop off to sleep again, I opened my eyes. Or dreamed I opened my eyes. And there was a young woman sitting on the floor next to my bed. She had her knees drawn up, and her arms wrapped around them. She had honey-brown hair that flowed long over her shoulders like a waterfall. She never looked at me or acknowledged that I was there.

I blinked a few times, and by the third blink she had faded. And I really was sitting up in bed, looking at what I thought I'd seen in the dream. So maybe all of it *was* the dream. Clearly it was not all reality. But I was left wondering if it might have been part dream and part something else. Some other experience that science—much as I respect science—dismisses and belittles because it can't quantify it.

As I stared at the spot where she had sat before fading, I knew it was my mother as a young girl. Not as young as I was, but young. Sixteen or seventeen, maybe. I had seen pictures of her from her youth, but I did not entirely base my conclusion on that type of knowledge. I knew because I knew.

In time I got back to sleep, and as far as I know I haven't seen my mother since.

In the morning Gabriel told me I'd been crying in my sleep, but I have no firsthand knowledge of that.

Chapter Twenty-One

Wake Up, Wake Up, the Sky Is Dancing

You know those documentaries about Mount Everest where you get to watch the weather change in what feels like the time it takes to blink?

First the climbers are out doing their training runs. Acclimatizing. The sky is blue, and the wind doesn't so much as ruffle their outerwear. Sometimes they even have their parkas off, because the sun radiating up off the blinding white snow makes it strangely warm during all that exertion.

Then it's an hour later, and they're huddled in their tents with the wind buffeting them so hard you think they'll blow right off the mountain.

Well, the weather outside Inuvik was like that for us, but in reverse.

In the morning, after a breakfast of hot chocolate and instant oatmeal, Gabriel and I trudged our way through the daunting process of getting ready to go outside. When every inch of us was bundled and the sat phone zipped into my pocket, when we had snowshoes strapped to our boots and rifle and bear spray in gloved hand, we headed out on the same hiking route we had taken the day before.

But this day it was beautiful.

We didn't know what time it was—we never did anymore—but the sun glowed near the edge of the horizon. The sky was a lovely cloudless pale blue. The air was perfectly, windlessly still.

We waddled our way up toward the lake together.

We didn't say a word to each other, but not for any uncomfortable reasons. There was simply nothing that needed saying.

Though we didn't discuss it out loud at the time, the wilderness was changing us. I liked the changes, but I could also feel why they caused a lot of people to break out the sat phone and ask to come in early.

We were becoming a whole different kind of animal. Not different from each other—we definitely changed together, in unison. And of course we were still very different from all the other animals who inhabited this wilderness. But we were also a different animal than the one we'd been when we arrived.

We didn't speak because we flowed together, naturally.

Gabriel and I had become a herd.

Once he saw a bald eagle swoop by overhead, and Gabriel nudged me with his elbow and we watched together. And that's communication, of course. But we still felt no need to talk about it in words.

When we had struggled our way up to the summit of a long and gentle slope, we saw the lake stretched out below us. It was covered with a thin film of ice that glittered in the now partly risen sun.

How did I know the sheet of ice was thin from so much distance? Because a herd of caribou gathered at one of its banks, and a very large male with very large horns was battering the ice at the edge of the lake with one cloven hoof, presumably so he could drink. I know the ice was thin because I watched him break it fairly easily.

A moment later he dropped his head and drank, and the rest of the herd picked up the signal. Some moved in and drank at the spot where he had shattered the ice, while others created their own breaks.

There were forty-two of them, I determined with a quick scan.

We watched until they were done drinking, and the biggest male was the first to turn around to leave. As he turned, he saw us there, standing on top of the hill in silence. For a fraction of a second he seemed to freeze and assess. Then he bolted, and, as he bolted, the whole herd bolted as one.

That's the thing about herds, I was thinking. They don't stop and make their own judgments. They don't wait and assess the danger on their own to see if they agree with their herd mates. They just act together, almost as one mind.

But the truth is, I'm not sure if I thought that, exactly. I think I just knew it in that moment. It was simply a thing that was there to be known.

———

"I loved the way we hiked together and didn't talk," I said as we huddled before our fire in the woodstove. "But now I'm a little curious about what you were thinking."

"It was so still out there," he said. "It was so perfect. I felt like words would only ruin it."

"What about now?"

"I don't feel like I *need* to talk. But I can. What were *you* thinking?"

"I guess I was feeling like we've turned into a different kind of animal than we were before we got here, and that we were moving together like a herd."

"Hmm," he said, and nodded a few times. "I can see that. I was thinking about this man my uncle used to know. He was a recovering alcoholic and drug addict and he had years and years of homelessness in his past. He told my uncle that homelessness is addictive, because nobody expects anything of you. You have no appointments. No responsibilities. I didn't understand that at all."

"But now you do," I said.

"Yes. Now I do."

It was the last time we spoke that day, and the second-to-last time we spoke while out in that wilderness. We went to bed in the middle of the day, because we wanted to be awake all night. We didn't even talk out the plan. We just knew.

———

Gabriel shook my shoulder to wake me, and when I opened my eyes it was dark. But the view was brilliantly green through the high windows. The sky was swept wide with the aurora, and the lights were dancing.

I rose quickly, and we struggled into all that outerwear. We were pretty good at the routine by then.

We stepped outside into the still, freezing night. We did not bring the rifle or the bear spray, because we knew we were going to climb straight up to the roof without much wandering around first, and we needed both hands for the railings of the ladderlike steps. We didn't expect to see any wild animals ranging freely up there anyway.

Though, again, we didn't discuss any of this out loud.

Gabriel had pulled two stout wool blankets off one of the beds and hung them over his shoulder, and we climbed up to the railed platform, where we knocked snow off the metal chairs with our huge gloves.

Then we sat on the blankets and watched the show for hours.

There were a few trees around the dome, but they were short, scrubby little things, and we found ourselves looking down at the tops of them. There were no obstructions to the sky in any direction. No matter where we looked, we could see from the apex of the world to the horizon.

And the lights filled the sky.

I don't claim they filled the entire sky all at once, or at any given time. But we were up there for several hours, and, given that space of time, I think I reasonably can say they left no area of the sky untouched.

And they danced. And danced. And danced.

They slid and flowed and jumped and shimmered. Within every wide band of green, brighter vertical bands rose and fell like the digital readout on a sound recording.

It seemed like the more excited we got to see them, the more excited they were to perform. But of course I know that's not really true. I'm just saying it felt that way in the moment.

We watched for most of the night in perfect silence, and then we had the last brief wilderness conversation we would have.

Gabriel said, quietly, "Now I'm wishing we'd thought to bring a camera."

Without any pause or thought I said, "No."

"You don't think it would be nice to have pictures of this?"

"I think pictures are for later. People want to take pictures so they can experience the thing later. But meanwhile it's happening. It's happening now. And fiddling with the camera just helps you miss it in the now."

Besides, I was thinking, would I ever again close my eyes and think about this trip and not see them dancing there inside my eyelids? I knew I would not. They were printed there for whatever time my eyes had left on this earth.

I almost said as much to Gabriel, but I knew he agreed and was probably thinking it right along with me.

Have you noticed how much time human beings waste saying things they know the other person will agree with, just to hear the agreement? I've noticed that.

We stayed up on the roof until the eastern edge of the sky grew vaguely light, even though the aurora had faded at least an hour earlier. But it was still a view of stars and snowy tundra and treetops, and that was also good.

Then without a word we climbed back down and went to bed. We slept the day away, in case there was another performance that night.

———

We stayed two more nights in the dome, just as we had claimed we would. And we never had another conversation out loud, though our communication was nearly perfect.

The aurora staged multiple-hour performances each night for those two more nights.

It would be a slight—but not a wild—exaggeration to say that we grew feral over those four days. But, though this may sound strange, that was only true in the most pleasant and useful of ways. We didn't lose any part of being human that would have been a good thing to keep. We just spent so much time around wildness that we saw what wildness had to offer and took the best of it.

It's not the easiest thing to describe, but I think the parts we found worth taking were as follows: Staying utterly in the moment. Maintaining a near-complete situational awareness. Not overthinking our lives. Being amazed at all times.

———

We were sleeping when Gerry's big utility vehicle pulled up nearly to the door, but it woke us immediately, because it was a thing out of place. By then the sound of a motor vehicle was as foreign to us as the trumpeting of an elephant or the screeching of a herd of howler monkeys might have been.

We sat up, and looked at each other, and in Gabriel's eyes I saw both his disappointment and the mirrored reflection of my own.

It's not that we had wanted to stay out there forever. It was always meant to be a four-day excursion, and we had no desire to amend the plan. We were just sorry that the four days were over.

Gerry thumped on the door a few times.

"You decent in there? Can I come in?"

I said, "Yeah, come on in, Gerry."

I can't tell you how strange it felt to use my voice, especially at some volume.

She threw the door wide and stood there in the open doorway for a moment, letting the cold in. She had a look on her face that bordered on amusement. She was smiling at us with her eyes while her mouth stayed neutral.

"Oh good," she said. "You're alive. When I didn't hear from you I figured you were either dead or the exception to the rule. Happy to see it was option number two. I called your pilot and he'll be at the docks in two hours to pick you up, so gather up your things and let's get going."

———

We didn't talk much on the drive.

At one point Gerry looked over at us, briefly taking her eyes off the road.

"You're being awful quiet," she said. "You okay, you two? Did you have an okay time out there?"

"It was the best thing I've done in my life," I said.

Gabriel nodded almost solemnly. "What *she* said," he told Gerry, indicating me with a flip of his head.

"Well, I probably shouldn't be surprised," Gerry said. "It's the young ones and the old ones who do the best, psychologically speaking. They're the most open. The ones in the middle are the problem. They think they've got better things to do, and they can't shut off their brains. They're the ones who have all the trouble. And it's too bad, too, because it's the very young and the very old who almost never get the credit they deserve."

After that we fell into silence again.

Now and then a car came toward us, traveling in the opposite direction toward Tuktoyaktuk, and we found ourselves shrinking back against the truck seat, as if being charged by a lion. I suppose I shouldn't say how it appeared to Gabriel, but I could definitely feel him flinch.

I don't think it had occurred to us that there would be an uncomfortable sense of decompression as we reentered the world. It definitely hadn't occurred to me. But it hit us in the face soon enough.

A plane flew overhead as we cruised down the Dempster Highway, and I covered my ears as though my eardrums were injured by the sound. But in truth the noise didn't exactly hurt my ears. It did, however, challenge and insult them.

As we got back into Inuvik, the houses looked to be a strange shape—what with all those right angles—and there were too many of them pressed too closely together. That was an odd way to feel about the smallest town I had ever visited, but I felt it.

I'm not trying to exaggerate and pretend I'd forgotten the world existed. Only that the world felt like a memory far more distant than four days. And maybe, just maybe, it was a little bit as though I had wanted to forget the world, and tried hard to forget it, but hadn't entirely managed to pull it off.

———

"Where's that sat phone?" Gerry asked as we stood on the dock together.

"Oh," I said. "Right. Sorry. It's zipped into the pocket of my parka."

"Good girl."

I handed it to her, and found myself missing it slightly, even though I had never so much as turned it on.

"You didn't make any calls on it, right? I should have mentioned it's not for chatting. Those minutes are expensive."

"No," I said. "It was powered off the whole time."

"Good girl."

Meanwhile Gabriel was staring off into the distance with some brand of complete fascination, as if hoping to prove the round-Earth theory by watching a ship appear over the horizon. An odd thought on my part, I suppose, but that was what flitted through my mind.

"If you need to go . . . ," I said to Gerry.

"I'm not leaving you standing out here in twenty below until I see that plane coming with my own eyes."

We turned back to the water and, as if Gerry had summoned it, we saw the plane taxi across the frigid lake in our direction. Or maybe it was the Mackenzie River. I wasn't really clear on that point. But in any case he was using that body of water to come get us and bring us back to Yellowknife. The sound of his motor felt more intrusive and more disturbing the closer he got to the dock.

He was in a smaller plane than the one in which we'd flown to Inuvik, but we could definitely see the pilot, and he was definitely the right pilot.

I turned to Gerry, suddenly overcome with emotion, and threw my arms around her. She seemed surprised, to say the least.

"Thank you," I said. "Thank you thank you thank you. Thank you so, so much."

"Oh my," she said, half-reluctantly returning my embrace. "You really did have a good time out there, didn't you?"

"It changed everything."

I let her go, and Gabriel stepped in and gave her a much briefer and more restrained hug.

"What *she* said," he told Gerry as he stepped back again.

"You give Gladys my regards," she said. "Tell her I send my best. I'll fly down and see her by and by."

I thought it was a strange thing to say, and Gabriel seemed to notice it too. I watched his brow furrow as she said it. How could she fly down and see Gladys "by and by" if Gladys was in the Northwest Territories for less than two weeks total, and had been here nearly a week already?

But we really had no chance to sort it out, because it was time to board the plane and leave that place forever.

———

"I just have one stop to make," the pilot said, seconds after takeoff.

Gabriel and I did that thing again, the one where we spoke simultaneously, like a beast with two bodies but only one mind between us.

We said, "Good."

The pilot didn't ask what we meant by that, and we didn't clarify our thinking to each other. But I just know we were on the same page.

In our minds, Yellowknife had grown into a booming metropolis. It was noisy and crowded and artificially lighted, and about as far from wilderness conditions as one could get and still be in the Northwest Territories.

We had no choice but to go there, and yet we were in no way ready to be there.

The more time we spent floating over Swiss-cheese lakes, the happier we would be.

Chapter Twenty-Two

Having Misplaced Our Grandmother, Sir . . .

The stop was on one of the larger Swiss-cheese lakes, at the shore of a small island with a single dock.

"Is this where we dropped off that man and his son?" I asked Gabriel.

"Maybe," he said. "Not sure. These islands all sort of look the same to me."

As we taxied closer to the dock, we saw them. They were sitting waiting, their canoes by their sides, their backpacks and fishing gear stacked all around them.

"How about that?" I said quietly to Gabriel.

The pilot tied up to the dock and, maybe because it was a smaller plane, began strapping their canoes to racks just above the plane's floats. Meanwhile the man and his son climbed on board.

Their faces were windburned. When they pulled off their toques their hair was wild and unbrushed. But they were purely happy.

When they saw us, they both grinned widely. They were clearly happy to see us. They clearly shared our view that this was a happy coincidence.

But they never said a word.

I remember briefly wondering if they were dominoes in our lives, and, if so, why?

They sat and buckled their seat belts, but never spoke to each other. The father just looked at his son, and the message came through, and their hands moved together, and their belts clicked at the same time.

"Look at that," I said quietly to Gabriel. "They're a herd."

They grinned at us again.

They might have overheard us. It was an awfully small plane. But, if so, they never asked us what that meant.

Then again, it might only have required an explanation for those who were not a herd.

———

Gladys met us at the dock on the Great Slave Lake in Yellowknife. Picked us up in our own Jeep.

We expected her to drive straight back to her brother Darryl's house, but it didn't go the way we expected.

Instead she drove us up to a lookout point, poised over that city built on rocks, looking out over one of the world's ten largest lakes. I swear it had more ice at its edges than when we'd last seen it.

We sat with the engine running, the heater blowing on high.

"What are we doing here, Gladys?" Gabriel asked.

"I need to tell you somethin'," she said.

"Okay," I said.

"I don't think you're gonna like it."

I glanced at Gabriel, sitting in the back seat, and caught his eye. Neither of us spoke. A silence fell that was probably three or four seconds long, but felt endless. In my head I was thinking, *Just say it, Gladys. Just get it over with.*

"I'm not goin' back to the States."

"Oh," Gabriel and I both said at once.

"If I go back, I won't get back home here again before I die. I just can't afford to leave this place. I'm sorry."

We sat listening to the heater blow for maybe a minute.

"That's why you brought those huge suitcases," Gabriel said. "We wondered why you'd bring so much stuff for just a two-week trip."

She never answered.

"What about all your other stuff?" I asked her, thinking about her cluttered house in Montana. "What about your house and your truck?"

"A guy I worked with is gonna pack it all up and ship it for me. Not the furniture. The furniture'll stay, and I'll rent the place furnished, and he wants to buy the truck, and that'll be some income. I can stay with Darryl and Evelyn, so that's all the income I need. I'll get by."

More silence.

"Look," she said, "I know you wanted me to get you across the border. I saw your passports. I know you're underage. And I'm sorry, but it's just gotta be this way. Maybe you can pick up somebody else who's goin' to the States. A hitchhiker or somethin'. If not, I'd go with the same story we used comin' in. Your grandma hauled you over the border to show you the town she grew up in, but then she threw you a curveball and sent you back alone."

Gabriel and I exchanged another glance.

If the weight of the world had been so light as to be nonexistent in the wilderness outside Inuvik, it had returned with a vengeance now. It rested on us harder and heavier than at any point in the trip. Maybe than at any point in our lives.

"It just would have been nice if you'd told us you were only going one way," Gabriel said.

"Would've been nice if you'd told me you were minors crossin' the border," Gladys said. She allowed a long silence, then added, "I'll still pay your gas back. I said I'd pay gas and I won't break my word on that."

I looked at Gabriel, longer this time, and he looked back. It was clear in that look that we weren't really angry at Gladys. We couldn't be. She was dying. She was also right. We had withheld our details and she had withheld hers.

"You shouldn't have to pay our gas if you're not going," Gabriel said.

"But I promised."

"We'll split it," he said.

"Done," Gladys said. "Now let's go home. I'll have Darryl show you how to put on those tire chains before you go. You might need 'em. And because you'll have to stop at night, we're givin' you an ice scraper for your windshield. And Darryl says you can keep the parkas and the boots. We don't want you to die drivin' back alone. But you definitely need to drive back alone."

———

We left that place very early the next morning. Just the two of us, headed south.

"Maybe we should stay in Canada," Gabriel said when we were well outside the city.

"Forever?"

"No, not forever. Till I'm eighteen."

"How long till your birthday?"

"No idea," he said.

"You don't remember your birthday?"

"No, I know *that*," he said. "I just don't know today's date. I've completely lost track, and we didn't think to ask anybody. But we could stay until summer, when the puffins come ashore in Newfoundland. Then I'll be well over eighteen, and we could cross the border and you could be my little sister and I could be the adult in charge."

The snowy tundra rolled by the window as I thought over what he'd said. A pair of musk ox grazed through the light snow by the side of the road, and Gabriel slowed in case they bolted suddenly. Instead they only lifted their heads lazily, almost disinterestedly, and watched us pass. They had massive curled horns that looked like a solid mass of hair parted in the middle on their foreheads.

"Do we even have enough money to cross Canada west to east?" I asked, still watching them in the side mirror.

"No," he said. "We'd have to work."

"I think we got lucky with that job in Montana," I said. "He was desperate, and he paid us under the table, and he didn't ask a lot of questions. But I would think most jobs would want ID, and maybe even do some sort of background check. And it might even be illegal to work in Canada without a visa, even if all those other problems weren't there."

He never answered.

We drove through mile after mile of cold white world, not talking. We were worried, and we had reason to be. And we were still decompressing from our wild state, which I think made us both especially vulnerable to the pressure of those negative feelings. It was something like having to do complicated math to save your own life seconds after being rudely awakened from a deep sleep in the middle of the night.

What I said next I maybe should have said sooner. It might have been one of those things like not telling Gladys we were minors, or her not telling us she wasn't coming back. Or maybe Gabriel knew it just as well as I did, or better, and it hadn't required saying at all.

In any case, it was time to find out.

"I think we need to consider this thing from the angle of your legal liability," I said. "I worry about you first turning eighteen and then us crossing the border. That makes you an adult male traveling with a girl under fourteen. I'm not sure I like how that's going to look. Even crossing a state line with a minor girl . . . I think that's some kind of legal offense."

He didn't answer for a long time.

When he did, he said, "Fair point."

I figured that meant we were headed for the border and crossing it, but we didn't discuss it beyond that.

We drove for an unthinkable number of hours that day. Probably close to fourteen. I knew Gabriel wanted to make miles so we wouldn't waste too much money on motel rooms, and maybe for some other reasons. Neither one of us would truly relax until that border crossing was in our rearview mirror.

Several hours after dark, he gave up. I mean, he had to sooner or later.

"I'm exhausted," he said.

We stopped in a town in Alberta with the appealing name of Peace River, and gave over ninety-six dollars of our precious gas money to sleep without freezing.

But we didn't sleep much.

———

In the morning, Gabriel pulled the curtains open while I was brushing my teeth.

"Holy hell," I heard him say.

I opened the bathroom door, but I couldn't see what he saw, so I moved closer to the window, still brushing.

All I could see was a blanket of white snow. And our window looked out over the parking lot, not an undisturbed field. Still, the cars were just vague mounds under that white blanket.

Everything was gone but the snow.

———

"I think you need to wait for the plow," the desk clerk said. "I mean, chains are all well and good, but by the time you dig your car out enough to even put them on your tires the road'll likely be plowed anyway."

So we ate their free breakfast of juice and fruit and cold cereal and yogurt and oatmeal and hot chocolate. And we waited. And waited. And waited.

We had to wait so long that we had no choice but to sleep over another night, south of Calgary. And maybe it was just as well, we figured. Maybe it was better to be fresh and alert and hit that dreaded border crossing in the morning.

———

We pulled up to the booth, aware of the tantalizing view of Montana, USA, just beyond. I could feel my heart pounding, apparently in my throat.

The border guard who stepped out looked a lot friendlier than the last one.

I took that to be a good sign.

Gabriel powered down the window, and the freezing morning flowed into the Jeep. It was a sensation like being plunged into a glass of ice water.

Gabriel handed him our passports.

I wasn't sure if he was going to offer the man an explanation or wait to be asked for one. And I'm guessing he wasn't sure either. He looked frozen, and possibly unable to speak.

I flashed on that scene from the first Star Wars movie, and tried to silently will the man to believe we were not anyone who interested him. That we were not anybody he was looking for.

Over and over again I imagined him waving us through, as if pressing it to happen just that way using only my mind.

He stared at our passports for a long time. It would not be entirely unreasonable to say my life flashed before my eyes.

He looked up at us, curiously.

"And you're traveling unaccompanied?"

That broke the ice that had formed on Gabriel, and he spoke.

"We came into Canada with our grandmother," he said. "She took us to see the place where she grew up. Yellowknife, NWT. But then all of a sudden she decided not to leave, and we had to drive back on our own."

"That's quite the trip for two young people your age."

"Yes, sir."

"And did she call your parents and tell them? So they had a choice of meeting you, or bringing you home some other way?"

We both opened our mouths at once, but neither one of us managed to say a word.

It was a question we had never anticipated.

It was the end of everything.

"I see. I'll need you to just pull over here and park," he said, indicating a spot to leave the Jeep. "We'll go inside and figure out the best next step to take from here."

We pulled over into the spot he had indicated. I could hear us both breathing. It had a desperate sound, like two people gasping to stay alive.

I saw Gabriel look through the windshield at the road as it extended into Montana, and I knew what he was thinking. Or maybe "thinking" is the wrong word. But he was having a panicky urge, and I could see it in his eyes. Then I saw him wisely put it away again.

"We wouldn't have gotten far anyway," I said.

Before we stepped out of the Jeep he looked at me for a long moment, and of course I looked back. We held each other's eyes like a lifeline.

"I guess that was that," he said.

"Yeah," I said. "I guess so."

"Was it worth it?"

"Oh hell yeah," I said. "A hundred times over. But I should be asking you that same question."

"A thousand times over," he said. "Hell yeah."

———

We had no phones. We had no watches. There was no clock on the wall.

I would estimate we spent forty-five minutes in that misery. Then again, misery being what it is, it might have been fifteen.

What we had was a hard wooden bench, and big, nearly floor-to-ceiling windows on either side of where we sat. The view out the windows on one side was Canada. Out the other it was the US. They were marked with flags, so it was impossible to forget which was which.

We looked out the windows, waiting for anybody to tell us anything. We never once looked into each other's eyes. I think we were instinctively afraid of what we might see there, either as a gauge of the other person's panic or as a mirror reflecting our own.

We weren't alone. That would have been too easy. There were uniformed officers sitting at desks, and coming and going from the snowy outdoors. Just not the guy who had left us here.

When "our" border guard finally, finally came back, he stood over us for a few seconds in silence.

I expected him to ask us a barrage of questions, but he never did.

"Here's what I know so far," he said. "You're no relation to each other. Neither one of you has a living grandmother. And you've both been reported as runaways. Anything you want to add to that?"

"No, that pretty much sums it up," I said.

I wasn't feeling casual, and I wasn't trying to be a smart-ass. It was just what came out.

He shook his head and unclipped two pairs of handcuffs from his belt. I was sitting on Gabriel's left, with the armrest of the wooden bench on my left side. He handcuffed my left wrist to the armrest, leaving my right hand free. He cuffed Gabriel's right wrist to the armrest on the other side.

Then he left us alone for another extended and quite miserable period of time.

The bench was a three-seater, so Gabriel and I had been forced somewhat apart. But, without a word of discussion, we slid back together as best we could. It involved keeping one arm weirdly extended, and then leaning.

I set my head down on his shoulder and he rested his cheek on the top of my head.

It wasn't the least bit comfortable, except to the extent that it definitely was.

"It's going to be okay," he said.

"How do you figure?"

"I don't know. I just think it's going to be okay."

I said nothing for a time, but eventually my curiosity got the best of me.

"Anytime soon?" I asked him.

"Now *that* I couldn't tell you," he said.

Then we waited a great deal longer, though we had no idea what it was we were waiting for.

Chapter Twenty-Three

I've Been to Heaven and That's How I Know This Is Hell

This, girls, is what I think of as the beginning of the dark ages.

About an hour later two Montana state troopers walked through the door, one male and one female. Or maybe it's more proper to call them the highway patrol. Not that it really matters.

The border guard uncuffed us from the bench, which was a relief, and the Montana state police handcuffed our hands together, which was not.

Not handcuffed us to each other. That I would have found comforting. Just our left hands to our right hands.

They led us outside, where I was surprised and disappointed to see two patrol cars instead of one. The male trooper put Gabriel in the back of his and the female officer put me in the back of hers.

Just as she closed the door I looked over to try to see Gabriel. The officer had one hand on the top of his head, the way they do when they put someone in the back of their squad car, so they can't be accused of hitting anybody's head. He looked back at me, and his eyes had that look people get when they're pretty sure all is lost.

From then on I had two images imprinted on the inside of my eyelids, so that all I had to do was close my eyes to see them. The aurora borealis and this.

And then, just like that, we were lone wolves. We were no longer a herd. We were in a different kind of wilderness, operating on half a mind each, utterly unequipped for the captivity that lay ahead.

————

It was a lengthy drive with that trooper to . . . wherever we were going. I didn't know at the time. I'm still not sure I know. Some kind of precinct for life outside the big cities. A police station of sorts, I guess.

Maybe twenty minutes into the drive she decided to talk to me.

"I feel for your situation," she said. "I ran away with my boyfriend when I was . . . well, not as young as you. But I was too young."

"He's not my boyfriend," I said.

My voice sounded completely without energy to me. Devoid of life force. Which was no surprise, as that was exactly how I felt.

She eyed me in the rearview mirror. She was short and slight, with close-cropped, unusually curly dark brown hair. Really tight little curls. Her eyes were dark brown and piercing. They skewered me.

"If you say so, you say so," she said.

Then I got a little mad, which was good. In a way. At least it helped me feel less dead.

"That doesn't *mean* anything," I said.

"Oh, it means something," she said, sounding quite sure.

"It's just tautology," I said. "All you're saying is that if I said it, then that means I said it. You're not saying that proves it's true."

Her eyes met mine in the mirror again. This time they seemed to contain a hint of mirth.

"I know," she said.

Then I shut up for a bit, because the phrase did mean something, and now I knew what. It meant she didn't believe me.

A few miles later she spoke up again.

"Must be hard," she said. "Being so smart. Feeling like you're forty but everybody treats you like you're thirteen."

"How do you know how smart I am?"

"Other than your use of the word 'tautology,' which I've never heard out of the mouth of any thirteen-year-old I've ever known, we talked to your aunt. She said you were attending a high-prestige university when you took off."

"Oh. Okay. Well, then you should know nobody treats me like I'm thirteen."

"We're treating you like you're thirteen right now. If you were forty, you wouldn't be in custody. There would be no problem."

"Oh. Right. Where did they take Gabriel?"

"No idea," she said.

"You really don't know? Or you don't want to tell me?"

"I really don't know. He'll have to be detained overnight, but where they decide to put him was yet to be determined when I last talked to anybody. Then he has an arraignment in the morning."

The word set up a wash of ice in my chest and belly. What had I done to Gabriel?

"And after that?" I said through the numb shock.

"Nobody knows *that*," she said. "It depends on the judge."

"Do *I* have an arraignment in the morning?"

"No. We're just turning you over to your legal guardian. Your aunt."

"So he's being punished and I'm not. Oh, wait. Scratch that. I have to go live with my aunt in Kentucky. I'm not sure what punishment could possibly be worse."

But I was deeply afraid that what the law had in store for Gabriel was worse.

She had no comeback, and we didn't talk for the remainder of the drive.

———

I sat on a hard wooden bench at the station. It was no more comfortable than the hard wooden bench at the border station. Well, in a way it was, because they didn't handcuff me to it. The officer took off my handcuffs and just left me to sit there on my own. Probably because I was in plain view of at least three officers at all times.

The view out both windows was Montana. Canada was a thing from my past. I had been there earlier that morning, but it felt like a years-old memory.

A few minutes later she came back and stood over me.

"Your aunt will be here to pick you up tomorrow," she said. "Here are your two choices for tonight. We can take you to a juvenile-detention facility for girls, and they'll give you dinner and a bed. It's like three hours each way, but we'll drive you there if you say that's what you want. Or you can sit on this bench all night with us. Well, not us. We'll be going off shift. But with the night-shift officers."

"If I sit here do I get dinner?"

I had already missed lunch, but probably that was not their concern. And it wasn't like I'd said so out loud.

"Sure," she said. "We order in. We'll get you something. We're not gonna starve you to death."

"I'll just stay here," I said.

The devil you know is always better than the devil you don't know. Or at least that's what they say. I doubt whether it's always better or not, but I don't doubt that it's almost always the devil we choose.

———

When the food came I had to ask permission to go to the bathroom and wash my hands, and a female officer had to accompany me there. Which was silly, because you could see the door to the bathroom from where I sat. You could see everything from everywhere.

She didn't come inside or anything. It wasn't that bad. She just waited outside the door for me to be done and then escorted me the whole fifteen feet back to my bench.

Dinner was Greek souvlaki and gyros, of all things. Not that I have anything against it, but I remember thinking, *Sure. Doesn't everybody come to Montana for the Greek food?*

Anyway, it was good, though I expect it might have tasted better without the side of abject misery.

The shift of officers was entirely different now, and I wasn't sure if I was supposed to talk to anybody or not. Nobody was talking to me.

But my question felt important, so I blasted out into a room full of authority-figure strangers.

"What happened to Gabriel?" I asked.

Nobody answered, and I thought they were simply ignoring me. One of them, a big, heavy, mostly bald male officer, started clattering on his computer keyboard, but I didn't take it to have anything to do with me.

"They took him to Bozeman," he said.

"And . . . ?"

"That's all it says right now."

That's also all *we* said. Any of us. All night. I mean, they talked to each other, and they talked on the phone. But that was the last time they talked to me.

———

When I saw it was dark outside the windows, I curled up on my side on the bench and tried to get comfortable. Ever tried to sleep comfortably on a hard wooden bench? Let me save you the trouble of experimentation: it can't be done.

I had to roll over every few minutes because it pinched a bunch of nerves against my hip bone. Every time I managed to doze off to sleep the phone would ring, and an officer would answer it and begin a conversation in a voice that sounded like shouting. Every time someone came in or went out, a blast of cold accompanied them, and I had taken off my parka because it was the only pillow I had.

I would guess I got maybe an hour of sleep, though not all together at one stretch.

While I was lying awake on that horrible bench, I remember thinking, *Now I can honestly say I've been to both Heaven and Hell. Heaven is a viewing platform on top of a geodesic dome outside Inuvik, NWT, Canada, under the aurora borealis. And this is Hell.*

And I wasn't even in Kentucky with Aunt Bitsy yet. Things could only get worse from there.

———

Speaking of Aunt Bitsy, which I'm always loath to do . . . it was morning, not all that early. I was so tired that I guess I had managed to drop off to sleep, even in the midst of all that noise and commotion. I was sitting up, my head drooped down toward my shoulder.

When I woke up and tried to straighten my head again, my neck was in a state of serious crick.

Aunt Bitsy was standing over me. I didn't know how long she'd been there. I didn't want to know.

Suffice it to say she did not look happy.

I wondered if her sheer fury and disapproval had wakened me, because I didn't think she'd spoken a word. But it was just a theory.

"There's a cab waiting out front," she said. "The meter's running, and it's not cheap, so get up and get going."

"What about my stuff?" I said, my mouth thick and dry from hanging open in my sleep.

"It's in the cab. They already released it to me."

"Oh," I said. "Okay."

I rose stiffly, feeling much the worse for wear after that night on the hard bench. I struggled into my parka and followed her out to the cab, blinking into the blinding-bright morning.

She put me in the back first, as if expecting me to be a flight risk. Then she climbed in after.

"What happened to Gabriel?" I asked as we pulled away from the curb.

"I didn't ask," she said, "so I don't know, and the reason I didn't ask is because I don't care."

"*I* care," I said.

"So he *is* your boyfriend."

"No. He's no such thing and he never was. He's my friend."

She had no reply to that. She seemed to have lost interest in the conversation.

A few miles later she said, "They tell me you were in Canada of all places."

"Yeah," I said.

"How far up into Canada?"

"Almost to the Arctic Ocean."

"That's a long way."

"Tell me about it."

"Just to get as far away from me as possible?"

"No," I said. "Not *just* that. We had some things we wanted to see. We were on an adventure."

"Well, I hope you saw everything you wanted to see, because the adventure is over now."

We hadn't, of course. We hadn't seen the Atlantic puffins. But I didn't tell her that, because Aunt Bitsy was the last person on earth with whom I'd be comfortable sharing my dreams.

"Yeah, I sensed that," I said.

Another dozen miles rolled by in silence. I caught her glancing at the meter at regular intervals. The fare was up over $200 already.

She must have seen me looking.

"This cab ride is expensive," she said. "The last-minute plane fare is expensive. You will pay me back out of your mother's estate."

"I thought she had no estate."

"You think she made no plans and had no security? She wasn't a vagabond, you know. She was an adult who handled her finances properly. It's not a fortune, but there are some funds to be distributed to you in time."

"She told me the medical bills were eating up the money really fast."

"That was when she thought she might live for another six months or more," Aunt Bitsy said.

"Oh," I said.

I noticed that, what with the adventure being over and all, the whole orphan thing was getting very real very fast.

More silent miles slid by.

Then the driver turned off the highway into a tiny regional airport.

This time I was the one to break the silence.

"Why do you even *want* me?" I asked her.

"I don't," she said. "But I promised your late mother I'd make sure you survived in spite of yourself, and that's what I'm going to do."

Chapter Twenty-Four

Toto, I Think We're in Kentucky

I had only been to my aunt Bitsy's house in Kentucky one time, when I was four. As far as I could tell, nothing had changed. Literally. Nothing. Even the tablecloths and towels were the same. The sheets were more worn, of course, but as far as I could tell they had not been replaced.

It was clean, though. Painfully, obsessively clean. The kind of clean that seems to indicate mental issues on the part of the cleaner.

She led me by the guest room without stopping.

In the hallway just past it, there was a trapdoor in the ceiling. She pulled hard on a rope and a set of stairs came down. She indicated with her hand that I was to use them.

"This is your room," she said.

"This is the attic," I said.

"And that's your room."

"I thought I was going to be in the guest room."

"But you're not going to be."

"Any special reason?"

"Because I might have a guest."

"Silly me," I said. "I thought *I* was a guest."

"Oh heavens no."

I sighed and walked up the stairs.

It was clean, but there was little else to be said for it.

It had a slanted roof, high in the middle and smack-yourself-in-to-concussionland on each side. There was one small window looking out over the front yard, and a bare light bulb with a hanging string.

As for furnishings, Aunt Bitsy had provided a single-size cot made up with sheets and blankets, a bedside table with one drawer, and an open set of shelves with cubby-like storage areas.

The only thing that might qualify as a decoration was a framed photograph of my mom.

I stared at the photograph for a long time, trying not to let it in. Trying to hold the whole thing at bay, the way I'd more or less managed to do while traveling with Gabriel.

It didn't work.

I started to cry, and the more I tried to stop the tears the more momentum they gained.

I heard a slight noise behind me, and I knew Aunt Bitsy had come up the stairs.

"Why did you put that here?" I asked her, indicating the photo.

"I would think it would be a comfort to you."

"Well, it's not. It just reminds me that she's gone."

I was trying to keep the tears out of my voice. I doubt I was succeeding.

"She *is* gone," Aunt Bitsy said. "You might as well accept that."

I could hear and feel her footsteps, and I knew she was right behind me.

"Here," she said.

I didn't want to turn around and see what was being offered because I didn't want her to see me crying.

"What?"

She held it over my shoulder and I took it into my hand. A laminated card of some sort.

"What is this?" I said, though I suppose I could have read it just as easily.

"It's a bus pass. You start at the community college tomorrow."

"You've got to be kidding me."

"Why would I kid?"

"I could *teach* community college. I could train their professors."

"You have to go to school," she said, "so cut the histrionics and tone down your ego. The university your mother had you going to recommended you to a couple of other more eastern universities, neither very close, and they're both willing to take you, but not until the beginning of the next semester. In the meantime, learn what you can. And listen to me well for a moment . . . I'm not going to lock you up, and I'm not going to watch you every minute."

"Glad to hear it," I said, still not turning around.

"But I'm telling you now, and I'll only tell you once. If you run off again and you don't get caught, there's nothing I can do about that. I did my best. If you run off and you do get caught, I'm not coming to pick you up, and I'm not taking you back. You can just stay in juvenile detention until you're eighteen. You can train all their teachers. It'll give you something to pass the time. I can only do what I can do, and besides, I only promised your mom I'd help you survive. I didn't say I'd house and entertain you no matter how many boneheaded decisions you make. You can survive incarcerated if you can't stay put."

She paused, in case I had any snarky comments to get off my chest. I didn't. I was still faced away from her, still staring at the picture of my mom and trying not to cry. I had nothing but defeat, and it didn't lend itself well to words, even if I'd had any.

"Dinner is at six," she said. "Be there, on time and clean."

Then she retraced her steps back down the attic stairs and she was blessedly gone.

———

The next morning I was sitting at the back of a classroom—like those people I used to be unable to understand—at the community college.

The class was an introduction to trigonometry, which was silly, because trigonometry and I had already been introduced.

I leaned over to scratch my calf, and just for a burst of a second I had a flashback to that experience I had the day my mother died. Nearly bumping into someone who wasn't . . . technically . . . you know . . . there.

I swung my head around, but the space was empty and still.

I felt it as a letdown.

It was nearly time for the bell to ring, and I was looking forward to that. I was bored out of my mind and there were no windows.

"One last practice problem before we wrap up," the instructor said. "Open your books to page one forty-one."

Then she looked around to make sure everybody did. But I had just dropped onto campus for the first time less than an hour and a half earlier, and I had no book.

"You," she said, and walked up the aisle to me. "Are you in my class?"

"I am now," I said.

"You're monitoring?"

"No. My aunt enrolled me. But I missed the beginning of the semester."

"Let me get you *my* book," she said.

She moved back toward her desk again before I could tell her it was a waste of time. That all this was just a waste of time.

A moment later she dropped the book on the desk in front of me, open to the correct page.

The practice problem read as follows:

"A mounted camera on the ground is watching a hot air balloon rise vertically. If the camera is placed 100 yards from the balloon's launch site, at what angle must the camera be mounted to capture a picture of the balloon when the balloon is 50 yards off the ground? Provide your answer in radians, rounded to two decimal places."

I raised my hand. She was on her way back down to the front of the classroom and didn't see me. I had to hold it up there for a long time.

I'm sure she figured she had plenty of time before anyone volunteered an answer.

She reminded me a little of Ms. Stepanian, except she was maybe a decade older. Which still was not old as teachers go. She had blond hair that trailed in a long braid down the middle of her back, and she wore the same blazer-and-jeans look.

I almost put my hand down because the muscles in my arm were getting tired. But just then she looked up and saw me.

"I don't know your name," she said.

"Ru."

"What's your question, Ru?"

"It's not a question. I'm volunteering the answer."

"That was fast."

"It was all the time I needed."

"Okay, go. Tell us the answer."

"It's 0.46," I said.

"Oh. Well, that's a nice try, Ru. But the answer is in the back of the book."

"Yeah, I saw that," I said. I had looked. It said 0.56. "But that answer is wrong."

"Wait. What answer is wrong?"

"The one in the book," I said.

"You're telling me there's a mistake in the textbook?"

"Yes. I'm telling you that."

Meanwhile the other students had taken to craning their necks around so they could look at me in a way that reflected how much they were wondering what was wrong with me.

"That seems unlikely," the teacher said.

"I can't speak to the odds of the thing," I said. "But it's wrong."

"I'm not sure what to do with that," she said. "The people who wrote this book know a lot about trigonometry. They don't tend to get it wrong."

"I don't think they *did* get it wrong exactly. Whoever wrote this . . . I think they got the right answer but typed it wrong. I think they just hit the key next door and nobody caught it in the proofreading. The five is right next to the four, of course. And that's not uncommon. Most books go to press with at least one small typo. It's harder to catch this kind of typo than a mistake in spelling or punctuation, because it has no real context unless you solve the problem yourself from the beginning."

She stepped up to a desk in the front row and turned a student's book around, staring at it for a long time. Weirdly long. Long enough that students began to shift uncomfortably in their seats.

She looked lost, so I said more.

"The ratio of the vertical distance of the balloon from the camera divided by the horizontal distance of the balloon to the camera is 1/2. We're looking for the angle of the camera, so we can use the inverse tangent function to tell us that the answer should be arctan (1/2), which is 0.46 when rounded to two decimal places."

Finally her head came up and she stared straight through me, as if trying to pin me to the wall behind my desk with a laser gaze.

"I'll be damned," she said.

And then, just at that moment, the bell rang.

Everyone more or less sprinted for the doors, but I was culled from the back of the herd.

"Wait," she said, and took a little piece of the fabric of my sleeve in her fingers.

"What?"

"I just want to talk to you."

"Am I in trouble?"

"Not at all. I just have some questions."

She sat down at her desk and I stood in front of it, rocking on my toes, my thighs touching the front of the desk so I couldn't fall forward.

"Do you have this trig book at home?" she asked me.

"No, I've never seen it before."

"So your eyes just fell on the page and you knew it was wrong?"

"I thought about it for a few seconds."

"And you're how old?"

"Thirteen."

"I guess I just have one question, then. What are you *doing* here?"

"Define 'here,'" I said, still rocking. "If by 'here' you mean planet Earth, I wonder that myself all the time."

She burst out laughing. When that was done she looked less puzzled and more amused.

"I meant in this college."

"Do you mean why am I reaching up to this college when I'm only thirteen, or why am I reaching down to it when I'm obviously freakishly smart?"

"That second thing," she said.

"I was going to Wellington, in California. But I got bumped out of the state unexpectedly. My aunt enrolled me here. I tried to tell her it was a waste of time, but you really can't tell her much."

"She's not interested in getting you into a top university like Wellington but closer?"

"She did get two universities to agree to take me on. With a lot of help from some people at Wellington. But not till next semester. She didn't tell me which two they were. She probably thinks all information is dangerous in my hands."

"Somebody needs to advocate for speeding up the process."

"That would be nice," I said.

"I'm on my way to administration," she said. "Walk with me."

We stepped out into the light, and I noticed her cell phone. It was hanging in a case, clipped to her belt with a carabiner like the kind climbers use.

We fell into a side-by-side formation and walked, blinking our eyes against the painfully bright morning.

"I need to ask you a really big favor," I said. "Kind of rudely big."

"Okay, I guess. So long as I can say no."

"Can I make a call on your phone? My aunt leaves hers locked up."

"You don't have a cell phone?"

"Technically I do. But it's in the metal pouch of a rusty kangaroo sculpture in the deserted parking lot of this defunct diner in Nevada."

She glanced over at me skeptically. I think it was dawning on her that a kid can be smart and have a wild streak at the same time.

"Is that a joke?"

"No, it's a true story. I'll tell it if you want, but you'd need to have a big block of time on your hands."

She unclipped the phone and handed it to me without comment.

"It's to a California number," I said.

"Doesn't matter."

I called Gabriel's mother's phone number by heart. I didn't want to talk to her. I wanted to talk to Gabriel. But I couldn't call Gabriel, because his phone was in the metal pouch of that same rusty kangaroo sculpture in the deserted parking lot of that same defunct diner in Nevada.

She wasn't home, or didn't answer, and the call went to voice mail.

"Hi, Mrs. Gulbranson," I said. "It's me. Ru. I need to know if Gabriel's okay. If he's there with you, safe at home, or . . . you know. In trouble. I know you're probably not my biggest fan right now, but please tell him I called. Please. I'm worried he got in trouble, and how much, and what kind, and stuff like that, and I can't even eat or sleep because I don't know. Please have him call me. Please. I mean, if he's . . . you know. A free person. And in a position to make a phone call. I'm at my aunt's in Kentucky but she won't let me use the phone, so . . ." I paused, realizing I had not thought this out well. "So I guess just have him call me back on *this* number. Thanks."

In my peripheral vision I saw the teacher glance in my direction with raised eyebrows. I clicked off the call.

"Sorry," I said. "That was not my best thinking. I didn't mean to do that without asking your permission, but all of a sudden I realized I didn't know where to tell him to call me. Can you at least ask him if he's okay? You know. If he calls? And then you could just tell me he's okay?"

"I suppose I could do that," she said.

"Thanks. I really appreciate it."

I handed her back the phone, and we walked without talking for a minute or two.

"You've got a lot of long stories in there," she said, "don't you?"

"You have no idea," I said. "Seriously. You do *not* want to get me started."

Chapter Twenty-Five

Will Work for Burner Phones

Somewhere deep in the bowels of that administration building was a room the students knew nothing about. Not that they would have been all that interested, had they known. It was nothing so fancy as a proper teachers' lounge, but it served as such. It was a place where a handful of them hid out between classes when there wasn't enough time to drive home.

The furnishings consisted of rolling typist's chairs, stacks of boxes, and filing cabinets that served as desks for people's laptop computers.

There were maybe six or seven teachers who used the place, and two days later they all knew me, even though I was only in classes with three of them.

When Ms. Bolt—that was the name of the trig teacher who'd let me use her phone—stepped into the room, I was taking an informal pop quiz given by one of the teachers who had already decided to give me an A.

Suffice it to say that my aunt Bitsy was the only person on the planet who didn't see that attending classes would be a waste of time. I hadn't been to a class since that first morning, and everybody but Aunt Bitsy knew it, and nobody who knew it failed to support the decision.

The teacher quizzing me was Mrs. Jankins, my anatomy teacher. And honestly, it really wasn't a test in any genuine sense of the word. I was asked to perform like a trained seal at regular intervals for the delight of the staff, but I make it sound like a bad thing and it really wasn't. At least, not entirely. It had an element of weirdness to it, but I also got the distinct impression that they liked me and enjoyed my company. And that—let's face it—was a missing element in my life at that juncture of events.

Mrs. Jankins presented me with a chart of the human cranial nerves. It had a clear plastic overlay with the names of each nerve, but she had that folded back. Otherwise it wouldn't have been much of a challenge, right?

"Okay," she said. "For the A grade I've already basically given you, name six nerves that exit the cranium, and the location from which they exit."

"Sure," I said. "Whatever. I was thinking this might be more challenging, but okay. From the cribriform plate, the terminal nerve and the olfactory nerve; from the optic foramen, the optic nerve; from the superior orbital fissure, oculomotor, trochlear, abducens, trigeminal; from the foramen rotundum, trigeminal V2; from the foramen ovale, trigeminal V3; from the stylomastoid foramen—"

"Wait," she said. "You were supposed to do six. How many is that?"

"Nine nerves so far."

"You were supposed to do six," she said again.

"Extra credit?"

I was approximately half joking. The truth was that I'd been something short of bored for a split second, and I didn't want the moment to end.

That was when I saw Ms. Bolt, my trig teacher, come in. She looked amused by me, but then she generally did. Not at my expense or anything. It seemed to read like a somewhat twisted compliment.

"This just in," she said. "Ru Evans gets an A in anatomy but flunks math."

I was shocked. So shocked, in fact, that my intended question about phone calls got knocked to the back of the line.

"Wait, you're flunking me?"

"It's a joke. I'm suggesting you can't properly count to six."

"Oh," I said. "Got it. I'm better at math and science than I am at jokes."

"Yeah, I'm picking up on that."

"Any calls?"

"Nope. Sorry."

I sat still a moment, letting the sting of that news settle in. Reminding myself that he might not have been in jail. He might just have been home with a mother who wouldn't give him my messages. But I didn't *know*, and I hated not knowing. Especially when it was so incredibly important.

One of the teachers spoke up suddenly.

"I'll give you fifty bucks to grade my papers," he said to me.

Everybody else laughed, but I honestly didn't think he was joking.

"I'm not even in your class," I said.

"I know it."

"I don't even know what you teach."

"Geometry," he said.

"Piece of cake."

"Wait," Mrs. Jankins said. "You're serious? You think she can correct your papers?"

"She could correct your textbooks," Ms. Bolt said. "But still. It's the principle of the thing. Isn't that something you should do yourself, Jack?"

"Hold on," I said. "Don't chase this idea away so fast."

"Well, I suppose if you really need the money . . . ," Ms. Bolt said.

"Not really," I said. "I mean, you can never have too much money. But what I really need is a phone."

The teacher who'd made the offer—I didn't know his name beyond the "Jack" I had just heard—seemed to backtrack when he heard my suggestion.

"Never mind, I'll grade them," he said. "Phones costing hundreds of dollars and all."

"You can get one of those cheap disposable phones for like twenty dollars," Mrs. Jankins said. "I get them for my stepkids all the time."

"You mean like the burner phones the drug dealers use on TV shows?"

"Something like that," Mrs. Jankins said. "You could get one and load it with some limited minutes for what you just offered her."

"Hmm," he said. "I guess that *would* be hard, not having a phone."

"Oh, she has a phone," Ms. Bolt said. "Tell him, Ru. Tell him where your phone is."

"It's in the metal pouch of a rusty kangaroo sculpture in the deserted parking lot of this defunct diner in Nevada," I said.

"There's got to be an interesting story behind that," he said.

I opened my mouth to answer, but Ms. Bolt beat me to it.

"Do *not* get her started," she said.

And that, girls, is how I ended up with a drug-dealer-style burner phone during my time in Kentucky. I kept it in one of the file drawers in that impromptu lounge, where my aunt Bitsy could never find it.

I called Gabriel's mom five times over the next two weeks.

No one ever called me back.

———

After the aforementioned two weeks of phoning into the void, I took to writing letters. Of course, having lived there for a time, I knew Gabriel's address at his mother's house by heart. Or . . . actually . . . where did that expression even come from? I didn't know that address with my heart. I knew some things with my heart, like the fact that Gabriel and I operated together as a herd, and that millions of stars against an unusually dark sky are good for the spirit. But the address I knew by brain.

I was sitting in the impromptu teachers' lounge, writing to him longhand on a yellow legal pad someone had left lying around.

"Dear Gabriel," I wrote. "I've been trying to call you for weeks, but I never hear back. I don't even know if you know I'm calling. I have no choice but to call your mom, what with our phones being stashed you-know-where. I think maybe she's not giving you the messages.

"Then again, there are three possible explanations for the thing, and I think I'm stuck on her not giving you the messages because, of the three, that's the one that feels most livable. I mean, it's frustrating as all hell. We're a herd. You don't break up a herd, right? But it's not all that disastrous compared to the other two. At least that one could be true and I could still get to sleep at night.

"Here are the options that keep running through my brain. They're wearing tracks in there and I'm getting pretty tired.

"One: You're in jail, and it's all my fault. And it's a terrible time for you and I'm not even there to help it be less terrible, like you always did with me. Two: You don't want to have anything to do with me anymore."

It was the first time I had allowed those words into my brain. The feeling of it had been there all along, but I'd been careful not to pin it down into language.

I tried to just keep writing so the feeling would go away.

"Now do you see why your mom ignoring my messages feels like a good choice?

"Anyway, I decided to switch to letters because I realized it's mean but basically legal not to give somebody a phone message. But the law is quite picky about US mail, and hopefully she knows that."

I stopped writing, because I suddenly realized that I didn't know the specific laws regarding US mail.

I looked up and saw that Ms. Bolt had come in and sat down. I looked at her and she looked back.

"Pen and paper?" she said. "You don't strike me as the Luddite type."

"As opposed to what other options?"

"Your aunt won't buy you a computer?"

"She hasn't yet."

"When you get to a genuine university next semester you'll need a computer."

"Tell *her*," I said. "Don't tell me. So listen. What do you know about the laws that govern the US mail?"

"Not too much," she said. "But I have my laptop and I can look it up."

"Yes please."

Mrs. Jankins came in and sat down, pulling a wrapped sandwich out of a brown paper bag.

"What are we talking about?" she asked.

"Mail theft," I said.

"Wait," Ms. Bolt said. "Why am I looking this up? I thought you knew everything."

"I don't know everything. Only everything I've seen, read, or heard."

"Oh. Well, thank you for that very important distinction," she said, in her half-amused, half-sarcastic voice.

In the pause that followed I had a realization, and it was not a happy one. As previously realized, I had spent my whole life being a smart person, except for that magical time when I was a person. And now it was blazingly clear to me that the time of magic was over. And I knew I would miss the half of me that had just been left behind.

It was the best half.

"What specifically do you need to know?" Ms. Bolt asked, ready to type.

"Is it against the law to open somebody else's mail and then not give it to him?"

She repeated the words out loud, almost exactly as I had said them, as she typed them into a search engine.

"Short answer," she said. "Yes. Opening or destroying mail that is addressed to someone else is a crime called 'obstruction of correspondence.' It's a serious felony and it can lead to prison time. The only thing is . . . I don't know, I'm still trying to find it, but it seems like that might apply to another *adult's* mail. Not sure about a person under eighteen."

"Gabriel is eighteen by now."

"Uh-oh," both teachers said at almost exactly the same time. But I think it was just a coincidence. I don't think there was anything herdlike about them.

"What?"

"That's gotta be dicey," Ms. Bolt said.

"What's 'gotta' be dicey? And also it's a good thing you're not my English teacher."

"You being thirteen and your boyfriend being eighteen."

"He's not my boyfriend," I said.

"Seriously?"

"Seriously. Why would you even think that?"

"Because you seem so obsessed with him."

"He's my friend," I said. "My best friend. My only friend."

"We're your friends," Mrs. Jankins said.

"It's different, though," I said. "No offense. But he's my herd."

"Your what?" they both said. But not exactly synchronized.

"Never mind. You wouldn't understand. And anyway, I have to finish writing my letter."

I put pen to paper again.

"But maybe she doesn't know that," I wrote, "about the whole mail thing. So, Mrs. Gulbranson, if this is you reading this, opening or destroying mail that's addressed to someone else is a crime called 'Obstruction of Correspondence.' It's a serious felony and it can lead to prison time. I'm just saying.

"Now, if it's Gabriel reading this . . .

"You can write back to me at the return address I'm going to put on this envelope. It's a community college in Kentucky. I'm putting down the name Lucinda Bolt instead of mine, and the address at the college. That's my trigonometry teacher. I don't think you should send mail to my aunt Bitsy's house because I don't think I'd get it. Maybe that law only applies to adults, or maybe she just doesn't care.

"I'm so scared not knowing if you're okay, Gabriel. Please write back soon. Even if you don't want to hear from me, maybe just to tell me you're okay? Or if you're Mrs. Gulbranson and not Gabriel, could you please just take pity on me and tell me he's okay?

"I'm sorry I got you/him in trouble. —Ru."

I looked up, trying not to cry.

"Where does a person get a stamp around here?"

"My purse," Mrs. Jankins said.

So maybe I really did have some friends in Kentucky after all.

———

In the roughly two months I spent semi-attending that community college in Kentucky, I wrote seven letters to Gabriel.

I never received a reply.

Though I swore no such thing could happen, I think something inside of me just . . . sort of . . . gave up.

———

The holidays came and went with little fanfare from Aunt Bitsy. There were no presents. There was no tree. Not that these were the most important things to me, but it speaks to my aunt's level of commitment, so I'm pointing it out.

In the first few days of January, the new semester started at a very good university in North Carolina. I had been given my choice of the universities that would have me midyear and on fairly short notice, and I had chosen this one—ostensibly because it was the best. Maybe it was, but I had actually chosen it because it was the farthest.

I was to stay in a dorm like everybody else all week, and then on weekends I was to travel back to Aunt Bitsy's on my own, by bus or train. The whole thing was quite ridiculous, as it was six hours each way, and, owing to my age, required a note from my guardian. But I jumped at it anyway because it got me out of her house five days out of seven. And even that's not counting half a day on the bus.

It wasn't lost on me that she was allowing something my mother had not. My mother had balked even at the idea of me living in a closely supervised family environment during the week. In a million years she would never have allowed this. Then again, why be surprised? My mother had actually cared what happened to me.

The day before I was to show up on campus, I was given the exact address of my dorm.

I sat in my room, in front of my new-to-me used laptop computer, vacillating wildly.

Then I wrote Gabriel one more letter, just so he would have my new address if he ever changed his mind.

Chapter Twenty-Six

Six Knocks on My Dorm-Room Door

My roommate was a sweet, plump, mousy girl of eighteen with a serious substance-abuse problem. I'm not suggesting she hung out in back alleys and bought heroin or anything so hard-core as that. She just always smelled of patchouli oil, and had that hazy film across her eyes that marked her as being absent from the scene.

It was ideal for me, really, though I hope it doesn't sound mean to say. We got along fine, but it was a lot like having a room of my own. I'm not wishing problems on her. I'm just saying how it was for me, her constant state of highness being a given.

The dorm room was weirdly bare, and what passed for beds were just two hard wooden platforms with flat pads of "mattresses" barely three inches thick.

I wondered how the nonscholarship parents felt about that. Here they were paying tens of thousands of dollars yearly, and not even a couple hundred of those dollars went into treating their kids to average comfort.

I, of course, was on a full ride, or I wouldn't have been there. I was the poor orphan who had to catch what crumbs she was tossed.

I sound like I'm complaining, but it was not Aunt Bitsy's house in Kentucky, and I was thrilled.

As for curriculum, it was much like Wellington—more challenging than where I had been, but not challenging enough. I think I had more or less accepted the truth by then—that the world was destined to be that way for me, in every instance and at every time.

———

I was maybe eight days at the university when they decided to show me off at a cocktail party for the donors, like I was their one-girl parade. Fortunately, I had grown accustomed to balancing a ball on my nose in return for a tossed fish.

Pardon the mixed metaphor.

And I want you to know that, despite all my complaints about it, I'm not suggesting any bad behavior on the part of the board. I was there at no expense to myself or my aunt Bitsy, and it's certainly reasonable and fair to ask me to spend a couple of hours helping the university in return. I'm not saying otherwise. I'm just saying it was a tough couple of hours.

Also there was homework involved. Preparation. It quickly came in the form of people knocking on my dorm-room door.

First the dean came knocking. And you have to know that deans of fine universities don't spend a lot of time knocking on students' doors. I'm guessing in most cases they would send someone to fetch any student the dean wanted to see, so his in-person appearance would have struck me as an honor if I were the kind of person who viewed things that way.

He was a rumpled man, small in stature, with an oddly pinched little face. Maybe seventy. He looked as though he'd never heard of wash-and-wear clothing, or even an iron for the clothing he already had. He was carrying a light camel coat over one arm, though the days had been around fifty degrees.

He peered past me to my characteristically stoned roommate and frowned.

"Miss Evans," he said. "Take a walk with me around campus, please. You might want to bring a sweater."

So we did that.

I took it that I was about to be kicked out for some reason. When he finally spit out his big ask, I was much relieved.

"We'd like you to attend a cocktail party we're having for our biggest donors tomorrow evening."

"You know I'm not old enough to drink, right?"

"Of course. I do know that. In fact, we'll have a student escort to walk you to and from the event, for your safety, and a member of the staff will act as a sort of . . . well, not exactly a chaperone, but she'll make sure you always have access to juice or soda or some other appropriate beverage."

"Okay," I said.

"Good," he said. "Very good. I'm glad you're on board with this. Everybody likes a story such as yours. Child genius, bounced around by bad fates. Orphaned at an early age. And then our university taking you under its wing and giving you the education you deserve."

"Okay," I said again. I wasn't sure what else needed saying.

"So I hope you won't take offense if we bring up the tragic loss of your mother as we share your background with people."

"Well, I don't know that 'offense' is the right word," I said. "It's still a sore subject, but you'll do what you have to do, I guess."

"Thank you. And the part about running away with a boy and ending up in Arctic Canada? And being apprehended at the border?"

"I'm guessing you will *not* be bringing that up."

"Correct. And we'd appreciate it if you didn't either."

"Okay," I said for the third time.

"We can go heavy on the idea that your future medical research might change the landscape of health as we know it."

"Sure," I said. "We can do that."

I had slipped into a mildly amused parody of myself, but I don't think he noticed.

"Excellent," he said.

He stopped walking, so I stopped too, though I wasn't sure why. I focused on my surroundings again and realized he had led me around in a circle and walked me back to my dorm.

"Someone will knock on your door at a little before seven tomorrow evening. Have a good day, Miss Evans."

He walked away, forgetting to mention that other people would knock on my door between then and the knock in question.

———

Someone knocked on my door at seven the following morning. I was awake, but my roommate was not.

It was a woman who appeared to be in her forties, wearing a short haircut and a smart pantsuit.

"I hope I didn't wake you," she said.

"No, I was up."

But my roommate had begun mumbling cusswords, so I stepped out into the hall and closed the door most of the way behind me.

"Bella McGonigal," she said. "I'm a special assistant to the dean. I wanted to catch you before you went off to breakfast. Or class. I see you have chemistry today at ten, but we're going to ask you to miss it just this one day. I'm taking you shopping."

"Shopping," I repeated. As if she'd said she was taking me skeet shooting or alligator hunting or chasing down tornadoes.

"So you have the right attire for this evening."

"Ohhhh," I said, letting the word stretch. "I get it now. I hadn't really thought about what I was going to wear. I figured I'd just go as myself."

"And we want that. We want you to feel like yourself. Just . . . the very best version of you."

"Got it," I said. "So . . . somebody else entirely."

She laughed.

"You're a good sport," she said.

———

She knocked on my door again at ten. So that was three knocks.

On the drive into town, she more or less trained me—taught me what to say and how to say it. She pretty much did everything but bring flash cards.

But again, it was a small price to pay for a free university education.

The real cost came in the form of a yellow dress that made me look about ten.

"It's so . . . innocent," I said, staring at myself in horror in the dressing-room mirror.

"That's the look we're going for," she said.

"It makes me look like a child."

"That's—"

I didn't even let her finish the thought.

"Right," I said. "Got it. That's the look you're going for."

"Good sport," she said again. And winked at me.

Then she paid for the dress, tucked it in its bag under my arm, and drove me back to campus, where I finished my day of classes and tried not to think about the insult of that ridiculous yellow dress.

———

The student escort knocked on my door at 6:50 that evening. That was my fourth knock.

He was a burly young man of eighteen or nineteen, wearing jeans and a university sweatshirt.

"I'm here to walk you over," he said.

"Thanks," I said, and stepped out into the hall.

"You sure you don't want to bring a jacket for later?" he asked.

"I'm fine," I said. "It's not cold. This is not cold. I've been to the Northwest Territories, just a handful of kilometers from the Beaufort Sea, which is pretty much the Arctic Ocean. That was cold. This is not cold." A warmth spread through me as I spoke about the place. "But don't bring that up at the party," I added.

"Oh, I'm not going to the party. I'm just walking you over."

"Oh. Okay. But you know what? I *am* going to bring a scarf."

I popped very quickly into my closet and grabbed the wonderful multicolored scarf Darryl and Evelyn had given me. Not because I thought I'd be cold, but because I'd been talking about the Northwest Territories, and bringing something from my time there felt like a security blanket.

He held out his elbow like an old-fashioned gentleman, and I hooked my arm through his, and he walked me outside and through the campus.

"You look very nice," he said.

"I look like a clown."

"I don't think you do."

"I look like somebody else."

"Well, I don't know who you look like when you look like you, so I can't say. But I think you look nice."

He walked me right to the door of a building I didn't know. Then again, I was less than two weeks in. Most of the buildings on campus were buildings I didn't know. Bella McGonigal was waiting there for me, like I was the baton in a relay race. She led me inside by the elbow, unwinding the scarf from around my neck.

"We'll just hang this up with the coats," she said.

She didn't say straight out that it didn't match the dress or continue the desired look. But I knew.

She led me inside and left me with the dean, who began introducing me to people. Mostly older couples. We didn't move around the room. We held perfectly still, and they came to us. If they didn't, Bella McGonigal led them over, saying, "I just know you'll want to meet Miss Evans."

She also made sure I had my choice of "cocktail"—cola with two cherries and one wedge of lime—in my hand at all times.

Seven people told me I might discover the cure for cancer. I just smiled and said, "Well, you never know."

That seemed to please the dean.

Ten people consoled me on the tragic loss of my mother, and I had to thank them and pretend it hadn't really happened that way at the same time.

Mostly I didn't have to talk. Mostly my bona fides and abilities were rattled off for me, I assumed so I wouldn't sound immodest by listing them myself.

Still, it was exhausting. Everybody was talking at once, my face hurt from fake smiling, and I couldn't stop tugging at the skirt of that yellow dress, because I felt so uneasy in it. I didn't have a watch, so I didn't know how long the torture had been going on.

That is, until the dean said, "Well, it's nearly ten, and we should probably let our little wunderkind, Miss Evans, get a good night's sleep. She's just a girl, and that beautiful mind needs its beauty sleep."

Bella McGonigal led me to the door and outside, where I was met by the same student escort.

"How'd that go?" he asked as he walked me back to my dorm.

"I'm just glad it's over," I said.

"Oh, I'm sorry. Did it not go well?"

"No, it went fine. It was just exhausting. Being around all those people is just exhausting for me. It's draining. It's like running the headlights on your car with the engine turned off. You can do it. But only until you're out of juice. Know what I mean?"

"Not really," he said. "I feel my most energized when I'm around people."

"Oh. You must be more of an extrovert than I am."

"I guess. I only know how it feels to be me."

"Yeah," I said. "That's the universal, quintessential problem humanity faces."

I think that observation must have sailed past his understanding, because he walked me to my door without encouraging any further conversation.

———

The fifth knock came a few minutes later. My roommate was not home—I had no idea where she was—so there was no one to answer the door except me.

I had been so tired that I'd more or less fallen facedown on the bed and stayed that way. I hadn't even bothered to change out of the dreaded yellow dress.

"Hang on," I mumbled, with as much volume as I could muster.

I opened the door to see Bella McGonigal again.

"That went very, very well," she said. "The dean is quite pleased."

I opened my mouth to say something like "You got me out of bed for *that*? You couldn't have just told me that in the morning?"

Before I could say anything, she held up my precious scarf from Yellowknife.

"I forgot to give this back to you," she said. "Sorry."

"Oh," I said. "Thank you."

I didn't go into how much it meant to me, because I didn't know her that well or trust her that much, and I didn't figure she cared.

"Get some sleep," she said.

"Oh, I definitely will."

I closed the door, flung the precious scarf around my eyes, and fell facedown on the bed again. My only real commitment to comfort was to turn my head slightly so I could breathe. And that was the way I stayed until morning.

———

The sixth knock barely woke me. I mean, I heard it, but I was pretty deeply asleep and it hardly broke through. It didn't strike me as a thing that required any action on my part.

Next thing I knew, my roommate was shaking me by the shoulder.

I opened my eyes, and the morning sun shocked and burned them, making me wince.

"What?" I mumbled.

"It's for you," she said.

I got up and stumbled out of bed. I was vaguely thinking, *I was supposed to be done with this. I'll be done with this at some point, right? I'll get my life back soon, won't I?*

I was still rubbing my eyes when I got to the door.

"Maybe this can wait till I've had more rest," I said.

"Ru," a familiar voice said. "It's me."

My hands fell away from my eyes.

"Gabriel!" I shrieked.

He was standing in my hall with both hands behind his back. He apparently hadn't cut his hair since I'd last seen him. It was down well past his shoulders. He gave me what—to this day—I believe was the best Gabriel smile of all time.

As you must know by now, that's not an easy contest to win.

"Oh my gosh! Gabriel!"

I dove in and gave him a massive hug. He hugged me back . . . in one respect. I felt his long arms wrap around me. But he didn't touch me with his hands.

The door across the hall flew open.

"Oh my gosh!" a girl shouted, imitating my excitement. "Be quiet! We're trying to sleep!"

"Sorry," Gabriel and I both said at exactly the same time. Nice to know we hadn't lost that synchronicity.

The door slammed shut again.

"What's with your hands?" I asked, quietly this time, because I still couldn't feel them.

He stepped back and put them behind his back again.

"They're full."

"Of . . . ?"

"I brought you two little presents," he said, looking me up and down. "What's with this new look?"

I realized I had never bothered to change out of that silly dress.

"Oh. That. Long story."

"Short version?"

"This dress to me is what you dressing like a lumberjack to go see your father is to you."

"Got it," he said.

"What did you bring me?"

"Just little presents. I don't want to oversell them. Pick a hand."

I reached out and touched his left forearm and he pulled that hand out from behind his back. In it was a stuffed Atlantic puffin.

It was about the size of a real puffin, which is to say not all that big. It had green triangles of markings around its eyes, and an orange-tan-and-green beak. It had little flippery orange feet, and floppy little black wings with white underneath.

I actually, literally, put my hand against my heart and held it there, waiting to breathe again. And I had never in my life done that before. Not for anything.

"So now I've met a puffin face-to-face," I said.

"Oh, it's just a down payment."

He pulled his other hand from behind his back. In it was my phone.

"My phone!" I said, kind of whisper-yelling.

"I had to drive through Nevada anyway."

"But you were depending on me to know the mile marker."

"Yeah, that's the way we left it," he said. "But it turns out there aren't as many two-story metal kangaroos in Nevada as you might think."

"Did you get in trouble?"

"Go change back into you," he said. "I'll tell you all about it on the drive."

"Wait, what drive?"

"The drive I'm about to take you on. But I'm not telling you any more than that. It's a surprise."

Chapter Twenty-Seven

When We Were Two Pufflings in the Wild

Gabriel led me out of the dorm and into the bright sunlight, and we walked off campus to wherever he was parked.

"Oh, you're wearing your Yellowknife scarf," he said. "That's such a good memory."

"I know, right?"

"But it's not that cold," he said.

"No. It's really not."

"So it's mostly about the memories."

"Oh, it's all about the memories."

Before he could answer I saw his very yellow car.

"You got your car back!" I said. "I love this car."

"Me too," he said.

We climbed in.

"Did your dad ever get his Jeep back?" I asked as he fired up the engine.

"Oh yeah. They impounded it. But it was registered in his name, so they contacted him. It cost him some money. Fees and such. But he got it back."

"Was he mad?"

"Not really. I actually think he was proud of me for taking off like that."

He shifted into "drive" and we headed out on the road. To where, I had no idea. I wasn't even all that anxious to find out. I just figured if Gabriel wanted to take me there, I wanted to go.

"I have so many questions," I said. "I literally don't know what to ask you first."

"It's a long drive," he said. "Take a deep breath. We have plenty of time to catch up."

I looked down at my hands. The phone in one and the puffin in the other.

"I charged it for you," he said. "But I have no idea if the plan is still active."

"I assume you mean the phone, not the puffin."

"Right. The phone. And here's a question. What were we thinking with that nonsense about remembering the mile marker? I mean, it's a two-story metal kangaroo. Isn't that marker enough?"

I laughed and laughed and laughed. And then, just like that, I was crying.

"I missed you so much," I said.

I figured it would be a quick thing, the crying. A release of some small chunk of the grief I'd been holding.

I could not have been more wrong. I cried, and I cried, and I cried.

And Gabriel, being the most amazing person in the world, never tried to soothe me into stopping, the way most people would have.

All he did in response was to say, "It must feel really good to let all that out."

———

"My mom got me an attorney," he said. "And he got me house arrest instead of jail."

"Great!" I said.

"Well, it was. And then also it wasn't. He was . . . interesting."

"Good interesting?"

"No. More like that ancient Chinese curse 'May you live in interesting times.' He was kind of a pit bull. And don't get me wrong. I was really happy not to have to go to jail. I was eighteen by the time I got to court, and so close to it when I was arrested. It probably would have been adult jail, which is just utterly terrifying. I should be grateful, I guess, no matter what."

"But . . . ?"

We were headed east on the highway. I could tell that much by the sun. But that was all I knew. I just loved being in the passenger seat again, Gabriel driving. I just loved every mile that slid by my window.

"He told me the day before my court appearance to go completely as myself. No haircut, don't slick it back, keep the makeup and nail polish. I thought, *This guy really gets me.* But it turned out he was using the fact that I'm nonbinary to get the judge's sympathy. He pointed to me and said to the judge, 'You want to put *this boy* in prison with a bunch of hardened criminals? *This boy?* Why, that's just cruel. It would be kinder to turn a puppy loose on the freeway.' I swear those were his exact words. And it worked. But it was just so . . . I don't know. Everybody was looking at me like I was this . . ."

In time I gave up on the idea that he would finish the thought. Also, he didn't really need to. The feeling was abundantly clear without the words.

"I'm so sorry I got you into all that trouble," I said.

"You didn't."

"I really did, though."

"No. You didn't. You didn't hold a gun to my head and make me take you on the road. We decided together."

"I'm still sorry."

"Well, you shouldn't be," he said. "It was the best thing I ever did in my life."

We drove in silence for a few miles.

"So it was actually, honestly worth it?" I dared to ask.

"Oh, more than worth it. For an adventure like that? I had to be home for my sentence and wear one of those ankle monitors and go to school remotely. You know. Online. Big deal. All those days wearing bell-bottoms—that was probably the worst punishment right there."

I laughed, thinking that was funny. And then the laugh just died there in my throat, and nothing was funny. And I felt like nothing ever had been or would be again.

"Why didn't you write or call and tell me you were okay?"

"I didn't get any letters from you until this last one. I only know there were others because you said so in the letter. You said you'd written a bunch of times and called my mom, but I didn't know about any of that. I'd just gotten the monitor off, two days before I got your letter. It was my second in-person day at the university and somebody phoned in a shooter threat that turned out to be nothing. Probably some fool who hadn't studied for his exam or something. So they sent us all home. My mom was out shopping, and the mailman had just been there. I saw him walking away. So I brought the mail in. I didn't have your number, but then all of a sudden I had your address, and I was banking on the fact that I could get to you faster than a letter would." He fell silent a moment. Picked at the chipping blue polish of one thumbnail. "You know . . . the whole time I was stuck home, I asked my mom over and over if you had written or called. She said no. She said you must not care about me as much as I thought you did."

"That could never happen," I said. "I hope you didn't believe her."

"I tried not to," he said. "But it was hard to know what to believe."

"I get it. I kept wondering if maybe you weren't answering me because you never wanted to talk to me again."

"That could never happen," he said.

A few more silent miles slid by my window.

Then I said, "That was pretty cold of her."

"I think . . . I think in her mind she thought she was protecting me. But . . . yeah. It was. It was pretty cold."

"This *is* a long drive," I said, wanting to lighten the moment. "We'll be back tonight, right?"

"Oh yeah. I should have you back by dinnertime."

"Good. It might raise a red flag if I wasn't in my dorm room at night. Do we have to cross any state lines?"

"Nope. Not a one."

"Good," I said. "Because you're not a first offender anymore."

Fortunately he was able to hear that in the mostly tongue-in-cheek manner in which it was intended.

———

Two and a half hours of driving, and we arrived at our destination, which appeared to be a large zoo. How did I know it was two and a half hours? Because I had a phone! Glory hallelujah, I had a phone!

We parked in a lot so big that the different sections had animal signs to identify them. We parked in Giraffe, paid our entry fee, got our hands stamped, and walked inside.

Looking back, I should have guessed what the point of the trip was by then, but I was just blithely following Gabriel around, figuring he'd reveal his plans soon enough.

Gabriel was following some kind of map on his phone, and he led us into an Arctic exhibit, an indoor building with individual bird habitats behind glass. And I still didn't guess it. I just figured we missed our time in the Arctic and he was grabbing a piece of that back for me. We passed cormorants, and white-tailed eagles and auks and penguins. And then he stopped so suddenly I nearly ran into him.

"There they are," he said.

I looked into the exhibit in front of us and saw them.

"Puffins!" I shrieked. "You found puffins in North Carolina!"

"They're not exactly Atlantic puffins," he said. "They're horned puffins. But that's pretty close, right? That's good enough for now, isn't it?"

"*So* good enough!" I said.

There were eleven of them that I could see, though more of them might have been hiding inside their igloo house. They were much closer to the Atlantic puffin than the tufted ones they had in the Pacific Northwest. They had slightly less colorful beaks, but colorful enough— orange at the ends with a black-and-white spotty area behind that—and the "horns" were these fleshy little curved protrusions above their eyes. The rest of them were perfectly puffin-like. Just what I would expect.

"I love them," I said.

But, oddly, he was on the phone.

"Yeah," I heard him say. "It's me. Gabriel. The one who called you before. Okay. Thanks!"

A few seconds later a door I hadn't even noticed opened between exhibits, and a slender man of about forty with thinning hair stuck his head out.

"Come on back," he said.

I was a bit overcome, and I asked no questions. I just followed Gabriel, who followed the man down a long hallway. We ended up at a sort of rear door of the exhibit.

"I called him from the road," Gabriel said. "While I was driving to you. I just told him you'd had a really bad year and you wanted to meet a puffin face-to-face."

"But you had a bad year too."

"I didn't lose my only parent and have to go live with the worst relative on the planet. And, anyway, I get to go in too. But it's mostly for you."

I started to cry again, and really, for the most part, didn't stop.

I cried when the man handed me a bucket of fish, and the whole time we were picking our way out to this rocky area beside their pool.

I cried as they wiggled their way through the water to us, lifting up onto their back ends and craning their necks to see what was being offered, their wings out in such a way as to give them the appearance of broad shoulders.

I cried as they made little showers in the water with their hyperkinetic wings.

I cried as they jumped and fluttered into the air, flapping their little wings wildly.

I cried as they caught the fish I dropped into their amazing beaks and swallowed them down whole.

For several minutes they fluttered and waddled all around us, like we were old friends they hadn't seen in years. Because, I guess, when you're a puffin, any person with a bucket of fish is an old friend.

I fed them until the bucket was empty, and I never once stopped crying.

———

We were halfway back to the university, and it was dusky late afternoon.

"You never told me about the weird dress," he said.

"Oh. That. The university wanted me to put on a show for their donors."

"That's not a very long story."

"You're right. I guess it's not."

"How did you feel about that?"

"It was weird. But, on the other hand, sometimes you have to sing for your supper. And, I suppose, be glad that supper is not on a cash-only basis."

"That's a reasonable way to look at the world," he said.

I took a long, deep breath and asked Gabriel the dreaded question.

"I hate to even ask this," I said. "I've been putting off asking it because I know if I ask you'll answer. But . . . how long are you planning on staying?"

"Until you're eighteen," he said.

"Seriously? That's not a joke?"

"I've never been more serious about anything in my life. I'm a legal adult. I can live wherever I want, so I'm going to live here for as long as you have to live here. I'll get a job waiting tables or something. There's always bare-bones housing in a college town. I can apply at your university, or some other one within driving distance. It might take a while, but my grades are good. I'll get in somewhere. In the meantime, it's just sort of a gap year. Gap years are good, right?"

"Gap years are the best," I said.

I realized, as I said it, that I wasn't scared anymore. And that I hadn't been anything short of scared for as long as I could remember.

"Too bad you only got gap *weeks*," he said.

"Oh, but we packed a year of living into those weeks."

"We really did. But still . . . a college list is a college list, and when you're a legal adult and you can go wherever you want, I think we should go to Newfoundland or Iceland and see Atlantic puffins in the wild."

"The ones we just met were pretty cool," I said.

"Agreed. But we said we were going to see Atlantic puffins in the wild. And that's what we're going to do."

———

In the fullness of time, five years and many waiter jobs and undergrad degrees later, we kept that promise to ourselves, to each other, and to Atlantic puffins everywhere.

I'm not convinced that the puffins cared, but it sure meant a lot to me.

Chapter Twenty-Eight

Not Later but Now

Well, girls, you'll be glad to hear that I'm finally done. I hope you know I never would have told you a story like that in such detail—especially all in one sitting—if there weren't a few things I very much needed you to know.

So just on the off chance that it's lost on you why I told that story . . . this is why.

Thing number one: I want you always to believe me when I say I understand your pain. I will always know what it feels like to lose your mother. When I say I feel for what you're going through, I think you'll believe me now.

I don't believe we ever get over the loss of our mother. I don't mean that to be a pessimistic statement. I just think you're better off knowing that right out of the gate, as opposed to thinking everybody is getting over it but you. I'm not saying you'll always feel the way you feel now. You won't. In time you won't feel nearly so lost. You'll feel her "missing-ness," but you'll understand how to live your life around that absence. You'll find that when you think about her you'll think more about how good it was to have her and less about the downsides of having her, or the pain of losing her, or both.

But I need to make you a promise about the kind of guardian I plan to be for you. I will never tell you to grieve her loss more, and I will never tell you you're overdoing it. Your own grief is a path you know better than I ever will.

I support you with not so much as a word of advice. My only point on the subject is that I've been there too.

Thing number two: Because of everything I've told you today, I'm hoping you'll understand—maybe for the first time—why I took you. I hadn't really thought about children, my own or adopted. But when I learned about you losing your mother, and at just about the same age as I lost mine, my heart went out to you. I had to take you, and I had to take you both to keep you together. Because you're a herd, and you can't split up a herd.

There. See? I had to tell you every one of those details. Imagine if I had just called you a herd without the background story. You would have thought I'd lost my mind.

By the by, I did not tell you that story to encourage you to tell lies or run away from home. But it might help you to know I was not perfect at your age. Still not, but I've gained ground.

Thing number three—and this also goes to what kind of guardian I plan to be. But no, I don't just *plan* to be this for you. I *promise* to be. I hadn't even thought about this when I began my story, but now it's another thing I'd like you to take away. I was a child, but I managed to have a full life and experiences I'll never forget.

Adults do wrong to children in a number of different ways. At least, in my opinion we do. We talk to you, but we don't listen. We act as though you have nothing to say because you're children. We insist you sit quietly and listen to those who "know." But you know all sorts of things, and I'm genuinely looking forward to finding out what things those are.

Along those same lines . . . it may sound strange to say it, but please know that you're alive now. Right now. Your life doesn't start on your eighteenth birthday. It started a long time ago. Adulthood is not the first act of a play, and childhood is not the scene decoration and the learning of lines. This is it, girls. Welcome to your lives.

So if you want to be something, be it. If you then change your mind and want to be something else, by all means do that other thing. If you want to take a gap year and backpack around Europe, I'm all about gap years.

Trust your uncle Gabriel to be on board with all of this as well. He's been in places where he was accepted for himself and others where he wasn't. But it's been a long time since he had to live anywhere he wasn't fully welcome. This college town has been just the ticket for him in that regard, and that's why we stayed.

He'll be a champion for the real you.

Last, and probably most important, I wanted you to know that I learned to put intelligence in perspective. Yes, I have it. But I'm not my intelligence. And I'm not sure it's even the most important thing about me.

I appreciate the cooperative way you held still for some IQ testing, but I'm worried it might have given you the wrong impression. Even though I told you high intelligence was not my goal for you, I would understand if you didn't fully believe me. But now—now that I've told you everything—now I expect you will.

You're smart girls. That's what we found out. Well above average. But you're not off-the-charts geniuses. You're not freakishly smart. And, for that . . . I want you to know that I am so, so genuinely happy for you.

Now go ahead and get cleaned up for dinner, and I promise I'll never again make you digest that much information about the adults in your life as long as we all three shall live.

After this you can light up the world with your amazing lives. Either that or just enjoy some peace and quiet. Know that I'll love you whichever style you choose.

BOOK CLUB QUESTIONS

1. Near the beginning of the book, after Ru first meets Gabriel, they bond very quickly. When she asks him why he wasn't wearing makeup at lunch, he replies that he often must do things he's uncomfortable with in order to fit in and not cause conflict. Ru finds it odd that anyone would tell him not to do something that makes him feel like himself. Why do you think Ru so readily accepts Gabriel for who he is? And why do you think it's so difficult for the other people in his life to do the same?

2. Gabriel has Ru do a small experiment and asks her to point to herself. Ru points to the spot between her eyebrows. Gabriel explains that a study shows that most people point to their hearts. How much do you think self-perception affects a person's choice when doing this activity? Why does Gabriel suggest this exercise?

3. Ru's astrophysics professor tells her, "If you want a piece of advice, always choose to live your life in a way that promotes awe." What do you believe she meant by that, and how is her definition similar to or different from yours?

4. Ru rushes to see her mother before she dies, with hopes of some last moments to bond. When she arrives, she realizes she's missed her opportunity. As she watches her

mother struggling to breathe, she marvels at how much suffering we're willing to allow at the end of someone's life. What is your position on this concept? What is your opinion on whether people should have more control over their end-of-life decisions?

5. After Ru's mother's death, circumstances leave Ru feeling remorseful and angry. Grief manifests in many different ways. Was Ru's reaction justified, or could she have handled things differently?

6. As Ru processes the loss of her mother throughout the book, Gabriel says, "I figure, we used to be part of our mother's body . . . She breathed for us, and pumped blood through us. And there's only one person in the entire world we can say that about." In what ways might this special bond a mother and child share affect the grief process?

7. While staying in the cabin in the deep snow, Ru and Gabriel have a life-altering moment when they view the aurora borealis, the vastness of the stars, and nature around them. Have you ever had an experience in nature or in life that affected you deeply? In what ways do you think it changed you and redefined your world?

8. After Ru and Gabriel run away, things often just seem to fall into place as they go on their adventure. Even when they face the challenge of crossing the Canadian border, circumstances conveniently align to allow them to cross safely. Ru believes that life has a way of letting events drop into their perfect slots at the right moment. However, she states, "there's a catch to that kind of living. You have to be doing it right." What does Ru mean by "doing it right," and do you agree with her?

9. Ru and Gabriel are able to communicate without using words, and they have a deep understanding of each other.

After experiencing the aurora borealis, Ru feels their connection is like being part of a herd: "We were in a different kind of wilderness, operating on half a mind each, utterly unequipped for the captivity that lay ahead." How likely is this kind of dynamic with another person to occur? Why did the author choose this analogy to describe their connection?

10. When Ru and Gabriel are caught coming back home from Canada and face being be separated for many years, Ru reflects on why it was all worth it. Why do you think they were so brave and willing to risk it all for this adventure, even knowing what was at stake?

ABOUT THE AUTHOR

Catherine Ryan Hyde is the *New York Times*, *Wall Street Journal*, and #1 Amazon Charts bestselling author of well over forty books and counting. An avid traveler, equestrian, and amateur photographer, she shares her astrophotography with readers on her website.

Her novel *Pay It Forward* was adapted into a major motion picture, chosen by the American Library Association (ALA) for its Best Books for Young Adults list, and translated into more than twenty-three languages for distribution in over thirty countries. Both *Becoming Chloe* and *Jumpstart the World* were included on the ALA's Rainbow Book List, and *Jumpstart the World* was a finalist for two Lambda Literary Awards. *Where We Belong* won two Rainbow Awards in 2013, and *The Language of Hoofbeats* won a Rainbow Award in 2015.

More than fifty of her short stories have been published in the *Antioch Review*, *Michigan Quarterly Review*, *Virginia Quarterly Review*,

Ploughshares, *Glimmer Train*, and many other journals; in the anthologies *Santa Barbara Stories* and *California Shorts*; and in the bestselling anthology *Dog Is My Co-Pilot*. Her stories have been honored by the Raymond Carver Short Story Contest and the Tobias Wolff Award and have been nominated for *The Best American Short Stories*, the O. Henry Award, and the Pushcart Prize. Three have been cited in the annual *Best American Short Stories* anthology.

As a professional public speaker, she has addressed the National Conference on Education, twice spoken at Cornell University, met with AmeriCorps members at the White House, and shared a dais with Bill Clinton.

For more information, please visit the author at www.catherineryanhyde.com.